Storms

Books by Chris Vick

KOOK
STORMS

STORMS

CHRIS VICK

HarperCollins *Children's Books*

First published in Great Britain by
HarperCollins *Children's Books* in 2017
HarperCollins *Children's Books* is a division of HarperCollins*Publishers* Ltd,
HarperCollins Publishers
1 London Bridge Street
London SE1 9GF

The HarperCollins website address is:
www.harpercollins.co.uk
17 18 19 20 LSC/C 10 9 8 7 6 5 4 3 2 1

Text copyright © Chris Vick 2017
All rights reserved.

ISBN 978–0–00–821533–0

Typeset in Bembo Std 11.25/16.5pt by Palimpsest Book Production Limited,
Falkirk, Stirlingshire
Printed and Bound in the United States of America by LSC Communications

For Julia, Lucy, Steve and Janine. You know why.

PART ONE

BEFORE THE STORMS

Forecast

Winds: light-variable

Conditions: calm

Waves: clean, fun, 2ft

Blue skies, calm seas.

No major swell, people. A few 2 or 3 ft peelers on the more exposed beaches.

But hey, it's summer. The sky is blue.

Enjoy the balmy weather.

Get on a longboard.

Drink beer.

Have fun.

Jake

THE PLAN WAS to get to the beach for a sunset surf, then sit round the fire with some other idiots and their girlfriends, talking shit and sinking beers. When he'd had his fill of it, he'd fall on his sleeping bag, drunk. After a few hours' kip, he'd be woken by the dawn, and the crash of waves.

Surf. Party. Dawn surf. Home for Mum's fry-up. That was the plan. Not falling for some girl.

*

He got there late. People were already arriving for the party, lugging blankets and cases of beer across the sand to the nook below the rocks. There were surfers in the water, getting some half-decent waves.

'Bastards!' Jake dumped his gear on the rocks, changed quickly and pelted into the water.

3

The surf was good. Summer-small, no more than chest high, but clean and peeling nice, giving long, smooth rides, with a fast, steep wall before they died on shore.

He surfed till he was out of juice and it was near-dark. At the back of the beach, tucked in a crescent of rock, a large bonfire was burning, with a smaller fire nearby, for cooking. Gangs of people stood around them. Fag and spliff-ends lit the dusk like fireflies. The air was filled with laughter, music, the sizzles and smells of fish and burgers cooking. It was going to be a good night.

As he walked over the sand he saw a girl. She was sitting by the smaller fire, taking mackerel out of a cool-box. Her blonde hair hung down, hiding her face.

'All right?' he said, as he walked past.

'Hi,' she said, looking up. 'Good surf?'

'Uh, yeah.' In the light of the fire he saw her eyes. Oval sea-pools. He reeled, like he'd been thumped. The girl's eyes had delivered the punch. Those eyes, and her sunshine smile.

He climbed on the rocks, in the near-dark, to find his gear, thinking, *What just happened?* No girl had ever done *that*. Not with one look, one smile.

Jake watched her from the shadows. He felt like a stalker, but he couldn't help it. She had freckles, a tan, silky straight hair. She dressed plain. Jeans, hoody, a T-shirt, flip-flops. She had a slim, tight bod. She was gorgeous. Some girls wore prettiness like a new dress, like they knew what they had and needed to show it off. Not this one. She looked a good sort too. Kind. Could he tell that just from how she looked? Yeah, maybe.

He *forced* himself to stop bloody staring. Hung his suit on a rock and towelled his hair.

He should have gone over and said hi. That would be normal. But he didn't feel normal. He felt nervous. Like he might fall over, or say something stupid. Or, worse, nothing at all.

He thought he'd best think about it a while. Get the courage up.

Or . . .

Set about necking beers. There was Goofy, by the fire. *Exactly* the guy to drink with. Goofy, with his bird-nest hair, copper tan and crazed blue eyes.

'All right,' said Jake.

'All right, you daft fucker,' said Goofy, putting an arm round Jake's neck and squeezing him tight. It still seemed odd, to hear a gruff Welsh accent come out of Goofy's mouth. He didn't *look* Welsh (whatever Welsh looked like). He looked like a caveman.

'Too dark to surf, eh?' said Goofy.

'Yeah. Got a beer?'

'Always, man.' Goofy let Jake go, grabbed a bottle, cracked the lid with his teeth and handed it over. Then he dived into a story: 'Some daft tourist put pics of Eagle Point on Instagram. Place'll get rammed now. Reckon I'll not surf it till September, when waves are bigger and crowds thin . . . Oy!' He slapped Jake round the back of the head. 'You listening, man?'

'Eh?'

'What you staring at?' Goofy scanned the crowd. 'Oh, I see.' Goofy winked. The blonde girl was near now, handing out food, shining that super-beam smile on everyone she talked to. Getting closer. 'That's Perfect Hannah. Miss Goody-Two-Shoes they call her. Rough press if you ask me. Folk are jealous cuz her family's loaded. She's dead nice, really.'

'You *know* her?' said Jake, thinking: *You* know *her and you never told me.*

'You wanna meet her?' Goofy waved at the girl.

'No,' Jake whispered. He elbowed Goofy in the ribs. But his mate had an evil spark in his eye.

'Hannah!' Goofy shouted.

Hannah turned and smiled, holding Jake's gaze as she walked over.

'Hi, guys. Hungry?' she said, offering a plate of prawn skewers.

'Love one,' said Goofy. 'Hannah, Jake. Jake, Hannah . . . Is that Rob there? Bastard owes me a tenner.' Goofy sloped off, muffling a snigger.

'Hi, Jake,' said Hannah.

'Hi,' said Jake, grinning, nodding like an idiot and wondering what the hell to say. 'So, er . . . how d'you know Goofy?'

'He works for my dad now and then. Cottage maintenance, fixing boats.'

'Oh, right. Who you here with?' he said. Then mentally kicked himself. He might as well have said: *You got a boyfriend, or what?*

'Some people,' she said. 'We've just finished our A's at St Hilda's. We've been locked up studying for months. It's kind of a celebration.'

She smiled again. He noticed how close she was. So close the air was thick between them.

'Right. Off to uni, then?' he said.

'A bit of fieldwork, then uni. Marine biology, specialising in cetaceans . . . that's whales and dolphins.'

'Right. Cool. I see dolphins, surfing some of the quieter spots.'

'Really?' Those sea-pool eyes grew wide. 'Tell me where. I'm part of a research group. We spend our weekends on cliff tops doing surveys. Bit sad, really.'

'No, that's cool. I see them all the time. Do you know Eagle Point?'

Once they'd got chatting, he relaxed. She was so smiley, so damn *nice*. It was easy to be with her. Really easy. They talked for ages: about dolphins, about surf. It was all good. Right up to when she said:

'So, what do you do?'

'Um . . . er . . .' he stammered. This girl was educated, well-off, going somewhere. Everything he wasn't. Truth was, he'd already told her what he did. He surfed. A lot. All the work in bars, on boats: it was all to fund surfing. Or help Mum out. He didn't really *do* anything else.

Silence filled the air between them.

'Got any plans?' she said, trying to help him.

'I'm saving, to go travelling,' he said. A lie. He *wanted* to jet off surfing, but he was broke.

'I'm going travelling. With the fieldwork I mentioned. Before uni.'

'Anywhere nice?'

'Internship, studying humpies . . . I mean, humpback whales, in Hawaii.'

'Hawaii! Jesus. Can I come?' he said. Eager. A joke. Just a joke.

Hannah weighed him up, looking quizzical, then smiled.

'Maybe,' she said, teasing. He grinned back at her. It was awkward, how much they were smiling at each other.

Goofy returned with a tray loaded with shot glasses and quarters of lime.

'Fancy one?' he said.

'What is it?' said Hannah.

'You're kidding,' said Jake. 'You never did a shot of tequila?'

'Nope. Never did,' Hannah said, with a shrug. 'Want to show me how?'

It was sweet how innocent she was, how keen.

Jake liked this girl. It wasn't just her looks. It was how she was.

He liked her a lot.

Hannah

SHE WOKE SLOWLY in the grey light of just-before-dawn. Memories seeped into her head. The lovely boy, Jake. His brown eyes and mischievous grin. His scraggy beard and sun-weathered face. His strong hands.

The tequila and beer. A lot of it.

Hannah smiled, waking slowly, softly, still feeling the warmth of the boy and the night.

She sat up gently, but wished she hadn't. Her brain sang with pain. Her mouth was sandpaper.

Happy or not, she had a monumental hangover.

She was alone, covered by a damp, open sleeping bag and blankets, lying at the foot of a dune.

Some twenty metres off, was the carnage of the night: Still-smoking fires. Bodies in sleeping bags, like landed seals. A dog licking grease off a grill.

'Oh God,' she said in a thick voice.

A vague memory of Bess and Phoebe begging her to leave. Her telling them she'd be fine. Sneaking to the dunes, away from fires and drunks. Making their camp of sleeping bags and blankets. His firm body, and those hands. On her. How they had explored her body. (Had they had sex? No, she'd remember *that*.) They'd done a lot, though. A lot. She hadn't been able to help herself. Because he was gorgeous. And kind. And fun. And good with those hands. *Really* good.

What a night.

So, where was the boy now. Run away?

No, he wasn't that kind of guy. She was sure of it.

Still. Where was he?

Hannah looked around. A bottle of water was wedged in the sand next to the bedding. She grabbed it and drank. No water had ever tasted so good.

There was a white enamel cup too and, in it, a toothbrush and toothpaste.

And next to the cup: her flip-flops and clothes, folded. Jeans. Hoody. She was wearing her T-shirt, but . . . Her hand reached down and found only her bare bum . . . Where the hell were her knickers?

She scrambled about under the sleeping bag and blankets with hands and feet. She found her pants, hooked them with her big toe, put her hands down and slipped them on.

'Jesus.' She cursed herself for the tequila, and maybe also for not leaving when she could have. For going too far.

What would Dad say if he found out she wasn't at Phoebe's? Oh God.

But then . . . She smiled. After all that studying, all that stress, she'd gone off like a firework. She'd had a good time.

There seemed to be two Hannahs now. One normal, and another who was – apparently – a tequila-necking hussy.

Not-so-perfect Hannah Lancaster now.

She giggled, and realised she might still be drunk.

Knickers safely on, she got dressed. As she stood, brushing, gargling, spitting, she saw, lower down the dune, scrawled in the firm sand:

I AM HERE.

An arrow pointed to the edge of the dunes, to the sea.

Hannah picked up a blanket, wrapped it round her shoulders and walked slowly down, following the direction of the arrow. She came round the dune and saw the sea. It was high tide.

And there he was, in the shore break, surfing the waves of a silky milk-coloured sea.

He was on a wave now, spinning all over it, graceful and strong. Even at this distance, she could see his body, lithe with muscle. Like some animal.

He came off the wave and paddled out again, but not before he'd checked the shore. He waved. She waved back. Then she walked down, nearer to the sea, and sat on the sand with the blanket round her.

Her face tingled from the gentle breeze. She shivered on

the cold sand. But a warm glow, a soft fire, was growing inside her. Her throbbing head didn't matter now.

Beyond the shadow of the land, a sheet of blue approached, reaching to where Jake was surfing. The summer sun rose, slow, in the sky.

The boy carved the waves. Was he showing off? Probably. From what she remembered, he didn't do much other than surf. Lucky he was good, then.

A surfer. She'd fallen for a surf dude. What a cliché.

As she watched, she wondered about Hawaii and the weeks between now and then. About the boy, Jake. Which was crazy. She didn't know if they'd have breakfast, let alone a *relationship*.

But somehow . . . she did know. They would have breakfast. They would see each other again. She wasn't kidding herself. This was quick, but real.

She wondered what Dad would make of him.

Jake

HE LIKED THIS. The girl sitting on the beach, him surfing the high-tide breakers.

The waves were big enough for him to chuck the board about. But not so big he'd get punished for it.

He pulled tricks: sharp bottom turns, up the wave, smack the board off the lip, drop back down into the power pocket. Up: float over the white crest, run back on the green. Pump the board for speed. Tuck in a tiny barrel as the wave closed on shore.

He took a bigger one, got some speed till the wave was almost closing, launched off the top and spun in the air, then tried to stick the board back into the wave. It was crazy to try a 360. He needed onshore wind that wasn't there. He nose-dived the board in a foot of water, somersaulted and head-butted the sand.

He stood, spinning.

The girl – Hannah – laughed. Jake spat sand. He regretted making a tit of himself. Hannah stopped laughing and gave a sympathetic 'argh', then clapped and whistled. Her eyes were smiling. She wasn't taking the piss.

'I don't know much about surfing,' she said, 'but that looked great.'

'Even the wipe-out?' he said, and winked. He walked up, leant over – careful not to drip on her – and kissed her.

She stood up.

'My dad says you've got to fail and fall. And then get up again. In order to learn.'

'A surfer is he?' said Jake.

'More of a yachtee.'

He put the board down. She opened the blanket and closed it round them both.

'I'm soaking wet,' he said.

She pushed against him and the warmth of her was like an unmade bed. Her hair was messed, her eyes raw and sleepy.

God. She was beautiful.

Her lips met his. Her tongue too. She tasted of toothpaste.

He wanted her. She writhed a little under the blanket, feeling him there. She unlocked her lips from his and leant back, meaning: *Enough. For now.*

He picked up his board.

'So. What happens next?' she said.

Did she mean right this second, or something else?

'Um, breakfast?' he said.

Hannah looked up at the blue-filling sky.

'What time is it?'

'Early. Won't be anywhere open yet. Goof might have brekky stuff. Coffee leastways.'

She frowned. Her perma-smile dissolved.

'I need to get a signal. Send some texts. I wasn't exactly meant to be out all night.'

'Where you supposed to be?'

'Phoebe's. In her spare room. It's no biggy. Just parents, you know. They'll want to know I'm okay.'

'What will you tell them?'

'That I'm at Phoebe's. They'd freak if they thought I was out all night. With some boy. Who they don't know. That's three big bads. Besides . . .' She frowned, and acted a gruff voice, '. . . Pete Lancaster's daughter doesn't sleep on a beach.'

'Hannah . . . Lancaster. Goofy does stuff for your dad . . .' It all clicked inside Jake's head. 'Pete Lancaster's *your* dad?'

'Yes. Is that . . . er, okay?'

'Of course. I'm just . . . well. He's a big cheese around here. He's got a . . . rep, you know?' Jake couldn't find the words. Not honest ones. He'd never met the guy. But he knew plenty who had. *And* there was the time Lancaster had tried to buy their cottage off their landlord. That had been ugly. Too ugly to tell Hannah about right now.

'He'll want to know I'm okay,' she said. 'If I can get a message or two out, we can, you know, spend some time together? . . . If you're not busy.'

'Sure. I'd like that.'

Her smile came back. The sun, from behind a cloud.

They walked back to the dunes. Hannah sat on the bedding while Jake searched the sea of bodies.

Goofy was lying on his board bag. His jeans and pants were halfway down his bum, his mouth wide open and snuffle-snoring.

'What a sight,' said Jake. He picked up a seagull feather and wedged it down Goofy's butt-crack.

'Gerroff,' Goofy slurred. 'You've got your wetty on. You've been surfing and you didn't wake me. Bastard. How is it?'

'Decent. It's got a bit of—'

'N'er mind. What happened with you and that Hannah? Vanished, you did.'

'She's sat over there.'

Goofy looked over, and nodded his approval. 'You be nice to this one, you hear?'

'I'm always nice.'

'Right. While it lasts.'

'Listen, man, can you drive us? Hannah needs to get a signal, and we need some breakfast.' Jake lowered his voice. 'Away from this lot. Bit of privacy, like.'

'Course. Gissa few minutes.'

★

They piled into the front of Goofy's knackered van.

They'd drive to Penzeal, and get a signal over the moors. Then head to a café soon as one opened.

'Quick brekky, then we'll have you at your friend's before they even wake up,' said Goofy. 'Don't you worry 'bout nothing.'

'Okay, great,' said Hannah. She was looking at her phone. Concentrating on it.

'You all right?' said Jake.

'Yes.' She kept her eyes pinned to the phone. It lit up. Notifications streamed on to the screen. She scrolled through. Paused.

'Shit. Dad's coming to Phoebe's to pick me up. We're going to brunch with family friends.'

'When?' said Jake.

'Now. Goofy, can you drive me there?'

Jake put a hand on Hannah's arm. 'It's early. He'll wait till you're awake and you've sent a reply, right?'

'Not Dad. He'll just turn up.' She was sitting bolt upright, looking at the screen. Frowning again.

'Don't stress,' said Jake. 'You haven't done anything wrong. He'll be okay, as long as he knows you're all right. Let's go for coffee: we can drop you in a bit.'

Hannah shot him a look like he didn't understand. Like he didn't have a clue.

'No. I know we – I – haven't done anything wrong. Look, I just don't want to do a whole lot of explaining. We have to get there before him. Goofy, I'll give you directions.'

★

They parked outside the drive of Phoebe's house. *What now?* Jake thought.

Number swaps. Arranging to meet. But *definitely* meeting up? Or super-casual, yeah-I'll-text-you vagueness?

Not this time. He wanted to see her again. He wanted her to know it. Fuck playing cool.

Hannah glanced up and down the road before turning to Jake. She opened her mouth to speak. But before she could a sleek, blue Merc sped round the corner and pulled up in front of the van.

Hannah's father got out and stood square in front of the windscreen, hands on hips, looking from Goofy, to Jake, to Hannah.

He wore pressed jeans, deck shoes and a white shirt. He was tanned and smooth, but serious-looking.

'Look, maybe you guys should go,' said Hannah.

'Why?' said Jake. She smiled, weakly. Clearly, he still didn't understand.

'Can't just scarper, can we?' said Goofy. 'I know your old man. Be rude not to say hello.'

How *would* it look if they just revved out of there? Like they were running away.

When Hannah got out, Jake followed. Goofy got out of the driver's side.

'Dad. Hi.' She kissed him on the cheek. 'We just went to get some . . . things for breakfast. The boys came over this morning.' Her voice was high and forced. She was a bad liar.

'So where are the breakfast things?' said Hannah's dad. He didn't move, or raise his voice, or blink. Hannah shrank in his gaze.

'The shop was closed,' said Jake.

'You know Goofy,' said Hannah. 'This is Jake.' Pete Lancaster looked him up and down.

'All right, Mr Lancaster,' said Goofy.

Lancaster nodded at Goofy, then turned his eyes back to Jake.

'Good party, was it?' How he said it. It was a simple question, but loaded.

'Yeah, we had a great time last night,' said Jake. Hannah bowed her head.

'Hannah, you don't look like you had much sleep,' her dad said.

It was true. Gorgeous as she was, she looked washed out. Party-broken.

'I'm fine, Dad.'

'Anything you need to get from the house?'

'No. The girls are asleep. I can get it later.'

Pete Lancaster turned back to the car, opened the passenger door, then went and stood on the driver's side, waiting.

Jake hadn't had a chance to say goodbye. Now he had to do it with this guy watching.

'Bye, then,' said Jake.

Hannah looked to her father and back to Jake. She put her hand on the door, about to get in.

Then she bit her lip, thinking for a second, and ran to Jake. She kissed his cheek, bringing her lips close to his. Lingering. She whispered her number in his ear.

'Got it?' she said.

'Yes,' he whispered back.

Hannah and her dad got into the Merc, and it slid quietly away.

'Pen, paper, phone. Quick,' said Jake.

'Why?' said Goofy.

'Her bloody number, that's why.' He went into the van, searching his sleeping bag and rucksack, saying the number out loud to himself. Repeating it over and over while Goofy laughed.

Hannah

SHE'D FALLEN FOR Jake.

It had only been a couple of weeks. But this was like some drug taking over her mind, her body and her every waking thought. Her dreams. Deeper every day.

Two weeks of cloudless summer days.

They lay on the sand till they baked. They cooled down in skin-biting water. Walked cliffs with her sheepdog, Beano.

In the evenings Jake worked shifts in the Queen's Arms. Afterwards, he walked her home.

More than once she saw the curtains flicker in the shadows. She wanted them – Mum at least – to meet him, to see what she saw. But for now she wanted to keep Jake safe. From questions. Because there would be a lot of them.

★

So they visited Jake's family first.

It was away from the village, at the end of a terrace of cottages, near the cliff tops.

All the other cottages gleamed smart. Not Jake's house. Later, Hannah told Bess, it had 'ramshackle charm'. In truth, the roof slates were loose and covered in moss and the walls were stained grey by summer sun and winter storms.

But the weedy lawn was freshly mown, and in the corner of the garden Jake had built a pretty pink painted shed for his sister. There were stickers and dream-catchers in the windows. The house was run-down, but it looked like a home.

They'd hardly got through the door when a boy and a girl appeared.

'You're the dolphin lady,' said the girl. Hattie was ten, with dark ringlets, and round eyes like Jake's.

'Yes, I suppose so.'

Sean was fourteen. Runner-bean skinny, with straw-blond hair to his shoulders. He was grinning madly.

'You must be special. He don't normally bring them home.'

Jake took a firm grip on his brother's nipple, and twisted hard.

'That hurt!' Sean yelped.

'Good.'

Hattie laughed, and poked Sean, joining in.

'Stop. Now.' Jake's mum stormed out of the kitchen. She was plump, younger than Hannah expected, with long dark hair and dressed in jeans and a shirt. She glared at her sons, wiping her hands on her jeans, then the hair off her face.

'I'm April.' She grabbed Hannah by the shoulders and kissed both her cheeks. 'Come in, love,' she said, walking back to the kitchen. Jake and Hannah followed.

The walls had paper peeling off in the corners, showing patches of mould. Wind whistled down the chimney. The kitchen was clean, but crammed.

'We're having curry,' said April.

Hannah spied the pile of veg and the joints of chicken on the sideboard.

'Yes. Lovely.'

'Mum,' said Jake. 'She only eats fish. I told you.'

April sighed, heavily, like that was one thing too many to remember.

'Get Sean to cycle down the Co-op for a bag of prawns.'

'I'm fine,' said Hannah. 'I can just take the meat out. Let me help.' She ran to the sideboard, pushed some letters out of the way and grabbed a chopping board and knife.

'Oh,' said April. 'Um, okay.' She tidied quickly, so Hannah had some room. But she wasn't so quick that Hannah didn't see the bills. One, unopened, was from the gas board. Another, open, had FINAL DEMAND printed in ugly, red letters. April saw Hannah's face. Saw that she had seen, and gave a small, embarrassed smile.

★

The evening went well. Hannah was determined it would. She liked Jake's family and home, and she worked hard at being liked, herself. She answered Hattie's questions about dolphins. She teased Jake, with Sean. They ate the curry and drank beer and wine.

Sean and Hattie watched her all the time, carefully curious about everything she did. She forced herself not to lift her little finger off her wine glass, and to use just her fork to eat, in her right hand.

They asked Hannah about herself, her family.

'Pete Lancaster's your dad, isn't he?' said Sean. She'd heard those words before. Sometimes they made her nervous.

'Yes. He is.'

'He tried to kick us out of here,' Sean said, stuffing rice into his mouth.

'Sean!' said April. 'What my oaf of a son is getting at is that your dad wanted to buy this place.'

Hannah looked at Jake. 'Really? Jake never said.'

Jake turned to Sean. 'I *told* you not to say anything.'

That mad grin was splashed over Sean's face. He was buzzed by the trouble he was causing.

'You didn't want to sell?' said Hannah.

April laughed. 'Bless you. We don't *own* this house. Your dad tried to get us out so he could buy it from the owners. But we have tenants' rights. And that counted, no matter how hard he tried to *persuade* us.'

The way April had said 'persuade', it could mean anything.

Hannah focused on her food, picking at it with her fork. She'd lost her appetite.

'Sorry. About my dad. I don't know much about his business.'

'We didn't want to leave, you see,' said April.

'Yeah,' said Sean. 'We told him where to stick his offer.'

Jake stared at his brother. Unblinking.

'Well . . . good . . . for you.' Hannah searched for words. 'You did the right thing. I'm glad you stayed.' She smiled at Jake.

April poured Hannah more wine. 'Sorry, love. We didn't mean to embarrass you.'

'I'm glad we stayed too,' said Sean. 'We're the only ones that did. All our neighbours are grockles now. Saps. This place is empty in winter.'

Hannah felt awful. She hadn't done anything, but she felt blamed. Guilty.

'Shut your mouth, Sean,' said Jake.

Sean beamed his crazy grin at Hannah, then at Jake. 'Make me.'

Jake leapt up and had his brother on the ground so quickly it made Hannah jump. It looked serious. She thought he was going to punch Sean, till she saw – with relief – that Jake had Sean's forearms under his knees and his brother's nose between his thumb and fingers, squeezing. He was playing, but making a point. The kid was hurting, but laughing too.

'Say sorry for being a dick,' said Jake.

'Get off me or I'll fart,' Sean shouted.

'No, you will not!' said April.

'Dare you,' shouted Hattie.

Jake squeezed Sean's nose hard, then his ear. Sean trumped, loudly. Hattie shrieked with joy.

April rushed to the cupboard, came back with a broom, and started prodding at her sons as Jake tortured Sean, and Sean wriggled to get free.

Hattie was holding her nose and waving her other hand to get rid of the smell. She was near helpless with laughter.

It might have disgusted Hannah. This scene. What Mum would call *a display of vulgarity*.

But she didn't mind. And that surprised her.

She stood up and stepped back from the awful stench, giving April room as she poked and shouted. April looked at Hannah, pleading: *What can I do with them?*

Hannah shrugged. Soon, she was helpless with laughter too.

★

Later, Hannah helped April with the washing-up. April said she would do it herself, but Hannah insisted.

They worked, April humming, elbow-deep in suds, Hannah busy with the tea towel.

April had been so nice, but Hannah still felt bad, like there was a mark against her. After a while, she put the damp towel down and put her hand gently on April's arm. She waited till April looked at her.

'I'm not my dad,' she whispered. 'And I really like Jake.'

'I know, love. I know.'

★

She sent him a text one morning:

*Jake, Yr turn to see my home. As yr not wkng 2nite, wld u
lk 2 come over for dinner?*
Hx
PS M and D away. Will have place 2 Rselves

★

At a café in town, she showed Phoebe and Bess the text.

'Well,' said Phoebe. 'I think we know what "place to ourselves" means, *don't* we?'

'It means more than frottage on the beach, Hannah Lancaster. Right?' said Bess.

'What does *frottage* even mean?' said Hannah.

Her parents would be away. Hannah and Jake would be together. Not fumbling on a beach blanket, in some den between the rocks.

Jake would be in her bed.

Jake

HANNAH'S FAMILY LIVED in one of the old merchant houses on the cliffs near Whitesands Bay.

Jake got a good look at it as he walked down the drive in the evening sun. It was huge. Three storeys high, a covered porch, freshly painted white walls and a tall hedge surrounding the gardens. You'd need a sit-down mower for a lawn that size.

Amazing, the money you could make, owning boats and renting out cottages.

Jake knew there was no one there apart from Hannah, but he still felt on show. Watched somehow.

The security camera over the porch door didn't help.

He rang the bell, and waited.

He was wearing jeans, but they'd been ironed. Mum had cleaned his shoes with a damp cloth. His shirt was crisp and white. He'd even trimmed his beard into trendy stubble. He had a bottle of wine in his hand, notes for a cab home in one pocket and condoms in another. Just in case. He didn't expect it. But . . .

They hadn't shagged yet. Almost, but not quite. The beach was no-go. His place was a dead end; even if Mum was cool, Sean would listen through the walls.

Tonight they were alone. It might be different.

He rang the doorbell, again.

'Helloooooooo!' It was Hannah's voice, through an intercom. 'I've been watching you.' He looked up, smiled at the camera.

The door opened. She was wearing a green Roxy summer dress, light and clinging. She had smoky eye make-up on. And lippy.

'Wow. You look proper . . . I mean . . . Amazing. You *look* amazing.'

'A change from shorts and a T-shirt, right?' she said, curtseying. 'You dressed smart.'

'Um, yeah.' He felt like an arse. Like he'd tried too hard.

'You look *great*, Jake. Handsome. I'm glad you made the effort.' She smiled, kissed him and took the wine. 'Sancerre, niiice. Come on,' she said, and led him into the house.

He'd known the family had money, but this? Bloody hell. Just the hallway was massive. In a corner was a large bronze statue of a nude girl. On the walls framed photos of the family sailing, a huge modern-art painting of the nearby cliffs, an ancient drawing of a girl selling fish at the quayside.

It wasn't just money. It was taste.

His shoes thunked on the chequered marble floor as he followed Hannah. The kitchen was huge too, with black granite surfaces, a wooden work station and a breakfast bar. At the far end of the kitchen was an old oak table, set for two.

Nu-folk music drifted out of unseen speakers. He smelt herbs and candles. Good smells. Hannah's dog, Beano, was sitting, strangely quiet in a basket in the corner, as though even he had to behave himself in this place.

'The house is fantastic,' said Jake.

'Um, yeah. I guess. I'm making you steak.'

'But you're a pesky whatsit.'

'Pescatarian. I'm having swordfish.' She smiled and waved her hand over the table, like a magician's assistant showing the final part of a trick.

'This is all a bit grown-up,' he joked. He felt out of place. Weirdly wrong about being there.

Hannah came up and stroked his cheek, then laughed.

'Don't *worry*, Jake. The folks aren't here,' she said. 'No grown-ups. Just us.'

'Yeah.' He relaxed. This *was* just him, and Hannah. They could do what they wanted.

He opened the wine.

'My dad collects it,' she said as he poured. 'That and boats. It's like an obsession with him. He's got loads. A cellar, full.'

'Can I see?' he said.

'If you like. Follow me.'

She led him back to the hall, then into another hall, down curving stone steps and through a smoked-glass door into a cellar.

Three walls were covered floor to head-high with racks. Hundreds of bottles.

'Holy shit,' said Jake.

'We can have some if you like. I'm not bothered, but if you want?'

'Maybe later.'

'Dad won't mind us taking one, as long as it's not one of those.' She pointed at the top row of the rack that was furthest from the door. 'The pricey ones.'

They all looked expensive to Jake. Everything about this place looked expensive.

★

They ate salmon pâté she'd made herself, on tiny squares of toast.

They drank the wine, with the steak and swordfish.

They talked, a lot. About surf, dolphins, the sea. His mates. Hers. The usual stuff.

But all the time Jake was working up the courage to ask about Hawaii. They'd never planned anything beyond the next day's picnic.

He knew they needed to talk about it – she was headed off in September.

He took off his shoes and stroked her leg under the table.

'So,' he said. 'You got your ticket yet? A date for going?'

'I told you. September.'

'You never said the date.'

'Why? Are you planning a leaving party?'

Hannah stared at Jake, looking a little scared. He stared back. The words *leaving party* had cut through their evening like a knife.

Neither of them spoke for a while. No one filled the heavy silence.

They hadn't talked about 'goodbye'. Or a future. Jake downed his wine and poured himself another.

'Jake.'

'What?'

'This is difficult. You don't know . . . look. Do you even know what I'll be doing there?' she said.

He shrugged. 'Going on boats looking for whales?'

Hannah sighed. 'Dr Rocca takes four interns a year. Hundreds apply. You spend five hours on the boat, every two weeks. The rest of the time you sit on a cliff watching for whales to dive so you can take photos of their tail flukes, to ID them. You listen to hours of whale song and make notes. You spend days at the computer filing ID shots. That's the fun bit. When you're not doing that, you scrub floors, you make food for Paul and his team. It's hard. You earn nothing. You sleep in a bunkroom with the other interns. You live it and you breathe it. You don't get time off.'

Jake couldn't believe how serious Hannah sounded.

'Why do it, then?'

'You get close to the whales. You get contacts, experience. A chunk of data for your degree. Do you know how many people want to be marine biologists? No one can get the experience you need. No one.'

'Why you telling me this?'

'Because . . .' She spoke slowly, carefully. 'If you came . . . Well, like I said, there isn't even time off, really. We'd never see each other. It wouldn't be fair on you.'

He took his foot off her leg. So that's what this evening was about. This summer was as far as it went. She was letting him know. Gently as she could.

'You don't want me to come?' he said.

Hannah dropped her fork, wide-eyed with shock.

'What? Jake, no! No. I didn't mean . . . I'd *love* you to be there. More than anything.' She reached across the table and grabbed his hand. 'But it's a big ask. We couldn't even stay together. We'd hardly see each other.' She sounded sad, talking about the reality of it. He had to admit it didn't sound like he'd imagined. Even so . . .

'Don't matter,' he said, shrugging. 'I can surf. It's Hawaii. That's a dream come true. Better seeing each other once a week than Skyping. Better than waiting six months. They'll have to let you see me *sometimes*.' He squeezed her hand back and smiled at her, noticing the softness in her eyes. The mistiness.

'You'd wait?' Hannah said. 'Six months? For me?'

'Yeah. Course.' He pulled his hand from hers, feeling oddly

33

shy. He coughed, and attacked his steak. 'I'd rather come to Hawaii, though.'

'Where would you stay?'

'I'd work it out.'

'What would you do for money?'

'I'd work that out too.'

'It's that simple for you, isn't it?'

He took a chunk of fat off his plate and threw it to Beano. He took another gulp of wine.

'Yes,' he said.

She watched him eat, her elbows on the table, resting her chin on interlaced fingers and gazing at him, carefully.

'Okay,' she said.

'Okay what?'

'Okay, come to Hawaii.' She shone her sun-smile at him.

'Yeah?'

'Yeah. I wanted you to. I just . . . needed to hear you say it.' Hannah stood up, came round the table and plonked herself on his lap. She snuggled her bum into him. On to him. And kissed him.

'Hawaii, yeah?' he said.

'Yes. Yes. Promise me.'

'I promise.'

They kissed some more. He had one hand on her thigh, another round her waist. His hand moved up her leg, and the dress moved with it. She put her tongue between his lips for a second. He felt himself, against her, stronger by the moment.

She wriggled out of his grip, and stood up. She reached for the wine bottle but it was empty. 'Go get another,' she said breathlessly. 'To celebrate.'

When he stood up, his head was spinning from the wine and from the warmth of Hannah. From the promise they'd made. They were going to Hawaii.

Jake walked to the cellar, swaying, like he was surfing the air. He was ready to grab a bottle and run back quickly, before the moment dissolved.

He stood, in front of the racks, a kid in a sweet shop, not knowing which to take. He picked one at random then looked around the cellar, up and down, as if there might be a camera there too. But there wasn't.

He still felt giddy. Drunk, and not just from wine.

He had an idea. It made his head spin even more. He picked a bottle off the rack on the far wall: one of the 'expensive' wines. He wiped the dust off, on his jeans, and replaced it with the one he'd just taken.

It felt bad and good at the same time. Naughty.

So what? he thought. A little payback for the grief Lancaster had caused Mum. Why not? Lancaster could afford it. He probably wouldn't even notice.

Jake toyed with the idea putting the bottle back. A twinge of guilt making him hesitate. Then:

'Fuck it,' he said, laughed out loud, and ran.

Back in the kitchen, Jake opened the wine and Hannah turned up the music.

They danced. She taught him moves she'd learnt at classes when she was young. She seemed pleased with how quickly he picked them up.

They slow-danced. Snogged.

He thought about Hannah as they danced. This smart, beautiful girl. The girl he'd be with in Hawaii.

'Why me?' he asked, as they swayed slowly, with her head on his shoulder and her breath against his neck.

'Why you what?'

'You could have *anyone.*'

They sat down, with her on his lap again. No wriggling away now. Her arms hung round him, pulling him closer.

'Those people Mum and Dad are with tonight . . . Their son, Simon, was my first proper boyfriend. It lasted a year. It should have been a week. The guys I meet in my world, they're like Simon. Too polite, too awkward. Or they're rugger-playing idiots whose total dream is to be a stockbroker with a Porsche,' she whispered in his ear, her hand on his chest. 'They don't interest me; they're not . . . real.' She took a glug of wine from the bottle, kissed his neck. 'I don't want to be some banker's wife. I don't want to end up . . . I hate myself for saying this . . . like Mum. You see this – this place. Think it's nice?'

'Yeah. It's . . .'

'It's a prison!' Hannah cried, suddenly angry-drunk. 'This life. Why do you *think* I'm going to Hawaii? It's not just whales. Not just that. I'm getting away.'

'Is that me, then? Am I an escape too?'

'No, Jake. I mean you are, but you're more than that. I'm drunk. I don't know what I . . . I'm just trying to say . . . You're different. You're strong and kind. You don't give a shit about things that don't matter.' She waved her arm at the kitchen, the house. 'You're all about *doing* things, being who you are, not just getting more . . . Stuff. You're free, like . . . I dunno. The sea.'

'The sea?' he laughed. 'What does *that* mean?'

'I told you. I don't know.' Her hand slipped inside his shirt. Their mouths locked, softly, and the talking stopped.

They stood up, still kissing, for a long time, then in one movement, he took the hem of her dress, lifted it over her head, and let it fall to the floor.

They came back together, knocking a chair over.

'Leave it,' she said, wrapping her arms round his neck.

They stumbled through the door and up the stairs, stopping to kiss, to feel, before staggering into Hannah's room. To her bed.

★

Afterwards, they lay together. The window was open. Jake watched the star-rammed sky, and listened to the sea on the rocks. Hannah fell asleep in his arms.

Hannah

HANNAH'S EYES FLEW open.

Why?

Something wasn't right.

The sound of the drive gate, clinking smoothly shut. The purr of Dad's Merc. The crunch of tyres over the gravel.

'Shit! Jake, wake up!' She grabbed his shoulder and shook him.

'Wassup?'

'They're back.' Hannah leapt to the window.

'Who, what . . .' His voice changed from sleepy to wide-awake in a second. 'They're not back till tomorrow.'

'That's what they said.'

'They gonna flip?'

'They knew you'd come round. They didn't know you'd stay. Shit.'

Hannah searched her memories, through the haze of wine and sex and sleep.

Plates and glasses on the table. Empty bottles. The chair knocked over.

Her dress on the kitchen floor.

'Oh no. Oh God, no.'

The front door opened, then clunked shut.

Voices. Sharp and loud.

Dad: 'I've known him for fifteen years. I've kept that bloody bank going.'

Mum: 'You didn't have to make a scene. Why don't you . . . Oh. My. God. Pete, come here.'

Mum was in the kitchen. There was no time to do anything.

Hannah froze at the window. Jake sat in bed. Both of them naked.

She covered herself with her hands, then pulled her dressing gown off the back of the door.

'Stay here,' she whispered, hurrying. If there was going to be a scene, it would be better in the kitchen, before Dad made his way upstairs. She ran down, took a breath before going in.

'Hi,' she said.

Dad and Mum stood by the table. Mum had the dress in her hand. Dad picked the chair off the floor and put it upright. Mum placed the dress carefully on the back of the chair.

'Thought you were back tomorrow,' said Hannah. They turned to her. Her gaze fell to the floor.

'What's been going on?' said Dad.

'Pete,' said Mum. 'It's pretty *obvious* what's been going on.' Hannah steeled herself, but kept her eyes on the floor.

'He *is* my boyfriend,' said Hannah. Quietly, politely.

'You said he might come round for a drink,' said Dad.

'Pete. *Come* on,' Mum said. Hannah looked up. Mum rolled her eyes, not believing Dad's naivety. Was she okay with this? Was she on Hannah's side?

'This is my house. I did not give permission for . . .' Dad looked at the dress on the chair.

'He came round for dinner, we had some wine.' Hannah felt a teasing pain in her hands, and noticed she'd clenched her fists. Her nails were digging into her palms.

'So I see,' said Dad.

'He's my boyfriend. We *can* . . .' She couldn't say it.

'Not in my house,' said Dad.

'You'd better get used to the idea. He's coming to Hawaii.' She didn't know where these brave words came from, but now that they were out there she felt reckless. She could still feel Jake's sweat, his warmth, the wine. It was all like armour, protecting her.

'How the hell can you make that decision?' Dad shouted. 'You've known him, what? A week, two?'

'Longer.'

He stepped towards her. She didn't move, though her legs were weak as twigs. 'And where is he? This boy who's flying round the world with you, who we don't even know?'

'I'm here,' said Jake.

He'd got dressed. He'd made himself presentable as possible. But he was barefooted, his shoes were still under the table.

'We met briefly, Mr Lancaster. I'm Jake,' he said, and held out his hand.

Dad looked him up and down. Dad, with his jacket and tie and slick hair. He shook Jake's hand, limply, but pulled the sides of his mouth down and raised his eyebrows as he did it.

He'd dismissed Jake and everything he was with one look. And Hannah hated him for it.

He picked up one of the empty bottles, took his glasses out of his shirt pocket and examined it. Reading it like a book, like there was no one else there.

'You said I could take some wine,' said Hannah.

'And so you did,' said Dad, still looking at the label. 'Do you know how much this bottle was worth?'

'Sorry, Dad.'

'Sorry?' he said, softly. 'You're sorry.' Jake stepped forward.

'Hey. We got carried away, drank too much. I was never even going to stay here.'

Her dad didn't look at Jake, only at Hannah.

'No. But you did, didn't you? Hannah, you know which bottles not to take.' He showed her the bottle, like she would recognise it.

Jake held his hand up. 'It's my bad. I went to get another bottle. Maybe I got one of the pricey ones by accident.'

Dad looked weirdly pleased by this news. Hannah shot Jake a WTF look.

41

'I'll pay you back,' said Jake. 'I promise.'

Dad looked at Jake now. Examining him.

'That might take longer than you think,' said Dad. 'You work in a pub, don't you?'

'There's no need for that, Pete,' said Mum. 'I mean, there's no need for Jake to pay for it. *Is* there?'

Mum never stood up to Dad, but she was now. Even Beano looked at Dad, like he was going to bark. Her father was alone.

He raised his finger and pointed first at Mum, then at Hannah.

'You'd better go,' Hannah said to Jake before Dad could speak. She leant over, ducked under the table, grabbed his shoes, and herded him to the front door.

'I'm sorry,' he said. 'About the bottle.'

'I'm sorry too. About Dad.'

They kissed. A reminder of their night.

She watched him disappear into the dark.

Jake

THEY AVOIDED HANNAH'S house after that. And her family.

They took long walks on the cliffs. Searching. Because Hannah had heard a rumour. The sighting of orcas. Killer whales.

'Not sure I want killer whales around, anyway.' Jake said after they got home one day. 'I'd freak if I saw one in the water.'

Hannah grinned. 'Worried it'd surf better than you?'

'Killer whales don't surf.'

'Yeah? I've *seen* it, Jake. I've filmed it.'

'Get out!'

'Wanna see?'

Hannah searched files on her laptop, a look of total concentration on her face. It surprised Jake when she got serious. She screwed up her eyes, sticking her tongue a little way out of the side of her mouth. It was cute. And sexy.

'Can't find it,' she said. 'I should give these files names, not just numbers. Listen to this, while I search. Sounds from a hydrophone we placed off the Scillies, last summer.'

Jake strained his ears. Bubbling, rolling currents, soft gurgles, washing white noise. Hisses and whispers.

Then:

Cik . . . cik . . . cik . . . Faster. *Cik . . . cik . . . cik . . . cik . . . cik . . . cik . . . Ckkkkkkkkkkkk . . .*

'Sonar,' said Hannah.

The air filled with waves of echoes, whistles, clicks and thuds. Jake's skin goosebumped.

'Voices,' he said.

'The sounds amplify through the hulls of ships,' said Hannah. 'Sailors used to reckon it was mermaids. Or the cries of drowned sailors.'

'What are they saying?'

'Hard to know, exactly. We match sounds to observed behaviour, and work out the combinations for feeding, hunting, calling. It's rudimentary language, which varies between communities. They have dialects, and they use sets of unique phrases for individuals.'

'You mean . . . *names?*'

Hannah shrugged. 'I guess so.'

'That's *incredible.*' He slumped in his chair, open-mouthed. Hannah saw, and smiled.

'Want to see incredible? Watch this.' She shifted the angle of the laptop, and moved her chair up next to his. He put his arm round her and rested his hand on the curve of her hip.

The footage was of sea and islands, taken from a boat he guessed, as the camera was swaying. The water was smooth and the day was crystal-blue, but at the edge of the island were huge breakers. As if on cue, a wave rose up on the screen. The wave held up, feathering white off the top.

A dark blur emerged inside the wave. Sleek, big and fast. An orca. It waved its tail frantically as it cruised through the blue, then erupted out of the face of the wave, flying backwards. A huge fish in its mouth.

Jake shock-laughed. He almost clapped. The cheek of the thing. The skill, the grace, the power.

She stared at him, watching his reaction.

'I've never seen anything like that,' she said. 'But I will again, one day. I'm going to study orcas.' Her eyes misted, seeing a dream. 'You know what's different about them?'

'Tell me.'

'Animals spend their whole existence hunting or fleeing, finding food, breeding, caring for young, keeping warm, finding shelter. That's their life. But orcas have evolved beyond that. They have no natural predators, they hunt easily and they're resistant to cold. So they just . . . play. Travel. They have large families they stay with for life. Run by the matriarchs. And pods and super-pods that meet up, once in a while. Tribes of the sea.

'They look after each other. They *never* leave a sick family member. They've got life sussed. They're free.

'A lot of people are like most animals, running around,

chasing their tails. If they're lucky enough to have a roof over their head and food to eat, they stress about exams or money or how they look.

'We could learn from orcas. They just like hanging around, eating, playing and surfing. They're a bit like you,' she said with a sly grin and a nudge to his ribs.

'You should see your face light up when you talk about this stuff, Hannah.'

Her dreamy eyes hypnotised him. The sun-smile, and freckled nose. How she was serious, but passionate too.

He showed her surf vids. She showed him more vids of dolphins and whales.

It was near dark when April, Hattie and Sean got home.

'Get these on,' said Mum, handing Jake frozen pies, peas and chips from her shopping bag. 'Hannah, sorry, love. I'll have to move you.'

Hannah had that look about her still. The sea-eyes, misted.

'That's okay,' said Hannah. 'Anything you want me to do, Mama orca?'

'Mama what?'

'It's a whale,' said Jake.

'It's a compliment, April,' said Hannah. 'I promise.'

PART TWO

SEPTEMBER – THE FIRST STORM

www.Eye-Sea-Surfcheck.com

Forecast

Winds: Raging westerlies, 30mph with up to 50mph gusts

Conditions: Heaving. Massive. Dangerous.

Waves: Big, bigger and also massive. Swell 12–15ft at 13–14 seconds wave period. Wave face 15 and up to 20ft. More.

Whooaa!!

Summer's well and truly over, folks. This is a biggy.

Once-in-a-blue-moon sheltered spots will be firing. The sea gods are giving us gifts. It's going to be special. It's going to be wonderful . . . if you know where to look.

Jake

THERE WASN'T MUCH to Brook Cove. A river that poured into a small harbour, a handful of fishermen's cottages and a café selling cream teas.

It was pretty in summer, but when autumn came the valley was dipped in shadow. The café was closed and the cottages empty.

It was a lonely place, but it suited Goofy. He lived above the café in a studio flat, with a kitchen at one end, a sofa-bed at the other and a separate bathroom.

Jake climbed up the steps to the flat, knocked and walked in. The place was a mess, with beer cans on the floor and pizza boxes and surf mags on the table. Three knackered surfboards leant against the wall.

Goofy was asleep on the sofa, fully dressed but, weirdly, holding a mug of tea.

'Bit late for sleeping,' said Jake.

Goofy opened an eye. 'Been for a dawny surf, haven't I? Catching up on the zeds.' He glanced down at his mug. 'This is cold, man. Get a fresh brew on.'

Jake walked to the kitchen end of the flat and got busy rinsing mugs and boiling the kettle.

'You come about the money?' said Goofy.

'Yeah. Need to get that Hawaii ticket sorted. Listen, mate –' he turned to look at Goofy straight – 'I'm sorry about this. I wouldn't if I wasn't desperate. I've had to help Mum out. More than I thought.'

Goofy picked up a pizza crust and threw it at Jake.

'Shut up, you daft twat,' he said. 'You helped me settle 'ere when I had nothing.'

Goofy *had* arrived in Cornwall with nothing. Less.

'How come you turned up here in the first place?' said Jake. 'You were in a bit of a state.'

Goofy sighed. 'Running away from shit, like always.'

'What?'

'Never mind. I'm here now, aren't I? And rich enough to lend you money. I'm due some dosh from Lancaster.'

Jake shook his head as he poured boiling water into the mugs. If Hannah's dad knew he was helping fund Jake's trip to Hawaii . . .

'Soon as you get work you can pay me back. Electric transfer or whathavya. Small problem, though . . .' Goofy let the words hang.

Jake brought the tea over and sat down. 'Problem?' he said.

Goofy stared at his mug, chewing his lip. He looked embarrassed, which was a first.

'I can only go three hundred. Not seven, like.'

'What? Three hundred? You're bloody kidding?' Jake felt bad as soon as he'd said the words. He wished he could push them back in his stupid mouth. But in one second he'd seen Hawaii evaporate, like steam from his mug of tea. 'Shit.' He put his head in his hands.

'All I can do, mate,' said Goofy, getting off the sofa, holding his hands up. 'I am so, so sorry, man. Lancaster owes me loads for bits and bobs, but he takes ages to pay.'

'Yeah,' said Jake. 'Three hundred's huge. Massive. I'll find the rest. Somehow.'

'Not being funny, like,' said Goofy. 'But you have had *all* summer to save, Jakey. Just saying.'

'Yeah, right.' He stared at the floor, wanting to lie down, and never get up again. He could barely speak; he felt like crying. 'I'm not . . . stupid, Goofy. I did have some saved. Thing is . . .' He sighed heavily. 'Like I say, I've had to help Mum. She's got debts. She couldn't make the rent. I didn't have a choice. *That's* why I needed to borrow. She's in a bad way. I need to get her sorted before I go.'

'Oh, I see. Look, chin up, mate. I'm still here for your mum – you know I am. And there's a while yet. We'll figure something out. Together. Yes?'

'Okay,' Jake whispered.

51

'I *said*, yes?'

Jake looked up. 'All right. Yeah, there's a bit of time, isn't there?' But there wasn't. Not really.

'Come o'er here,' said Goofy, waving him towards the window. 'See those clouds? There's a storm coming.'

They went and sat, looking out of the bay window at the sea and sky. Goofy rolled a cigarette and talked about the storm, about the wave-fest headed their way. But Jake didn't hear.

He was already going to be living off Hannah till he got work. How could he tell her he couldn't even buy his ticket? He imagined her saying it was okay, saying they'd Skype every day. That they'd make it work till she got back.

Yeah, right.

'How come Lancaster won't front you, anyway?' said Goofy. 'I mean, you are boning his daughter.'

'Watch your mouth, cheeky bastard. Anyway, that's *exactly* why.'

'He could pay,' said Goofy. 'Seriously. Easy. Make his daughter happy.'

'I wouldn't take his money.'

'Why not? The guy's made a wad with that fleet, breaking the backs of honest fishermen. And renting out cottages to tourists. He's got himself to a place where he can literally do what he wants. A better hotel in the Caribbean, another frock for the missus. You're a better use of the cash if you ask me. His life? It's all one big straitjacket.' Goofy tapped his head.

'How does his brain work? I've seen him down his boathouse. He pays people to mow his lawn, but there he is, on a Saturday, painting an already-white fence even whiter. Fucking nuts if you ask me. Done all right with his missus, though. See where Hannah gets the looks from. I would, you know. I definitely would.'

'That's my girlfriend's mum, you sicko.'

'Don't tell me you haven't thought about it.'

'I haven't thought about it.'

'You have now, though. You won't be able to stop thinking about it, next time you're with Hannah . . . ouch!' Goofy winced from the jab in the ribs Jake gave him.

'You are twisted,' Jake said. He was laughing, though. He couldn't help himself.

'I'm sure her mum'll give you the money, for a special payment.' He winked and rocked his hips.

'Shut up!' said Jake.

'See. You're laughing. Better already. Fancy a can?'

'Bit early.'

'Too late for sleeping, too early for beer. You want to be careful with these rules, Jake. You'll end up like Lancaster.'

'No chance of that,' said Jake.

Goofy went and got a beer. Jake slurped his tea. They watched the distant wall of cloud out to sea. Jake sank into arms-folded silence.

'A storm like this churns everything up,' said Goofy, clearly trying to change the subject. 'All sorts come out the water. I seen it back 'ome in Wales too. Old wrecks, dead dolphins. A live one once. You'd be amazed what I've found down coves. A crate of beer. A life jacket. A container full of top trainers, once. Offerings from the sea gods, like.'

'Where was that, then?'

'Oh, you know, various surf spots.'

'No. Where was "back home?"'

'Here. There. Moved around a bit, I did.'

That was Goofy. Dodging the question like always. Jake knew better than to push it.

'Look at that storm brewing,' said Goofy, pointing to sea.

Jake loved an autumn storm. The best surf all year. But he couldn't feel hunger for it now. He was gutted, too worried about not getting on that plane.

'You gonna surf it tomorrow?' said Goofy.

'Maybe.' He doubted it. He needed to talk to Hannah. He'd arrange to meet. He'd break the news.

Unless he could find a way to get the money.

Jake

IT HAD BEEN light for an hour, but it felt like night out there, with the sky caked with cloud, and the wind screaming.

Normally he'd lie in bed with a cuppa, listening to the storm batter the window.

Or go surfing.

But today he needed to talk to Hannah.

They were supposed to meet up for a walk, but what could he say?

So far he didn't have any ideas about how to get the money. Not even bad ones.

Maybe a surf would help him think.

'What the hell.' He poked an arm out from under the quilt, found his phone and texted:

Hi Gorgeous. Weather no good 4 walking. Give yrself lie in.
Going qk surf. Best in ages. Meet up later, yes?

He snoozed, waiting for a reply. When none came, he crawled out of the sack and tiptoed downstairs. He made a steaming coffee, thick as soup, and ate an energy bar. He put his wetsuit on, got a board from the shed and headed out.

It was cold. The wind and rain had bite. They meant business. It was more like winter than the end of summer. The wind was so hard he had to hold the surfboard tight under one arm and steady the front with the other, just to stop it taking off.

Ten minutes later he was there. It didn't look good from the cliff. Great white horses were rising out of the sea, raging and disappearing. Huge waves, bouncing and twisting with wild energy. Impressive, but no good for surfing. Maybe he'd wasted his time. He played with the idea of heading back. But then again . . . he couldn't *see* the cove, and the forecast website had said:

It's going to be special today, guys. It's going to be wonderful . . . if you know the right spots.

Wonderful. That was weird. Jake had never seen that word on a forecast before.

If it was bad: *Pony. Blown to shit.* Or: *Flat as road-kill.*

If it was good: *Cracking. Thumping. Off the scale.*

Something like that. But *wonderful*?

Wonder-ful. Full of wonders. An offering from the sea gods.

There was a steep path, tucked into the cliffs, leading past a boulder and by a stream. No one used it apart from brave dogs and nudey sunbathers in summer.

Jake took that path, chasing a promise. Except the path and stream were now a river. He waded and climbed, slipped and swore.

He almost fell into the surfer coming the other way. A short, craggy-faced bloke he'd seen at Praa Sands a couple of times. The dude was climbing through the waterfall.

'Wass it like?' said Jake. He always asked surfers coming back from a break, checking their faces for glassy eyes and stupid grins. 'Is it wonderful?'

Crag-face headed past, without saying a word, or looking at him. Maybe he hadn't heard Jake? Or *maybe* he didn't want to let on how great it was.

Only one way to find out. And it would give him thinking time. Surf could do that. Wash all your worries away. Clear your head. Just for a bit.

Hannah

HANNAH CHECKED HERSELF in the hall mirror.

Sunset-red Henri Lloyd storm-breaker jacket, brand new. A present from Dad. Black waterproof trousers. Hunter wellies.

'Sexy,' she said. A howl of wind rattled the door, threatening to blow it open. Rain hammered on the conservatory roof like a thousand tiny drumbeats.

'No such thing as bad weather,' she said to Beano. He was scratching at the door. 'Only a bad attitude and the wrong clothing. Right?'

Beano whimpered, keen to get going.

'Hang on, he'll be here soon.'

'Morning, Hannah.' Dad walked down the stairs in his dressing gown. 'Going out?'

'Beano needs a walk.'

'Want some company? I can be ready in five.'

'No. You're okay. I'm supposed to be meeting Jake.'

'Supposed to be?'

'He hasn't turned up . . . yet.'

'Ah.' Her dad smiled, raised his eyebrows and walked to the kitchen. As if just that one look said everything about Jake. Just that look. He did it all the time. It annoyed her.

She looked at her phone. Seven thirty. There was a message. He was going surfing.

Hannah smiled. Maybe it was a *good* thing if she went by herself. She needed to think.

Without saying goodbye to Dad, Hannah headed out along the path down to the village, through the streets and past the houses. When she came round the corner and started on the road to the beach, she got the force of what Jake called *the full Atlantic blast*. A shock of wind and stinging rain.

'Jesus,' she said, and sank her head deep into her jacket as she headed down to the sand.

It was only weeks before she was due to get on that plane. It didn't seem real. How could she be walking on a howling Cornish beach one day, and not so many later be photographing whales in crystal lagoons?

And with Jake? He wanted Hawaii as much as her. More than anything. Not just for her, but because it was Hawaii, the best surf on earth.

It was his dream too. It was just a different one.

How would it go when they got there? Her working long hours, him surfing. And he hadn't bought a ticket yet. He kept saying he'd sort it, but he hadn't. She had money, but if she bought *his* ticket and had to pay for them both when she got there she'd be stony broke, pretty quick.

She reached the sand and started walking.

What if he couldn't get the ticket? What if he didn't come?

It would be months. And she'd miss him, the same as she'd miss the Cornish storms. The kiss of needle rain on her face, and Jake's kiss when he put a smacker on her cheek. How she'd wipe away the itch of his stubble.

'Ugh. It's like being kissed by a badger's bum,' she'd say. Complaining, but not complaining. Then he'd kiss her on the lips and it'd almost knock her out. Like the shots of tequila the night they'd met.

'That's disgusting,' she'd said, reeling from the salt, the bitter shot and the sting of lime.

'You'll get to enjoy it,' he'd said, handing her another.

She had too. Hannah smiled at the memory.

How could she go without him? How could she even *think* it? But . . .

He'll drag you down.

She heard the words like they were said out loud. She heard them every day. From Phoebe, Bess, Mum. Dad. *He* said it every chance he got.

'Well, sod you, Dad,' she said into the wind and rain. 'He's coming!'

Then she saw something, through the sheets of rain, at high tide, on the sea's edge.

At first she thought they were rocks. Six or more. Huge, smooth, black boulders. Big as upturned yachts. Bigger.

They *were* rocks. They had to be. The storm must have stripped the sand off them. But, at the same time, she knew they *weren't*. They were too dark, too rounded, too perfect in their shape.

So what were they? Beano ran straight to them, barking.

Only when she got close did Hannah see the white patches like giant eyes, the dorsal fins like great black knives on the creatures' backs. The tail flukes lying useless and still on the sand.

Orcas. Killer whales.

She ran to the first one, the largest. It wasn't moving. Its blowhole was closed and its mouth was open, showing a row of perfect, shining teeth. Its oddly human tongue hung out of the side of its mouth, limp and dead. Its eye was human-like too. But there was no light in it. It stared, unseeing, at the grey sky.

She checked the next one. It was half hidden in orange fishing net and seaweed. It was smaller, with a short fin. A female. Also dead.

The third one had fresh scars on it. They were pink and gaping: the telltale cuts of a whale tearing its flesh to escape netting.

This was what a loose net could do. She imagined the whales, trapped, holding their breath till they suffocated. Struggling uselessly against the nylon nets.

Three hundred thousand whales and dolphins died this way, every year. One every two minutes.

'Jesus Christ,' she said. Warm tears, mixed with rain, fell down her cheeks.

She stood, useless and tiny, next to these great, dead whales. She'd always wanted to see orcas. Now she had.

'Fuck!'

Beano was standing fast by one of the smaller whales, barking at it, then running away, coming back, front paws and head down, pointing and barking.

'Beano, leave it alone,' she shouted. But the dog ignored her, growling and barking ever louder. 'I said, leave it alone!'

She wanted some dignity for the poor things. She grabbed Beano by the scruff of the neck, and yanked him away. It was a young one, this whale, half grown, maybe a year old. Its mouth was open, its tongue lolling. It was just as dead as the others.

She put a hand on the young whale's head, stroking the rubbery skin, and felt suddenly ashamed of being human. Of what humans *do*.

She looked into the whale's eye. 'Sorry.'

That black pupil moved. A huge, rolling marble. The eye looked at her, glinting bright and fierce. It set Hannah's skin on fire, being looked at this way. A loud *phoosh* sound burst through the wind and rain as the whale breathed out of its blowhole, filling the air with a fishy stench.

Even in that mad second Hannah had a clear thought. This

wasn't like a dog or horse looking at you. It wasn't like *any* animal, or human, looking at you. It was something else.

Beano was back, down on his paws, barking.

'No, Beano. Stay,' she shouted, letting the dog know to behave. Not to bark and run around. Not to make the whale more scared than it already was.

Then a cry came from the whale. A long, desperate whine. The eye swivelled, looking at the other whales.

'Bloody hell,' said Hannah, her voice trembling.

What to do now?

She stroked the whale, blown away by it, gazing at her. Like it was looking *into* her.

What to do?

She wanted to comfort it, to talk to it.

But that wouldn't save its life, would it?

'Come on, Hannah, come on. Think!'

She stood back and checked the whale over, the biologist in her getting to work. No net injuries. A female. Juvenile. It had probably followed the others in.

She reached into her coat for her phone. She'd call Jake and tell him to get help. Then she remembered: he was surfing.

'Damn you, Jake!' She'd phone Dad instead.

There was no service.

She'd have to start sorting this herself.

She took some pics with her phone, running around the group of whales, getting photos from all angles. Seven of them in all.

She saw two move, heard their *phoosh* breaths.

'Don't panic, stay calm,' she said. She tried to fight the tears. They wouldn't help the whale any more than words.

Hannah searched her mind for what she knew. For the options. The sea was just starting to go out. She could see the tideline. It'd be hours before the sea came back and covered the whales. The tide might free the live whales. But then they might stay with dead or injured family members. Or be so exhausted, so heavy and so robbed of the buoyancy of salt water that their internal organs would collapse.

If there was hope – any at all – Hannah would need people, trained MMRs: Marine Mammal Rescuers. They'd need blankets soaked in buckets of seawater to keep the skin supple. Floats, inflatables, boats. Fish? Would she need to feed them? How would they drink if they were out of the sea? Cetaceans desalinate water. How could they do that on land? There was so much she didn't know.

Even while she was working out what to do, who to call, what she needed, a part of her was panicking.

Why this? Why now?

Right, she told herself. *Get organised*. Steve Hopkins, her old biology teacher. He was an MMR. He'd done seal rescues and some dolphins. She'd call him as soon as she got back.

Please don't die, whale.

She knew people with boats. RIBs, rigid inflatables. Could they get pontoons too? All the rescues she knew about had been dolphins or seals. The young orca was bigger. But not *that* much bigger.

Please. Live.

Hannah stroked the whale's head again and looked into its eye.

'It's okay,' she said. 'It's okay.' It wasn't, though. Everything for the whale was as bad as it could be.

'It's okay.' Hannah said it anyway. To herself. 'It's all right . . .'

Don't say it.

'It's okay . . .'

Don't give it a . . .

'Little One.'

. . . name.

'I have to go. I'll be back, Little One. I promise.' She leant over, above its eye, and kissed it. Then ran, calling Beano to heel.

Jake

WONDERFUL?

Fan-freaking-tastic, more like.

There was no need to duck-dive the waves. There was a conveyor-belt rip current by the cliff that took him straight out, right past the breakers. He got out back, to the side of the break point, then slowly edged into the reef, keeping a careful watch on the horizon. Waiting for sets. Getting in the sweet spot. Paddling like crazy when the right wave came.

They were big. But the power in the water was organised. It was easy surf to predict, easy to catch, the waves seeming slow at first, but walling up fast once he was on them.

Solid glass ramps to rip up.

He made huge, carving turns.

He came off each wave while it was still green, before it

closed, then paddled into the rip and out again. A merry-go-round.

He could have surfed it for hours. Happily. Part of him wanted to, wanted to delay meeting Hannah, but he couldn't stop thinking about her. After a few waves, the thoughts and doubts seeped into his mind. If Hannah went to Hawaii without him . . . how long before she hooked up with some geek biologist? Someone with prospects and a nice tan. They weren't all going to be gay or ugly.

He mistimed a wave, so it went under him. Then another. His concentration was shot with all this damn *thinking*.

He'd done a few good waves. Time to get out. Start dealing with stuff.

He got a wave in and walked out of the water.

There was a cave to the left of the beach, tucked under the headland. A deep space filled with boulders, plastic bottles, floats, bits of net and chunks of wood.

The rubbish was always worse after a storm, but now the cave was filled with it. He could hardly see the rocks. It was ugly, but weirdly impressive. A mountain of stuff.

Something caught his eye. Among the orange plastic and old tin cans was a crate.

He remembered what Goofy had said about all sorts washing up. Gifts from the sea gods.

He put his board on a pile of seaweed, and clambered over the rocks.

There was something in the crate, no doubt about it.

He dragged it off the rocks. It was heavy.

He pulled it down to the small pebble beach.

Whatever was in the crate was covered in thick, sealed plastic. He'd need a knife to get inside it.

He didn't have a knife. Or anything. He looked around, and found a rusted can lid. It wasn't sharp, and his arms were surf-knackered, but he stabbed at the plastic hard, and after a few goes made a small tear.

Jabbing and yanking, he made the tear into a gash. Underneath was another layer of plastic. He cut again, curiosity driving him. He saw what was inside. Several packages of it. Something white, the size of large books, taped tight.

His mind drew a blank. There was no label, no brand. So could it be . . .

His heart burned with the answer, before he even thought it. 'Drugs. Holy crap.'

He got the fear, raw and strong, like seeing a beast of a wave rising out the sea and heading his way. He looked at the path. Up at the cliff. Out to sea. There was no one there. But he felt in the open. Naked.

He cut at one of the packages. White, crystal powder burst out, coating the rusted metal then melting in the rain.

He dropped the can lid and dragged the crate up the rocks and into the depths of the cave. High up. Higher. Deeper. Beyond the tideline, where the rock was light and dry. Where the sea never reached.

He covered it in rocks and rubbish to hold it there. Then he clambered back down, picked up his board, and headed off.

What to do now?

Tell Hannah? Mum?

No, he'd tell the police. Straight away. He'd make the news. *Local surfer finds haul of drugs.*

How much? What kind? What was it worth? Jake had no idea. He wasn't into pills or powders.

Yeah, he'd tell the police, and the local papers and TV news.

Hannah would be well impressed. Plus: brilliant excuse for being late this morning.

Halfway up the cliff path he looked back into the cove. It was dead on high tide. He kept looking. Had he seen something? A broken pole, thick as a mast, poking out of the sea. Had he? The water was a mess of thrashing waves at the shore break. It was playing tricks with him. But . . . There.

Ten metres out was the broken mast of a boat. It was exposed when the waves sucked back. And, just below the surface, a wreck.

That was where the drugs had come from.

'D'you know what?' he said to himself. 'You could always sell it, dude. Get rich.' Maybe this was a gift from the sea gods like Goofy had talked about? Maybe it was meant to be. If he sold the drugs, he'd be able to fund Hawaii, easy.

Jake shook his head. He laughed at his own joke.

Hannah

HANNAH HAMMERED AT the front door till it opened.

'Hannah, darling. Is everything all right?'

She threw herself at Dad, soaking his dressing gown.

'What's he done?' said Dad.

'Noth-nothing to do with Jake. There's . . .' Hannah forced the words through her sobs. 'There's whales. Killer whales. On the shore.'

'What?' Dad held her shoulders, looking into her eyes. 'What do you mean, whales? Why are you crying? Calm down.'

'They're stranded. Dead mostly. But there's a young one, alive.' She pictured its black, marble eye. She heard its cry, like it was real. Calling to her, above the wind and rain.

'Come and sit down. I'll make you a cup of tea. We'll phone the coastguard.'

Hannah pushed his hands off her. She went to the hall and called Steve Hopkins. She got his answerphone.

'Mr Hopkins. It's Hannah Lancaster . . .' She took a deep breath, trying to calm the trembling, to put steel in her voice. 'It's eight fifteen. There are several stranded whales, orcas, at Whitesands beach. Some dead, at least two alive. One's a juvenile female . . . I think. Call me. No . . . get here, please. I'll text you some pics.' She left her number, then used the phone again, punching the buttons with her finger. She got Jake's voicemail too.

'Jake. Call me!'

Why wasn't Mr Hopkins answering? Why wasn't Jake? Why was Dad doing nothing, apart from offering tea? It was like swimming through treacle.

'I need him and he's surfing,' she sighed heavily, leaning against the wall.

'Well,' said Dad. 'It's not the first time, is it?'

Hannah didn't bite. Now wasn't the time.

She phoned again, punching the buttons with her finger. Got an answer message, again.

'Call me, Jake. I need you.'

Jake

'YOU HAVE TO be kidding me,' said Goofy. He was sunk deep in his sofa, staring at the small jar on the table. It was a quarter full of white powder.

He stood up, went to the kitchenette and came back with a teaspoon, then opened the jar and scooped some powder on to the table.

They both leant over to examine the small mound of boulders and crystal dust.

'I thought you might know what it is,' said Jake.

'Oh, really. Why's that, then?'

'I thought you might have . . . I dunno. I just did. Could you could test it?'

In films, people licked a finger and tasted a dab. Goofy just stared at the powder.

'I come down 'ere to get away from that kind of shit. I don't care what it is.'

'I thought you came here to surf?'

'Mostly.'

Jake thought of all the things Goofy had said about his past. And not said. Maybe Goofy had run from something as much as to something.

'*Any* idea?' said Jake.

'Coke at a guess. MDMA, maybe. Smack, possibly. Why'd you want to know?'

'So I know what to do with it.'

'You don't *do* anything with it. You tell the law. I hate the bastards, but they have their uses. You don't want some kids finding it, do you?'

'Any idea how much it's worth?' said Jake.

'If it's coke, there's more than a few grams there. A grand? Two, three, maybe.'

Jake sat bolt upright. He thought of the *full* jam jar under his bed and the crate hidden on the beach. How much money was in there?

'A thousand quid, plus? For that tiny amount,' he said.

'Yeah. For that tiny amount,' said Goofy. 'Why, how big is the package it came from?'

'Big,' Jake said. The air in the room was suddenly thick, the roaring wind a million miles away.

Goofy stared at him, his eyebrows knotted. 'You don't

want to worry about this, Jakey. You're getting on a plane soon.'

'And how am I going to afford that?' Jake shrugged, and nodded. Suggesting something. It took Goofy a few seconds to twig what that something was.

'Oh no,' said Goofy. 'No, no, no, no, no. You *are* kidding.'

'Imagine it, Goofy,' said Jake in a forced whisper. 'All that dosh. Thousands. More.'

Goofy stood up, keeping an eye on the small hill of powder, as if it was a coiled snake waiting to spring up and bite him. 'This ain't a bit of weed, Jake. This is ten years in prison. More, depending on . . . How much is there?'

Jake didn't want to freak Goofy out. Not more than he already was. Better not tell the whole truth. 'The package is about the size of a bag of flour. Is that a lot?'

'No, Jake. *This* . . .' Goofy pointed at the table, 'is *a lot. That's* a small mountain. You're talking about the entire Himalayas. Tens of thousands, like. More possibly.'

'Enough to get us made. For life.'

Goofy started pacing the flat, rubbing his hands together, his voice getting louder. 'Enough to get *you* banged up with rapists and murderers till your hair's gone grey!' He marched to the door, and opened it, letting in a blast of wind and rain. He looked around, then came back in.

'Did you see anyone down there? Did anyone see you?'

'No . . . Hold on . . . one guy. Yeah, this surfer. He'd been down before me. Older bloke with a craggy face.'

'Anyone else?'

'No, why?'

Goofy didn't appear to hear the question. He walked to the table, picked up the jar, put it just below the level of the table and brushed the powder back in with his finger. He put his hand to his mouth, as if to lick off the white stain. He paused, then licked it anyway. He looked at the ceiling, thinking. Then nodded.

'That's high-grade cocaine, Jake.' He went quickly to the sink and poured the powder in. He put the tap on full, then rinsed the jar out.

'What you doing?' said Jake, standing. 'That's more than a thousand quid!'

'Bollocks. I've seen what this poison does to fellows. Girls too. It's not happening to you, brother. Coke is evil shit, Jake.'

He turned and held the clean jam jar out to Jake, beaming.

'What the hell? Look at us, Goofy.' Jake stood up and pointed at his mate, then at himself.

'What d'you mean?'

'Where we headed? What kind of future we got?'

Goofy looked down at his stained jeans, at the rented bedsit with its damp walls and fag-burned carpet.

'Where we going, eh?' said Jake.

'We do okay.'

'*Now.* Plenty of surfs, beers, laughs. But in a year. Five?'

Goofy just shrugged.

'I need to get on that plane,' said Jake.

'Hawaii's not that important.'

'It is. Hannah is. This is a chance, Goof. A gift from the sea gods, like you said. I'll get rid of a load of it cheap. Just enough for a ticket, maybe a bit of spends. To set me up. I've got it figured out. I want to be a board shaper.'

'So does every surfer. You have to be good, to get experience.'

'I *am* good. I'm good with boats and wood; I've shaped a bit with Ned. I know surfing as well as anyone.' He could convince Goofy. If he'd just listen! 'I get there, right? I work, for free, with Alan Seymour Boards. Learn the craft. I come back with a rack of boards shaped in Hawaii. Who else round here can offer that?'

'All right. It's a good plan. If anyone can pull it off, you can. But you ain't funding it like this. Not if I can help it.'

'You won't help me?'

Goofy folded his arms. He stood, biting his lip. 'I can't get involved in anything like that.'

'Come on, Goofy. I helped you when you needed it.'

Goofy looked at Jake sharply. Jake was reminding Goofy of when he had arrived in Cornwall. A crusty loser, with a surfboard. Who'd needed clothes, food, a place to stay. Time to call in that favour. It was a rotten thing to do, but he was desperate.

'You helped me get out of shit,' said Goofy. 'Not into it. *I can't help.* Look, go see yer man Ned. He might help you. He sells a bit more than boards.'

'Yeah, weed. He's known for it.'

'More than weed I heard.'

'Ned? I never knew.'

'Well, he doesn't advertise, does he? Any case, *he* might know someone. Or someone who knows someone. Good luck.'

'Thanks, Goofy.' He opened his arms wide for a bear hug. Jake's way of saying: *We still okay?* Goofy hugged him, then held him at arm's length, keeping a tight grip on his shoulders.

'I'm telling you about Ned for one reason, so you don't start trotting into pubs asking random folk if they want to buy drugs. You'd only end up arrested, beat up or ripped off. Possibly all them things. You still might. And be careful. Ned ain't exactly sensible. Open his head, and there's no brain, just dozens of tiny monkeys, dancing. I don't think he knows what year it is most of the time, he's smoked that much. Now get out of here. Go see that bird of yours. Seeing 'er might put sense in your thick head.'

Goofy slapped Jake on the back as he went out of the door.

The door closed behind Jake with a cold thud.

He was alone. He'd wanted Goofy by his side. No one would mess with him, then. You could rely on Goofy.

Ned was a different story.

Hannah

THE CLOCK ON the kitchen wall told her it was an hour since she'd made those calls. And so far, nothing. She paced up and down the kitchen, biting her nails.

'Hannah!' said Dad. 'Darling. Why don't you sit down? Take your coat off.'

Mum and Dad were sitting at the table. At one end, Mum had laid breakfast: china cups, a rack of toast, a bowl of freshly boiled eggs. At the other end, Hannah had piled up blankets, a bucket, a camera and a notebook. Beano sat at the door, watching her, unsure if he should go and lie in his basket, or if they were off for another walk.

'Hannah, sit down,' said Dad.

'The whales . . .'

'The whales will wait till this marine-rescue chap calls, or arrives. There's *nothing* you can do yourself, is there? It's best to wait here.'

She hated Dad being right. She hated his self-confident, *knowing-he-is-right*-ness. Hannah wanted nothing more than to pelt down to the beach. To see Little One. To try to comfort the young whale. That much, at least.

'Hannah, please eat something,' said Mum.

'I'm not hungry,' she snapped. Then quickly added: 'Sorry.'

'Okay, darling. I'll make up a packed lunch.'

'Thanks.'

'You pamper that girl,' said Dad.

The phone rang in the hall. It hadn't rung three times before Hannah answered.

'Hannah Lancaster? This is Steve.' She could barely make out his voice through the crackle and shrieking wind. She put a finger in her other ear.

'Our people are down here now,' he said. 'Sorry I didn't call earlier. I've come off the beach to get a signal.'

'Oh. Right. Great. I'm coming down.'

'You haven't told anyone about this, have you?'

'No. Why?'

'We don't want crowds – they get in the way. We need to keep the media away too, as long as possible.'

'I'm coming down. I can help,' she said.

'We have all the help we need. But if you want to come

and watch . . .' Steve's voice drowned in white noise. 'You're breaking up . . .'

'How are the whales?' The line was dead.

'Is everything okay?' said Dad. He was right beside her. So was Mum.

Hannah dodged past them, grabbed the bucket, shoved the blankets and notebook and camera inside it, and left.

'Wait,' Dad shouted through the open door, holding Beano by the collar. 'I'll get my coat.'

Hannah

HANNAH STOPPED RUNNING and stood on the sand, watching.

The whales were the same. Limp, giant statues. The sea had retreated to mid-tide, as though it had dumped the whales and run off, leaving them to die.

The rain had stopped. Two girls in hi-vis orange jackets stood inside a fence of yellow netting that had been erected round the whales. Outside the cordon, a small crowd watched as rescuers in waterproofs poured buckets of seawater on to blankets and towels that had been laid over the whales' bodies.

Hannah counted. Three with towels and blankets draped over them, and four without. That meant three alive, four dead.

Little One was one of the three. Hannah's heart sang. She ran to the cordon and dropped her bucket, ready to climb over, to go and see the young whale. But a young woman stepped in front of her.

'Sorry, Miss. Marine-rescue team only.'

'I've done training, I'm not qualified yet, but . . . is Steve here?'

The girl pointed. Steve stood behind the whales talking into a brick of a radio phone. Hannah waved. He gave her a quick smile. Hannah looked at Little One. The whale's head moved, slightly, its eye rolling around, and – she was certain – seeing her. Its tail lifted and dropped. The whale moaned. A low cry of despair that reached inside Hannah and tore at her heart.

She stepped towards the fence, ready to climb over.

'Hannah,' said Steve, walking over.

'What's going to happen?' she said.

'We don't know yet,' said Steve. His face was pale, his forehead creased with stress.

'Can I come in? I want to see the young one. When I found them I knew they weren't *all* dead, because she cried out to me.'

'You understand how this works, right? How serious this is.'

She did. She understood too well.

An older, serious-looking man was examining the whales. He had a stethoscope and a large oilskin case. He was a vet at a stranding, there to sort the living from the dead, the healthy from the sick, the ones that had hope from the ones that didn't. Inside the bag would be vials, some full of vitamins and minerals, others loaded with poison ready to be injected.

Hannah swallowed hard. She wanted to be a marine

biologist. She'd see plenty of dead, and dying, whales in years to come. She had to get used to it.

Steve got close, so no one would overhear. In the low tone of a doctor delivering bad news he said, 'That animal is not in good shape. Even if we refloat it, it won't leave its mother, who is dead. And if it did, it wouldn't survive out there,' he pointed at the raging sea.

'No. No . . . you can't.' Hannah wanted to be strong, but she felt like the wind might knock her over.

Steve shook his head. 'We're set up for seals and dolphins. We don't have refloat equipment for whales. If the tide is high enough in the next day or so, we *might* be able to dig a channel, and get the healthy adults out. But the highest spring tide is what deposited them here . . .' He shrugged. 'Emotion can't get in the way. We'll do what we can, but in the end putting these whales down may be the kindest thing we can do.' He looked deep into her eyes. To see if she got it. To see if she'd be a pain about this.

'That's it, is it?' she said, looking past him, at Little One She felt anger rising like a tidal surge. 'Dig a ditch, see if the whales swim out, and if they don't, kill them?'

'Keep your voice down,' said Steve, through his teeth.

'Why? You don't want people knowing the truth?'

'Hannah, sweetheart,' Dad appeared at her side, getting a hold on her arm, trying to pull her away.

She twisted her arm out of his grip. 'Don't "sweetheart" me, Dad.' She turned back to Steve.

'You don't have the equipment, right?'

'No.'

'Who does?'

'Sorry?' He gasped, exasperated by her naivety. He waved at one of his team and held a finger up. A sign: *One minute. Soon as I get rid of this girl.*

Hannah leant over the fencing and poked him in the chest.

'There's a team in Massachusetts, north-east USA, who rescue stranded pilot whales all the time. Their pontoons will be big enough for the smaller orcas. Get them.'

'Get them from America? You have no idea . . .'

'Get their equipment too.'

'That would take days and cost thousands.'

'How long can we keep these whales alive?'

'Forty-eight hours. Seventy-two at the outside. After a couple of days on land their internal organs will start collapsing. Their bones will start breaking. You can't get that equipment here that quick. Even if you did, it would *probably* be too late. *And we don't have that kind of money.*'

'How much?' Hannah folded her arms, staring at her old teacher.

'Ten thousand. Twenty if we had to charter a plane. Even if we could manage it, even if the whales didn't die before the team got here, in all likelihood the calf is the only one we could refloat and it would probably still die. No one's going to fund that.'

Hannah shook her head. 'She's a juvenile, not a calf. She

might join another pod. One of the others might foster her. It's happened before. North Vancouver. San Juan Islands. I'm calling Paul Rocca. He'll know.'

'You *know* Dr Rocca?'

'Yes. I'm one of his interns. Now, you going to let me in?' Hannah was making a powerful nuisance of herself. It felt good. It felt right.

Steve shrugged, sighed.

'Go home, make your calls. But you're wasting your time.'

Hannah looked at Little One again. A girl was slowly pouring water over the whale's back. Hannah had a strong, sick twinge in her gut. It was concern for the whale, but also a pang of jealousy. *She* wanted to care for Little One. *She* had found her on the beach. They'd found each other.

'I want to see Li— the whale,' said Hannah. 'Can I?' Not forceful now. Pleading. 'Steve . . . please?'

'No. And you know why. No emotional attachment. It doesn't help.' Steve looked to her dad for help. Dad took Hannah's arm and pulled her gently, but firmly, away.

Jake

JAKE STOOD OUTSIDE Ned's house. He checked his phone: another message from Hannah. Shit. He turned it off. He'd call her. Right after he got this sorted.

Ned's workshop was in his garage.

Above the main garage door, Ned had once painted a graffiti pic of Little Red Riding Hood holding a basket of spray cans, with the words: 'Fear makes the wolf look bigger.' But he'd painted over it now. Maybe it was a bit attention-grabbing for a weed dealer.

Jake knocked on the door. The rap music blasting out was so loud, he guessed Ned couldn't hear. So he walked in.

A long rack of surfboards lay against one wall. Against the opposite wall were shelves filled with foam blanks, rolls of material and sanders. The equipment of a dedicated board shaper.

Ned stood in the middle of the garage, leaning over a board

on a workbench. His overalls were stained, and his hair was hanging round his face. He was hand-sanding the tail of the board. Blowing on it. Sanding a bit more. Blowing again. Smiling at his handiwork.

Jake waited for Ned to look up. Ned turned the music down.

'Thought you'd be out surfing, Jakey boy. Getting practice for yer big trip.'

'Been already. You?'

'Nah, waiting till it calms down a bit. Got this fix to finish anyway.' Any talk with Ned started this way. About surf. Often it stayed that way. 'You here for a board to take to Hawaii?'

'No. That's not why I'm here. Is Rag around?'

'Little Bro? He's off with his mates.'

'Sue?'

'Sue's history, mate. Gave me the sack, the silly mare,' he said, grinning and winking. That was Ned. Always grinning, always smiling. He had an easy flow about him. A permanent smile, which might be due to his almost always being stoned.

'You don't seem too upset,' said Jake.

Ned shrugged. 'Why you asking about Rag and Sue?'

'What I need to talk about. It's sensitive.'

'Oh, right.' Ned went to the shelf, found a tobacco tin and gave it to Jake. 'If yer gonna distract me from my work, make yerself useful.'

Jake opened the tin. Inside were papers, cigarettes and a small bag of weed.

'I don't really smoke,' said Jake.

'Thass all right. Make one fer me.' He got back to sanding, frowning, focusing.

'Funny that,' said Jake. 'It's drugs I've come about. I've got a sort of . . . business proposition.'

Ned froze for a second before he blew dust off the board.

'Yeah? Thought persians weren't your thing?'

'I need some dosh for Hawaii. Quick. Money doesn't grow on trees.'

'Yeah? Whoever said that never tried selling weed.' Ned chuckled.

'I'm not talking about weed.' Jake dug in his pocket and placed a small foil pack on the board, in front of Ned. 'Can you tell me if this is . . . any good? I can get more. But I need help selling it.' Jake carefully opened the foil envelope, revealing the powder inside.

Ned went and turned the music off.

'How much did you pay for that?' he said.

Jake's brain scrambled for an answer. 'Um. Fifty.'

Ned shook his head. 'Dude. You've been ripped off.'

'Oh,' said Jake. 'Is there not fifty quid's worth there?'

'Oh, yeah. Fifty notes' worth of baby-milk powder, mixed with a bit of speed, probly. But not coke.'

'How do you know?'

Ned laughed at Jake's innocence. 'If that was Charlie, you'd have coughed up more than that. Who sold you this shit?'

'Never mind. If it's duff I'll take it back.'

'Dealers don't do refunds, you muppet. Anyway, why've you bought coke if you don't do it yerself?'

'Can you just give it a try?' said Jake, trying not to sound impatient.

'All right, just for you . . .' He rooted around his shelves and drawers, till he'd found a roof slate, a credit card and a ten-pound note. He set all this up on the table, next to the board he was working on. Using the card, he carefully scraped a small bit of the crumbly powder out of the foil and on to the slate, and set about chopping at the small boulders and lumps till he was left with nothing but fine powder. He used the edge of the card to form a line. He didn't snort it, though. Not at first. Ned licked the end of his finger, dabbed it in the end of the line of snowy powder, and tasted it.

Fun drained from his face. He looked at Jake, dead curious. And serious. He rolled up the tenner, leant over, and Hoover-snorted the line of powder. He stood up. Stick-straight, like he'd had an electric shock.

'Holy shit,' Ned wheezed.

'Well?'

'Holy shit!' Ned stood up, sniffing, blowing, walking around, like he was too big for the room all of a sudden. 'Holy shit!' Ned sucked in deep breaths, one after the other. He clicked his fingers, repeatedly. It was weird. 'Holy shit.'

'Stop *saying* that, Ned. What's it *like*?'

'Like a fucking rocket, that's what it's like. You paid a hundred for this much blow? The dude who sold it hasn't a clue. But

I'll bet he's got an *endless* queue of customers. Where d'yer get this?'

'Do you know anyone who'd want some? I can get quite a lot.'

'At that price? Yeah. I reckon I can find someone . . . Holy shiiiiiiiitt!' Ned was twitching, sniffing, shaking his head.

'What if I could get a *lot* more,' said Jake. 'A flour-bag full. Dirt cheap. And we made some money and split it?'

Ned stopped pacing, getting control of himself, blowing out deep breaths, focusing on Jake. There was no laughing now, no smiling. 'Listen, mate, I can take some and sell a bit, but I don't know *anyone* who could take that much gear.'

'I do.' It was a girl's voice. Jake spun round to see where the voice had come from.

A girl with long brown hair, wearing a biker jacket, was standing at the door. She had dark skin, dark eyes and dark make-up. She was smiling calmly, staring at the powder.

'Who the fuck are you?' said Jake.

'It's all right, mate,' said Ned. 'This is Tasha.'

'You said you were alone.'

'I said Rag and Sue weren't around. Don't panic. Tasha's cool.'

No wonder Ned hadn't been upset about Sue.

'You cut the music,' said Tasha. 'I figured you'd quit work and wanted to play.' She strolled to the table, licked her finger, dipped it in the powder and put it in her mouth. 'Ooh,' she said. Her voice was soft, sarcastic. And posh. 'That's nice. May I?' She took another dab.

Jake wasn't happy about this strange girl's appearance. But there wasn't a lot he could do about it. He shrugged.

The girl took another dab, then another. And another, rubbing the drug into her gums each time. She breathed deep. She kept licking her gums.

'Well, um, er, wow. *Woooow*. You *have* got something special here, um, what's your name?'

'Jake.'

'Jake. Hmm, right. Well, *Jake*. Did you say a flour-bag full? That's quite a lot of snow. But I might know someone who would be interested . . . if you can make it worth my . . . our while. Me and Ned that is. Do you fancy a bit yourself? Know what you're dealing with. Or in your case, just dealing. Or shall I polish it all off?' She smiled, lopsided, like she knew a secret he didn't. She grabbed the note off the slate and started rerolling it, then made more lines from the small hill. Jake watched, hypnotised. She offered him the note.

He took it off her. He didn't know why. He didn't even think. He just did it, and held the note in his fingers, looking at it.

Thoughts raced through Jake's head. Should he? Shouldn't he? What was so good about it? What if he liked it? Course he'd like it. People don't get addicted to shit they never liked in the first place.

What if he *loved* it? A *lot*?

Same.

And he had a virtually endless supply. He thought of what

Hannah would say, and what she'd do, if she knew what he was doing right now.

He gave the note back.

'All right, who do you know?' he said.

Tasha snorted some of the coke herself, then smiled at him again. There was nothing nice about it. She was like a cat. One that killed a lot of mice and birds.

Could he trust her? Did he have a choice? And was this actually, in any way, even *remotely* a good idea?

Was it?

Jake looked at the girl, Tasha, then at the cocaine, at Ned, who was still breathing heavily, and twitching.

He could almost hear the alarm bells. He had a bad feeling about all of this. Goofy had been right. As per.

'I must be nuts,' he mumbled.

'What's that, Jake?' asked Tasha, sniffing. 'Are you still not going to have some?'

'No. But thanks for helping me get a grip.'

'What?' said Tasha.

Jake's heart sank. Because he knew, in an instant, that he had to let it go now. He had to walk away, even if it meant not going to Hawaii, even if it meant waving Hannah goodbye at the airport. Because this, here, with Ned and the girl and the drugs, was insane.

Jake went to wrap up the foil, to leave. But Tasha put a hand out, stopping him.

'I'll need a sample, Jake. For the deal. Something to show.'

'Did you not hear me? D'you know what? Keep it. Sell it. Snort it. I don't care.'

Jake walked straight out of the garage and into the air.

He felt queasy. Genuinely sick. Dizzy. Like if he'd stayed in there a second longer he would have puked. He sucked sea-clean air into his lungs.

He took his phone out and turned it back on, ready to send a text to Hannah. To go and see her, quick as he could; to tell her all about this badly weird day. And to break the news about Hawaii.

It felt heavy. But it felt right too.

There was a message:

Come round later, early evening. I've got something to show you.

Hannah

'IT'S JAKE, FOR you,' said Dad.

She was still on the phone.

Jake skulked, hands in pockets. He looked like Beano when he'd been naughty. He looked tired.

Hannah finished the call: 'Okay, yes. If you can email the details . . . Great. Of course, yes. We'll find the money. I'll get back to you later. Bye.' She put the phone down. 'Where've you *been*?' she said to Jake.

'Your last text said to come round this evening,' he said, with a shrug.

'You could have called.'

'Did. Left a message.'

'Oh. Yeah. I have been on the phone and email a bit.'

'I needed time to think, any case. I've been trying to sort Hawaii.'

'And have you?' said Dad.

'*Dad.*' She glared at him till he disappeared. It was times like this – when he was questioning Jake and everything about him – that she wanted to say: *You almost made his family homeless.* But she never did.

'Sorry, babe. I'll explain,' said Jake. 'A lot's happened. It's been a weird day.' Jake smiled and opened his arms. She stepped forward, buried her head in the warmth of his neck, and waited for his arms to close round her.

'It's been a strange day for me too,' she said.

'Do you fancy a takeaway? We need to talk about . . . stuff.' He held her away, and looked into her eyes. He had a strange expression, neither happy nor sad. Searching. Loving.

'Are . . . you all right?' she said.

'Yeah, I'm fine.' He forced a smile, rubbed the tops of her arms.

'Okay. We'll talk. Later. But I've got something to show you.' She tore herself away from him and started pulling on her wellies and coat.

'What we need to talk about. It's important.' Jake was serious. Not being like Jake.

'It can wait, Jake. Trust me. Come on.' She grabbed her camera off a peg and slung it round her neck. Jake frowned with confusion.

'Where are we going?' he said.

'The tide brought something in. Something amazing.'

'What? Which beach?'

'Whitesands.'

His eyes narrowed. 'What did you find?'

'Jake, stop being strange. You'll see. Something amazing.'

★

The rain had stopped. The wind had died. But the sea raged on, a grey and white mess of crashing waves. The sky was darkening by the minute. But among the clouds patches of sky let through columns of dusky light. It was a sky to make Hannah stop and stare. A sky to photograph, normally. But now she could only think of whales.

When they got to the sand, she made him close his eyes. She led him by the hand.

Jake stumbled. 'Hannah, this is crazy. I want to talk to you about Hawaii. About a lot of things.'

'Hawaii's not important right now.'

'It isn't?'

'No. Don't you *dare* open your eyes till I say.'

'What you going to show me? Look, we *need* to talk.'

'*Come* on.'

In the half-light of a fading sky, she saw the whales. The sea had come a long way in, but not far enough.

Hannah wondered how the whales felt. Stuck in this alien world. With the sea – their home – so close.

The crowds had gone. There were just two girls now, tending to the live whales, pouring buckets of water over their backs.

When they got close, Hannah put a hand over Jake's eyes. She led him right up to the fence, before she took it away.

'You can open them now.'

Jake

AS HE WAS being dragged over the sand, Jake had planned how he'd tell Hannah about the drugs. How he'd almost been stupid. How he didn't have the money. How he'd given Mum what he did have. How even that wasn't enough. That he loved her, but he wasn't getting on that plane.

Perhaps she would understand. He'd tell her. Soon as he got the chance.

He waited, standing, listening to the sea, with her hands over his eyes.

'Right, you can open them now,' she said.

Words stuck in his throat. He stood there, stunned.

All sorts of ideas had gone through his head. She'd found drugs too. She was going to show him a pregnancy test, a wreck, a container full of trainers.

Not this. Not orcas.

He looked at the smallest one. Its eye regarded them, and he heard the *phoosh* as it exhaled.

It cried. A weak, haunting sound.

'Holy shit,' he said. 'Whales. Bloody whales. What . . . how?'

'We're going to rescue them, Jake. *I'm* going to rescue them. Will you help me?'

Jake was so shocked; so downright gobsmacked he couldn't compute what she was saying. He just stared at Hannah, then at the whale and back at Hannah, trying to take it all in.

A girl came to the fence and held up a hand. Before she could say anything, Hannah started:

'We're organising the rescue equipment. We need to assess the living whales.' Hannah waved her camera at the girl. 'Has Steve not told you? It's important. I have to report back this evening.' She sounded confident. Jake had never heard Hannah so determined.

The girl looked at them cautiously before pulling the plastic netting down and letting them climb over.

Hannah led Jake straight to Little One. She knelt down, eye to eye with the whale, patting its skin.

'Hi, Little One,' she said. The young whale cried out, then whistled and clicked. Its eye rolled, examining Hannah's face.

'It's like it's *talking* to you,' said Jake, and knelt beside Hannah. The whale looked at him too. He felt its naked stare burn into him. It whistled and clicked again.

'It is talking. *She* is talking.' Hannah stroked the whale's skin. 'Say hello to Little One.'

He knelt in the sand, beside Hannah. She took his hand and placed it on the patch above the orca's eye. How different this was from seeing an orca on a computer screen! This creature, shifting gently on the sand, its breath rising and falling, its rubbery, rough skin under his palm, was *looking* at him. It let out a long, gentle 'scraaawwwk'.

'Hello,' he said. Hannah put an arm round him, leant on him. Both of them had a hand on the whale. Jake felt a warm current running through him.

'Jesus,' he said, surprised by this feeling. The depth of it, the strength. '*How* do we rescue them?' he said.

'There's equipment can be flown over from America. Tomorrow maybe. The day after. But we need money.'

'How much?'

'Fifteen thousand.'

'Fifteen! . . . Jesus. Your dad?'

Hannah shook her head. 'He can't. Not that much. I've already asked. He's up to his limits with the marina project. Cash flow. I've got some, supposed to be for Hawaii, but it's a fraction of what we need.'

The thought of selling the drugs crept back into Jake's mind. He pushed it away. Forced it out.

Hannah continued, speaking low so as not to spook Little One, but sounding excited too. 'An appeal in the paper maybe. A rich whale-lover. There has to be a way.'

Yeah, he thought. *Some way*. Some*body* who had that kind of money.

'What happens if we . . . *don't* get the equipment?' he said.

'I can't say it,' Hannah whispered. She swallowed hard, breathed deep. He noticed that her hand, on the whale's black skin, was trembling.

The way she looked at the whale. Strong with determination one minute, weak with hope the next. Vulnerable. It was how she looked at him after sex; the way she'd looked when he'd first said: *I love you.*

'Will you help me, Jake? Will you help Little One?' Those sea-pool eyes were working on him. Gentle and wanting.

Little One called out again. Its head rose, and twisted slightly, as much as the poor thing could manage. It looked at him. It blew a breath from its blowhole.

Jake looked at the sky. It was getting dark. The wind was picking up again.

'Fuck it,' he mouthed, to the sky. To no one.

He had a sudden vision, of himself, waving Hannah off at the airport.

'Sorry about the dead whale,' he'd say. 'Sorry about Hawaii. Sorry about Mum being homeless too. But hey, can't be helped.'

'Fuck it,' he said, again to no one. 'Yeah. I will help,' he said to Hannah. The words fell out of him. 'Of course, babe. Of *course* I will.'

Hannah threw herself at Jake. She nuzzled her head into his neck.

'I'll get the money,' he said.

She kissed his neck.

'How, sweet boy? You can't even get the money for a plane ticket.'

'I can get it.'

'Where from? Did pirate treasure wash up in the storm? Is there fifteen thousand pounds in a sea-chest somewhere?' She burrowed in further, between his neck and his shoulder, and held him tight.

'I'm serious,' he said. 'I can get it.'

Hannah unburrowed herself. She looked at him. Hoping. Maybe even believing.

'I'm serious,' he said, again.

PART THREE

BETWEEN THE STORMS

www.Eye-Sea-Surfcheck.com

Forecast

Winds: medium southerlies 12–15mph

Conditions: calm

Waves: 5ft at 6–7 seconds wave period. Fun.

This is a gap, folks, just a little rest before things get serious again.

There's plenty of small surf on the north coast. Bigger on the south, but winds might mess it up a bit.

Surf the tail end of the storm. There's a fair bit to be had today, but tomorrow it'll go small. Storm was local, so not much swell generated.

If you like it easy: enjoy it while it lasts.

Longer term: there's a storm forming off Iceland and the US eastern seaboard that's gonna rewrite the rule book. Serious. Heavy.

UK landfall within days.

Jake

THE PUB CAR park was a quarter full. The cars were old and cheap. The motors of bar staff and morning boozers.

The Range Rover was old too. And dirty. But it still stuck out.

Jake looked around, and up. The car park was behind the pub, with high walls on either side. There were no windows. No security cameras.

Two people were sitting in the front of the Range Rover. Tasha got out, leaving the passenger door open. She walked up to Jake.

'He likes the sample. I'll wait in the pub,' she said, and walked off, leaving him stranded on the tarmac. He stood there, not moving, his heart thumping. Half of him wanted to scarper. The other half told him not to be a pussy. To get this done.

Jake tried to swallow, but he couldn't. His mouth was dry.

He took a deep breath, and walked to the car door. The man in the driver's seat was in his forties. A bit chubby, but strong-looking. Solid. He had short grey hair and wore a leather jacket.

The man looked at him, and raised his eyebrows as if to say: 'Well?'

Jake got in and shut the door. He thought he should offer his hand to shake. Or say something. But what? What do you *say* to start a drug deal?

'Where we going?' he blurted, pulling his seatbelt across his lap. His hand trembled as he plugged it in.

'We're not going anywhere,' the man said, in a soft London accent. He pushed the button on Jake's seatbelt. It zipped limply back across Jake's chest.

'Oh. Right.' Now what? A voice inside Jake's head told him to shut up, to not say *anything*. To not give away what a total kook he was.

'What do you want to do?' asked the man.

'Sell.'

'I know that. How much?'

Jake didn't know if the man meant the price or the quantity.

'How much do you want?' he replied. The man looked confused. He checked the wing mirror, then the rear-view mirror. He looked out of the window. Then at Jake.

'Tasha tells me you're a bit new to this. So, how about this? You meet me here later today, and we do the business. You give me your number. I'll let you know what time. You bring an ounce. I'll give you twenty quid a gram. You come with the girl, but you and me do the business. Okay?'

Jake's mind raced, calculating. That was hundreds of pounds, not thousands.

'Er, we . . . I want to sell more than that. A *lot* more,' he said, trying to sound confident. Again, the man looked at him like he couldn't figure him out.

'Do you trust me?' said the man.

Jake was thrown. He felt his face turning red. 'What?'

The man tapped the steering wheel. He sighed, impatiently.

'I said: Do you *trust* me?'

'Um. Yes?'

'Well, I don't trust you.' The man's voice was hard all of a sudden. *Not* friendly.

'Oh,' said Jake. This was going south. His hand moved to the door handle. He'd been mad to think he could pull off a drug deal. Time to go. He opened the door.

'Wait,' the man said. His shoulders dropped. He rolled his eyes. Then, speaking more softly: 'Close the door.' Jake did as he was told. 'Look, son. Point I'm making is this. I don't know you, do I? You don't know *me*. Not from Adam. So it's best to go steady. If we're both happy later on, we'll do it again. With a bigger amount. If that goes all right we talk about something serious. It takes time to organise cash, you know. How about that?'

'Okay.'

'Look, I know you haven't done this much. Mind if I ask if you've done this at all?'

'Not much. Really. Look . . . What you said sounds fine,' said Jake. It was fine. For now. How long would all that take? How much money would he make? Would it be enough? *Quickly* enough?

He gave the man the number of the pay-as-you-go Tasha had given him.

The man did another check of his mirrors. He looked at Jake, and gave him a quick smile and a nod.

It took Jake long seconds to suss that the meeting was over. He got out of the car and walked to the back door of the pub.

Tasha was sitting at a corner table. She'd got him a pint. He picked it up and necked a third of it, then sat down, collapsing against the wall. The whole thing had lasted no more than a few minutes. He hadn't been arrested, beaten up or ripped off, like Goofy said might happen. He was relieved.

'Well, *how* – did – it – *go*?' Tasha teased the words out. She sat close. In her tight black jeans and leather jacket, with her thick make-up and arms jangling with bracelets, she was half cat, half Cleopatra. 'I said, how did it go?'

'Okay.' And it had. Though it struck him now, how the man had decided *everything*. The price, how much he'd buy. Where and when. Jake didn't even have the guy's number, or know his name. 'We're going to do an ounce, then see. Get to know each other a bit. And he wants you there. The first time, in any case.'

'Great. Happy to help.'

Was she? She seemed too cool with it. A bit *too* pleased.

'Ah,' said Jake. 'Right. You want paying as well as what I'm giving Ned.' His heart sank. He knew he'd have to share the money. He'd promised Ned twenty per cent. But now Tasha was getting more involved. Maybe he'd be better off negotiating with her.

'I've said twenty per cent. For Ned . . . and you.'

She didn't blink.

'Is that okay?' he said.

'Oh, I don't want money, Jake.' The way she said it, it sounded dirty, secretive. What, then?

He realised, nodding.

'Right. You want some free coke.' Well, that was all right, he had plenty of that. Too much of that, and no money.

Tasha put up her glass for him to clink. He did, then downed the rest of the pint. Suddenly he had a thirst like he'd been surfing all day and it was Friday night.

There was more drama to come. This morning was nothing. But at least he'd made a start.

A bead of sweat snaked down his back, cold and unwelcome. *Think of the waves*, he told himself. Think of Hannah. Think of Hawaii. Blue skies and bluer waves. Think of the whale.

Soon they'd be on their way. Those dreams would be real, and skanky pubs part of a nightmare he could forget.

Hannah

'CAN YOU SLOW down? I feel sick.'

Dad liked to drive the Mercedes fast. Normally it was fine. It was fun. Now it made her queasy.

'It's because you've got your head in that thing,' Dad said, taking a hand off the wheel and pointing at her phone. 'You know you can't read and travel at the same time.'

'I don't have a choice, Dad. I'm waiting for an update.'

She was. *Any* update.

How were the whales doing?

Was there news from the US? (Which was crazy, because it was eleven in the morning in the UK and six on the eastern seaboard.)

Would they fly the equipment on a promise or part payment, or only on full payment?

How was Jake doing, getting that money? She'd find out today.

And why the hell hadn't she known she needed six months on her passport *after* her US exit date? And that she had to go to the post office to get her application fast-tracked?

She was seasick with these thoughts, crashing against the inside of her head like waves. She felt battered. Weak with hope for Little One. Still shocked by the sight of the giant corpses of Little One's family, lying in the sand. Tight-hearted with worry that the rescue equipment wouldn't arrive soon enough.

Seasick or not, there was no stopping this journey. Not for a while. She had to see it through.

The Mercedes ate up the coast road. She put her phone down, promising herself she wouldn't look at it again till they got to Penzeal, and stared through the window at the sea. Beyond the moor and cliffs, white horses lurched and pitched. The ocean rocked and swayed, restless in the aftershock of the storm.

It wasn't even proper autumn yet, but summer seemed forever ago. The calm azure days. The easy life of swims and lying on the sand. The storm had broken that dream, and woken her up.

'Dad,' she said, watching the rolling waters, 'why is life so easy one minute and hard the next?'

'Because it is.' He sighed. Hannah turned to look at him.

He was focused on driving. Intently. Lines and greyness marked his face. He looked tired.

'The marina, today?' she said.

'Yes, Hannah. The marina.'

It was Dad's big project. It would make more money than anything he'd ever done. They would be rich. Truly, finally, stupidly rich.

But it had consumed him that summer. Taken all his time. His energy. He hadn't even been sailing. Not once.

'How's it going?'

'We'll get there. It'll take more time and cost more money than the idiot project manager said. But we'll get there.'

For all his grouchiness, his seriousness, she admired him. Dad said what was going to happen and he made it happen. He had always been that way. The marina would open, and it would be a success. It was that simple. Dad saying, *We'll get there*, was just a way of stating that fact.

That was how she felt about Little One too. Never mind what Steve Hopkins said. She would be her father's daughter. She would make it happen.

'I'm dropping you at the post office,' Dad said. 'I'll pick you up in two hours. I know you need to get back to the whales, and to sort out this equipment. But before you go any further . . . Hannah.'

'Yes, Dad?'

'You are . . . *confident*, aren't you?' he said, carefully. 'That your whale and dolphin group, and your contacts, will get the money? That you will get this sorted?'

Hannah looked back out to sea. She imagined black fins arcing through the white peaks. Plumes of whale water-breath, puffing into the sky. One orca – smaller than the others – following, but managing to keep up. Just. She pictured the pod, heading into the deep blue. To a place far from land.

'We'll get there,' she said. Dad nodded his approval.

She hadn't told him that getting the money was all down to Jake. Lying, for now. She sneakily, *guiltily*, looked forward to seeing his face when she told him the truth.

She believed Jake when he said he'd get the money. Just like she believed Dad would make the marina happen. She didn't know how Jake would get the money. He wouldn't tell her. But she trusted him.

She loved him.

Hannah

THE APPLICATION DIDN'T take much time. She used the photo booth, filled in the forms and signed them. The new passport would arrive within five days. One less thing to worry about.

Now she had over an hour to kill. And Penzeal was a pleasant enough place to kill it.

The town centre was a maze of poky, cobbled alleys and small shops. A place that still had its own cafés, grocers and fishmongers, though fewer each year, as the supermarkets set up outside town.

Tourists swarmed there every summer. And left it deserted come autumn, leaving money in the tills, and too many gulls, fat from a summer feasting on chips and pasty scraps.

Dad's marina was supposed to rejuvenate the town by bringing people in what they called the 'shoulder season', either side of summer. Yachtees. Gin and tonic types with money.

Hannah thought about wandering down to the site, to see how it was coming along. But dense clouds were racing overhead, promising fresh showers. She decided to have a coffee in the Hillside Bay Café, and check her emails.

She didn't like the café much. It was a shiny blue and white space, more Bess and Phoebe's kind of watering hole. But it was quiet out of season, and it had a great view.

She walked in, went to the counter and ordered a coffee.

'Hey, stranger.' It was Phoebe's voice. She was sitting at a window table, sipping lattes with Bess. And Simon. Hannah's ex.

'Shit,' she said, under her breath. She didn't really *mind* seeing him. It was just bad timing.

'I'll bring your coffee over,' the woman said.

Hannah went and stood by the table, feeling awkward. 'Hi,' she said.

She hadn't seen Simon since the split, but he was still the same. The Barbour jacket. The hair: short at the sides with a bouncy fringe.

Phoebe leapt up and hugged her. Bess managed an embarrassed smile before focusing on her latte. Simon and Bess glanced at each other, as if they'd been caught at something. Maybe they had. Bess and Simon? *Well*, she thought, *good luck to them*. Bess had always liked Simon, she'd just hidden it. Badly. Hannah sat down.

'Look at you girls,' she said. 'The skinny latte twins, drinking skinny lattes.' It was a favourite joke, to make out they were twins. They had the same slim bodies and straightened dark hair. Today they both wore black jeans and knee-high boots. They had almost the same jacket on. One black, one navy blue.

'The elusive Miss Lancaster,' said Bess. 'Honey, we haven't seen you in yonks.'

'It was last week, airhead,' said Phoebe.

'Well, that *is* ages.'

'I've been madly busy,' said Hannah. 'You won't believe what I found . . .'

'Yeah, madly shagging that surfer. We hardly see you—' Phoebe winced, catching herself. 'Sorry, Simes.'

'It's okay. It's fine. How are you, Hannah?'

'I'm good. How are you? Did you get your grades?'

'Yes. Off to Oxford soon.'

'That's wonderful. No surprise, though. You deserve it.'

'And you. Getting ready for Hawaii?'

They chatted. Hannah relaxed, and felt a bit less awkward. She slipped into the old banter with Bess and Phoebe. It was okay with Simon too. Their families had been friends since the two of them were kids. Maybe it was good she'd run into him, so they could get through this. So they could get back to what they'd been before she'd made the colossal mistake of going out with him.

He was friendly too. Hardly the same guy who'd cried, called, begged.

She told them about the whales and the equipment.

'My sister's a researcher at South West TV,' said Phoebe. 'We should tell her. Get it on the news.'

'No,' said Hannah. 'Best to keep it quiet. It won't help the whales if there's a media storm.'

'Come on, Hann. Be real. It's only a matter of time before they find out. What harm can it do? It might help. They could talk about an appeal, for the money?'

'They won't do that unless they're sure the rescue will succeed. And they won't listen to me anyway. Steve Hopkins will tell them there's no chance. Besides, we need the money now . . .' Hannah paused, thinking. Maybe TV coverage *was* a good idea. If there was publicity, it would be harder for them to euthanise the whales. She thought of the vet, with his bag and his syringes. If there was media, they'd have to do *everything* they could, before they used those syringes. 'I dunno, Phoebe. It might be a good or a bad thing. Let me think about it.'

'I could help,' said Simon. 'With the money. Lend you a bit, till you get the full amount. I've got some saved.'

Bess snorted. 'Saved? You probably got fifteen grand from Granny for your birthday.'

'Thanks,' said Hannah. 'My boyfriend Jake is getting the money.'

'Oh, fine, then,' said Simon.

Phoebe glared at Hannah.

'Sorry, I didn't mean . . . Look, who knows. Yeah, that might be good. Thanks, Simon. Thanks for offering. Look, I've got to go. I'm meeting Dad. Great about Oxford, Simon. Girlies, I'll keep you posted.'

'You'd better,' said Bess. As Hannah stood to go, Simon reached out a hand and got a hold of her wrist.

'Hann. Can I talk to you?'

She felt a creeping up her spine. Memories of the break-up. His hand, a snake, about to coil round her and drag her down.

'I've got to go. Dad's expecting me.'

'It will only take a minute.'

Shit. She didn't want to talk to Simon about the past. But she didn't want to look like a bitch. She didn't want to be one.

'Okay. A minute.'

She marched out, telling herself to be strong. She had Jake and Hawaii as reasons why there was zero hope of her and Simon getting back together. She could use those reasons like weapons if she had to.

As soon as they were out the door, she turned.

'Look, if this is about how things ended—'

'I don't want to talk about us.'

There is no 'us', she thought, folding her arms. 'Oh, right. What, then?'

'I wanted to ask about our dads. What's going on?'

'What do you mean?'

'Their bust-up. The marina? I think that's what it's about. Dad's being secretive about the whole thing. Mum too. Did you not know?'

'I'm not just saying this, Si, but I have no idea what you're talking about. They had dinner not so long ago.'

'That's when they had this big argument.'

She remembered: the night they'd come home unexpectedly, to find empty wine bottles and a green Roxy dress on the kitchen floor. She'd been so wrapped up in that drama, she'd never wondered *why* they'd come home, instead of staying with Richard and Lottie like they always did.

'I don't know, Simon. I honestly don't know what's going on. Look, I really do have to go.' She turned, and walked quickly away.

'I meant it, about the money, you know,' he called after her.

'Thanks,' she replied, and kept going.

★

She walked down the hill, through the narrow roads, to the site where the new marina would be.

She'd seen the plans, the drawings. The sea-view apartments and restaurants. The artist's impression with gin palace yachts cruising in. She didn't much like the idea of it, but Dad said it would be good for Penzeal. He was probably right. What did she know?

The site didn't look like the drawings now. Not on a rainy, start-of-autumn day, with new jetties half built and the apartments not even started. When she'd visited in early summer, the place had swarmed with workmen. Now it was cold and grey and empty. Just a few blocks of concrete slabs, and steel girders. One truck. A crane standing idle on the dockside.

And no sign of Dad's Merc.

Shouldn't the place be busy? There were only three workmen, in hard hats and coats, slowly unloading crates from a truck.

'Hi,' she said.

'Yes, love?' said one of the men.

'Is Pete Lancaster here?'

'No, but I am, sweetheart,' he said, with a leering grin. His mates sniggered.

'This is Mr Lancaster's daughter.' Dave the foreman appeared from round the side of the truck. The men went back to their work.

'Hi, Dave, have you seen Dad?'

'He popped in for five minutes, then went off again.'

'Oh, right. How's it going?'

Dave took off his hard hat, and scratched his head.

'Not going much at all, to be honest. Waiting on materials, permissions and paperwork. That's what your dad says. Just getting a few odds and sods done in the meantime.' He sounded sad. Like a man who'd rather be busy than not.

'Okay. Thanks.'

She walked back up the hill to the post office.

When Dad picked her up, she waited a minute or two, till they were out of town, before she spoke.

'How's it going down at the marina?'

'Good,' he said. But his voice was heavy, his face clouded.

He seemed hardly there. Like there was a wall between him and the whole world. 'We'll get there,' he said. For once, he didn't sound like he believed himself.

She was going to ask more, but her phone bleeped.

Her heart leapt. An email, from America.

Hannah,

Re stranded orcas

After we spoke yesterday, we had lengthy discussions with Dr Rocca. He (and we) support your assessment. There is a reasonable chance of a successful rescue. The equipment will float a lighter adult female and the juvenile. Please note: the equipment will *not* float the live adult male. Unless he can be freed via a dug-out channel he will have to be euthanized.

The full cost is $15–$20,000.

We understand it can take time to organize that kind of money, and – as we know well – time is one thing you don't have in a whale rescue.

To help, we will fund $2,000 ourselves, and organize transport from this end.

You will appreciate we can only proceed with a solid guarantee, which you alone cannot provide.

To that end Dr Rocca has agreed to underwrite the commitment. What this means is that if – for any reason – you can't find the money, he is **personally** liable for the remaining money.

He is signing a contract to that effect.

Once in the UK, Steve Hopkins's team will have responsibility for the equipment.

We need a deposit of $2,500 via bank transfer to green light this. Bank details at foot of this email.

Please let us know if this all okay.

Good luck!

Adrenalin raced through her blood, her heart, her head. She sucked in a sharp breath, and quickly typed.

Yes, great, will transfer $2,500 asap.

Thank you.

Her thumb hovered over 'Send'.

'Dad, if I can get you two thousand quid, can you transfer it to the US, to start the rescue?'

He shrugged. Like she'd asked for twenty quid to buy a skirt. 'Sure,' he said.

She hit 'Send'.

Immediately, she typed in another email. To Dr Rocca.

Thank you, thank you, thank you, thank you!

Hannah XXXX

As soon as she had sent that, she received another email. This one from Steve.

Hannah,

Whales in good health. For now. However: more orcas seen offshore. Can't be coincidence. Must be same pod.

Do you have access to boat? Plan to go look for them first thing tomorrow: see how many and if in danger of stranding.

Too rough today.

S

Hannah felt a sea-surge inside her. Like being on a yacht, screaming through the swell, with the wind full in the sails.

Jake

THEY MET AT Jake's house in the afternoon.

Hannah let herself in. *Bounced* in. She flung herself at him. Her cheek was cool and wet from wind and rain. Fresh off the beach.

'I've been checking on Little One. Before that, I was in town. I've got so much news, Jake. The equipment's coming. I've said yes, we can get the money. There's more orcas at sea too.' She was babbling, bubbling. 'And . . .' she stepped back, sniffing, 'have you been on the beer?'

'Yeah. Celebrating, about the money.' He coughed. Laughed. Noticed how forced it sounded. Wondered how she'd react if he blurted out the truth: *I've been at the pub, selling cocaine.*

'It's brilliant, Jake. How?'

'Sorry, what?'

'Come *on*. Spill the beans. The big secret. You said you'd tell me today. *How* have you got the money?'

Jake froze, the words trapped somewhere inside him. He'd practised his story, in front of the mirror. But now, here? He'd never lied to Hannah. Not about girlfriends or money. Nothing.

For one crazy second he thought about telling the truth. Like it would be easier, *better*, to let it just fall out of his mouth.

'Um . . .'

'You said you'd tell me, Jake. Today, once it was sorted.' Hannah's face shone with hope.

He took a deep breath. 'You know I had a different dad from Sean and Hattie. And *his* mum, my gran, she died a while back. You know I never knew her. But when she died, we got a letter from a solicitor, saying I would inherit some money one day.'

'Yes . . .' Hannah's brow creased with confusion. 'But you said it wouldn't be for years.'

'Well . . .' Jake paused. He looked upstairs. There was Sean, at the top, skulking in the shadows.

'Sean, get down here.'

'I heard the door, I was just coming to see who it was.' Sean jumped the stairs three at a time, and stood, arms folded, chewing gum. 'Wass this about money?'

'Get lost,' Jake nodded at the door.

Sean crossed his arms. 'Nah.'

'I mean it, man. Give us some space. And I mean, *out*.' Jake pointed at the door.

Sean stuck his tongue out the side of his mouth and looked up to the ceiling, like he was thinking about it.

'Nah,' he said again.

Jake sighed. He thought about forcing him out. But Sean was getting tougher – and cockier – by the day. The little git *actually* liked scrapping.

Jake pulled the wad of notes from his pocket.

Sean looked at the wad, his head forward like a bug-eyed turtle. Jake peeled off a tenner and held it up.

Sean snatched the tenner. 'It's raining out there, bro.'

Jake peeled off a twenty. He grabbed the tenner back, and gave Sean the twenty. They waited in silence as he put his trainers on and left.

'You've got the cash already, then?' said Hannah, amazed.

'Er, not exactly. This is a loan, from Goofy. I'll pay him back, soon as I get the inheritance. I just thought you might need some upfront, like.'

'How much is there?' she said, biting her lip.

'There'll be enough for the rescue. More too.'

'More? Your mum's going to be thrilled. All the bills. The loans. April!' Hannah shouted, looking round for Jake's mum.

'She's not here, it's just us. Let's go upstairs.' He reached out and held her hands. 'To talk. Come on.'

In his bedroom, Hannah took her windcheater off, and threw it on the floor. They lay on the unmade bed, locked in each other's arms and legs.

'Come on, then, tell me.' She rubbed her hand on his chest.

Jake liked how she was so pleased. He warmed up, felt less 'stuck' about telling the lie.

'Well. Like I said, the will states if the house is ever sold I get a chunk of the sale.'

'But there was some kid, some relative and his mum living in it?'

'Right. I've been to see them.'

'Where is it?'

'What?'

'The house, where is it?'

'The Cape. Big place.' That much was true. But where it was exactly, what it looked like? He had no idea. 'They've agreed to let me have my share now. It'll be less than I would get in the long run, but I get it *now*. They're kind of buying me out.'

The words flowed. It was easier than he thought; to tell a big fat lie, but mix it with truth. The story about the house and the gran and the family he never knew was all true. But he hadn't been to see the house, or the people who lived there.

'I don't know what to say, Jake. It's brilliant. I can't thank you enough. But —' she grabbed a wad of his shirt in her hand — 'I don't *feel* right. You can't actually pay for it. You *need* the money. Your *mum* needs the money.'

'I'm not telling her about it till this is sorted out.'

'Why?'

'Just trust me, okay?'

'But Sean heard.'

'I'll deal with Sean.'

'It's not right, though. This is *your* money. I've had offers of help.'

'Who?'

She let go of his shirt. 'Simon.'

'Why'd you call him? I *said* I could get the money.'

Hannah shook her head. 'I didn't call him – I bumped into him. Bess and Phoebe too. I said no. Obviously. I just think, well . . . this isn't right. It's not fair on you.'

'It's fine. And what about the whale? This is the only choice we have, Hannah.'

'Yes, but . . .'

He put a finger on her lips.

'If we don't do this it's going to die, right? And you've said yes. To the equipment.'

'She would die, yes, but . . .' Hannah was struggling with this. But not that hard. 'We *are* going to need that equipment. The whales are doing okay, but there's more offshore, we're going to go looking for them at dawn tomorrow. So, okay. Okay. You're a hero. Thank you.' They kissed. She lingered, letting his tongue explore the space between her lips, accepting his body against hers. More than that; hungry for it.

'You'd better let me go,' she said. 'I'd better get back to things.'

'Let you go?' he said, like it was a stupid idea.

Her hand slipped under his shirt.

'It is raining outside, Mum and Hattie won't be back for a while. Just saying.'

She smiled. 'Well. Maybe I could stay a *little* longer.'

He looked at her, under the quilt. And felt sick. Desire and guilt at the same time. The wonder of this girl, who believed in him. Who trusted him.

He kissed her, felt her skin. The space between them vanished, and the whole world with it.

Jake

JAKE SNOOZED ON the bed after Hannah had gone. The quilt was still warm from her, and he still had the smell of her on his skin. On his fingers too. It made him stir, wanting her all over again.

The memory of sex drifted slowly away. And all those other thoughts and memories returned.

Lies. Money. Drugs.

The sex had been shelter from all that.

They'd gone back to what they were before. What they'd be again, when all this was done.

Being with Hannah had calmed him, had eased the madness in his head. The lie was something he'd had to get out of him. It had been as hard as meeting in pubs and doing drug deals, harder in some ways. He didn't care what Ned, or Tasha thought of him. But this was Hannah.

'Fuck, fuck, fuckity, fuck, fuck,' he groaned, into the pillow. 'I'm the biggest-ever shit, in the kingdom of shit.'

Better get up, do something, he thought. If he stayed lying on the bed, it would all just whoosh around his brain, not going anywhere.

He heard a footstep on the stairs, soft as a cat's.

Maybe it was Hannah, coming back to surprise him. He got up, grabbed a towel, wrapped it round himself, and threw the door open.

Sean froze on the stairs. Jake came out and blocked his way.

'What you sneaking about for?'

'I'm not.'

'Yeah, you are. You're clumsy as shit. Why did you sneak back in? What's that in your hand?'

Sean put his fist behind his back. He flattened against the wall, then tried to push past. Jake got hold of him, pulled his arm, grabbed his wrist and Chinese-burned him.

A small bag dropped on to the landing. Jake snatched it up.

'What's this?' said Jake. But it was clear what it was. Weed.

'Nothing.' Sean tried to get by. Jake blocked him again.

'Jesus, Sean. You're fifteen. What would Mum say?'

'You're not going to tell her.'

Jake sighed. 'No. I'm not.' That was the rule. Always. No matter what. Jake waggled the bag in front of Sean's face. 'I don't want this here. I'm not stupid, I know I can't stop you. But not here.'

Sean just shrugged. 'What's this thing about money? What Hannah said. You going to get this inheritance?'

'Not exactly. Kind of. Look, I'm not telling Mum yet, right?'

'Why not?'

'Because I don't *want* to. It's my business. I'll see right by her. All of us. I promise. Okay?'

'Okay . . . If I can have my weed back.' Sean put his hand out.

Jake pocketed the weed. Shook his head. He dug out a twenty-pound note. 'Go and spend it on, I dunno . . . cider.'

'It's harder to get than weed. You could buy it for me.'

'Don't take the piss.'

'If I can't go get stoned, I'm going surfing. Coming?'

'Nope. Can't.'

'Too big for ya?'

'Get one for me, yeah?' said Jake.

'Sure.' He grinned that idiot grin, and pushed past Jake to go and get changed.

Jake went to the bathroom to have a shower. And to flush the weed down the bog.

Jake

'OUCH!' GOOFY STUMBLED over a rock. 'Suicidal, this is. I can't see where I'm going.'

'Put the head-torch on,' said Jake.

'Not till we get off the coast path. Suspicious-looking, we are. Two fellows wandering around at stupid o'clock in the morning. Wetsuits and boards is one thing. But torches and rucksacks?'

'The boards are cover. We look like we're doing a dawny.'

'Why am I doing this, again?'

'For Hannah. For the whales.'

'Ah, right. For the whales. Well, it isn't for you, you daft sod, you can be sure of that. *And* I can't see. Why couldn't Ned do it? 'E's the one you're in cahoots with in this madness.' Goofy poked Jake in the shoulder.

'I don't trust Ned. Him and that girl are a way to help me

sell the stuff. I need you to help me get it somewhere safe. Now stop whining.'

They trudged the rest of the journey in silence.

When they found the path, they switched the torches on, and tackled the nasty climb down.

As he clambered, Jake looked out to sea.

The wind was dead now, and the ocean calm. The sea had done its worst, and laid off for a bit. But there were more storms heading their way. Worse ones. Jake didn't trust the sea not to ride up and wash the crate away. He couldn't risk that.

The cove was locked in dark and shadow, but out to sea the sky was clearing, and the stars fading in the lightening sky. A soft light was in the air and on the water; showing the yacht, exposed by the tide. Its mast was snapped. The top part lay on the deck, tangled in rope and sail.

The yacht reminded Jake of the beached whales. Once a magnificent thing but now lifeless, it listed right over, a gaping hole like a massive wound in its hull.

'That's a fancy yacht. Someone lost a bit more than their gear, didn't they?'

'We'll have a look when we've got the stuff. There might be more in there,' said Goofy.

Was there? It didn't matter. What was in the crate was enough. More than. But Jake was curious.

When they reached the cove, Goofy turned off his head-torch and took Jake's board off him.

'Let's just get on with it, shall we? I'll keep a lookout. You go and find the stuff.'

Jake followed the orange beam of his head-torch, clambering up the rocks, over plastic bottles and crumpled tin cans. He entered the cave. Water dripped off the ceiling in loud sploshes. His breath was spookily loud, echoing back at him.

The back of the cave was a mess of rocks and rubbish. Where had he hidden the crate? He pulled at boulders and junk, panicking. Had someone been there, found it, stolen it?

But then there it was. A corner of the blue plastic, under a chunk of wood.

He yanked and heaved till he'd unburied the crate, then dragged it out of the cave into the dawn light and turned off his torch.

Jake got his knife from the rucksack. He was about to cut the wrapping when a hand grabbed his elbow.

He turned. 'What—'

Before he got another word out, a rough hand smothered his mouth.

Goofy's face was inches away. His mad blue eyes were wide and alert. He took his hand off Jake's mouth and put a finger to his lips. Then he pointed to a dip between the rocks, just down from the cave.

Jake didn't need any other sign. His skin electrified, and his skull tightened with fear. He moved, silent and quick, till he was wedged tight, hugging the rock like he was trying to blend into it. Goofy squeezed in, right next to him.

'How many?' Jake mouthed.

Goofy held up two fingers.

'The boards?' Jake whispered.

'Behind a rock.'

Jake listened. After a few seconds, the squawk of a gull rang out. He looked at Goofy, questioning. Goofy cupped a hand to his ear. He was stone still. He had a large rock in his other hand. Jake was still holding the knife in his own hand.

He dared to breathe.

Then . . .

A gruff crunch of feet over shingle. A thud-squelch of boots on seaweed.

Jake looked upwards, to the cave. The crate was in the open. The rucksack too. If the men bothered to climb up, they would see.

Shit.

One set of footsteps thudded towards them, louder with every step. Goofy lifted his hand, with the rock in it. He tensed, ready to rise.

The footsteps stopped.

There came the sound of a zip, and the hiss of a guy taking a slash. So close, Jake could smell it.

'Could be it's still in the panels. Maybe it moved about a bit.' It was a Cornish accent. Nastily, scarily close.

'Yer man had a good look when he found her,' said the voice of another man, further away. This one a London, or Essex, accent. 'A fair bit's gone, he reckons.'

'She was covered in water then. Worth checking properly now. What if it washed out the boat? Could be hereabouts.'

Jake and Goofy looked at each other. Both mouthed: *shit*. Jake looked at his hand, with the knife in it. He couldn't feel his fingers. His whole hand was numb. And vaguely, distantly cold. Like it wasn't even his.

''E said he had a proper look round. If it's not still on the boat it must have come out when she went down. Out to sea or washed up along the coast. It's not 'ere. It's the big man's problem anyway, not ours. Let's just get on and get what's left of it, shall we?'

The other man zipped up and walked back to his friend. Jake let out a long breath. He heard slopping and splashing as the men waded to the boat.

Goofy let go of the rock. He shifted, turning round, to rise and look. Jake grabbed his arm and pulled him down, shaking his head.

'No,' he whispered. 'What if they see you? What if they've got guns?'

'Guns? Don't be stupid. I just want to see how big they are. Reckon we can handle them if we have to.'

Jake stared at Goofy, disbelieving. Goofy was grinning. He didn't seem scared. Not even worried.

Goofy had a careful peek, then dropped back down. Something had washed the grin off his face. He held up two fingers and a cocked thumb. He waved his hand about, then tucked it under below his armpit. He was miming a gun.

'No,' Jake mouthed. Goofy nodded, slowly. 'Oh shit. Oh shit.' Jake put a hand over his heart, just in case it thumped through his ribcage and splattered over the rocks.

The next sound was a high whine, like an electric drill maybe.

It went on for minutes before it stopped.

A couple more minutes passed, with the men talking. But Jake couldn't hear what they said. Then there came loud splashes as the men jumped back into the sea.

What if the men could see the boards from the water? What if they had to fight them? Or not. Jake imagined kneeling, with a gun pointed at his head. Begging, pleading.

He listened, carefully, to the thuds and clicks of boots on rock, as the men passed beneath.

They waited a good while before Goofy looked. Then Goofy crawled carefully down the rocks, keeping low.

'They're gone,' he said.

'Holy shit,' said Jake, standing up and leaning over, with his hands on his knees. 'I think I might chunder. One of them had a gun?'

'Yes, inside his jacket. Now get to work. Quick,' said Goofy, throwing his rucksack to Jake. 'I'll look out in case they come back.'

Jake scrambled up the rocks, knife in hand. He cut open the outer packaging and busily set to work stuffing the rucksacks with blocks of class A drugs, like they were groceries from the Co-op.

The second he was done, he climbed back down and gave Goofy his rucksack. Both their packs were near full.

'Let's get out of here,' he said.

Goofy held a hand up.

'Wait on, man. They might be at the top. We want to give it a while. Give them a chance to clear off, like.'

'Okay.'

They both turned to look at the boat.

'What do you think they were doing in there?' said Goofy.

'Getting the rest, they said.'

'Tide's coming in. Might as well have a look.'

Leaving right now was more dangerous than staying. For a bit at least. And Jake was burning-curious, wanting to see what the men had been up to.

Keeping the rucksacks over their heads, they waded into the sea.

The boat was fifteen metres offshore, leaning heavily in the shallows. The hull was on show on the starboard side, with a gaping hole in it. The keel was wedged deep in sand. They moved out of shadow, into the morning light.

Jake could see the name.

Pandora

Climbing aboard was easy enough. But the boat was leaning so much he had to keep one foot on the railing – the lifeline – and one on the deck just to stay upright.

The yacht had a modern fibreglass hull, with classic wooden fittings and deck. But the deck hadn't been varnished in a while, and the glass on the cabin doors was dirty.

It wasn't a flashy yacht, but it wasn't in any way dodgy, either. It was the kind of boat that could cross an ocean, but was more likely used for weekend trips to the Scillies. Or perhaps a jolly day trip to pick up a few crates of drugs, floating in the water with a GPS tracker attached to them.

It was perfect for smuggling.

The cabin was half a metre deep in water. The men had been busy. They'd cut panelling from the inside of the hull, presumably because it was impossible to unscrew it with so much of the boat submerged. An empty blue crate floated on the water.

Wedged on a shelf made for books were more packages. Jake counted ten. Identical to the ones they had in their rucksacks. There were three larger ones too, packed with green buds.

'Bloody weed,' said Goofy. 'Sacks of the stuff!'

'Why the hell haven't they taken it? It doesn't make . . . oh shit. This means they'll come back. They're carrying what they can and mean to come back for the rest. What do we do?'

Jake had been so relieved after the men had gone, he'd been almost high with it. Now the fear was back. Racing round his blood.

'Your turn to look out,' said Goofy. 'I'll deal with this.'

'Why, what are you going to do?'

'Just go and look, will you?' said Goofy, scowling.

Jake sighed, then climbed out of the cabin, into the air. He scoured the cove and up the path.

'I reckon we've got a while,' Goofy shouted. 'It's ten minutes to the top, fifteen to the nearest road. They'll be unloading what they carried before coming back.'

This didn't reassure Jake.

'What you doing down there?' he shouted. When Goofy didn't reply, Jake went back in. Goofy was heaving and puffing, forcing a massive bag of weed into his already packed rucksack.

'You're supposed to be the sensible one!' said Jake.

'Cocaine is a bloody, nasty business, Jake. The sort of business that ruins lives. It's for crooks and dickheads. Weed, on the other hand, is a natural herb what God has put on this earth to mellow us all out and make us a bit nicer to each other. There is no way I'm waving goodbye to that much smoke.'

'You arsehole! They'll *know*. They'll *know* someone's got their drugs.'

'So what? We'll be long gone.'

'Goof. You are aware the way out of here is blocked? By drug dealers. One of which, let's just remind ourselves . . . has a FUCKING GUN!'

Goofy just smiled.

'The sea is calm. We've got wetsuits on. And we're surfers. Muscled up from years in the water. We can get the boards off the rocks and paddle out with this pirate booty on our backs.' Goofy explained this casually, like he was planning a picnic. 'Paddle down the coast, come in at Hope Cove.'

'You're actually enjoying this, aren't you, you sicko? Anyway, it's a good idea.' Hope Cove was a long way, far too long for anyone to swim. But paddling boards they'd do it easy. An hour, hour and a half tops.

'In fact,' said Goofy. 'If they're going to know we've been we might as well leave a message.' Goofy's eyes shone brightly. He got a knife out of his bag, and before Jake could stop him had grabbed a bag of cocaine and stabbed it. Sheer-white, block-packed powder fell over his hands and spilt into the water. Goofy took a tiny bit on the end of his knife, put it to his nose and snorted.

'Just for old time's sake, like,' he said, then dropped the bag in the water, like he was tossing away a beer can.

Jake watched, gobsmacked, hyperventilating.

'What . . . are . . . you . . . doing?'

Goofy grabbed another bag, and pierced it deeply. Once, twice, again and again. Like a potato he was about to put it in a microwave. He took it outside and threw it, far as he could.

'Earth to Goofy. I repeat: What are you doing?'

'We can't carry this shit. I ain't leaving it for them to do damage with.'

Goofy went and got as many bags as he could carry, and did the same to them, piercing them with the knife and throwing them away. He worked hard and quick, till all the bags had been thrown. Over by the cliff, Jake saw the bags slowly sinking as they filled with water. A soft white cloud was billowing out from each of them, before dispersing in the current.

Jake stood, open-mouthed. He could actually feel his own face turning white.

'I think we might have some very, *very* pissed-off drug dealers on our hands. Let's go. Now.'

But Goofy hadn't finished. He took his knife, and, holding the blade like a pen, he scratched the shape of a hand into the cabin door: clenched, upturned, with the middle finger up.

He sniggered as he did it, then started laughing, fully. 'I'd love to see their faces. It'll drive 'em nuts. They'll be searching the cove and cliff top for hours. They won't imagine the truth. They came down the path. No one could possibly get a boat in, not even a dinghy. There's too many rocks. They won't have a clue.' He laughed again. Like a devil.

Jake cracked up too, giggling nervously. He couldn't help it. He felt madly high.

'You bloody mentalist. You'll get us killed. We need to be sensible, stay in control.' He couldn't stop giggling.

'Control is overrated. Come on,' said Goofy, with a wink. 'Let's get the boards, shall we?'

They climbed out of the cabin, leapt off the boat and waded to the shore, watching the path the whole time. Then got the boards and headed out, with the rucksacks on their backs, past the boat, over and between the rocks that filled the mouth of the cove.

Jake didn't calm his paddling till they were round the cliff and heading steadily down the coast.

Hannah

THERE WERE FIVE of them, on the beach at dawn. Herself and Steve Hopkins, plus Dan and Jo from his team – dedicated young whale-heads like herself, they were thrilled with the prospect of getting close to orcas. Neil Trevedra completed the gang. He was the leader of her local survey group, a long-haired, unshaven, often grumpy, sea dog. But no one knew the coast better, and he had a boat. A rigid inflatable with a fibreglass hull and buoyancy tubes running down the sides.

Strapped to the deck were plastic barrels filled with snorkels, cameras, binoculars, flasks of coffee, survey clipboards and jerrycans of fuel. Hannah wore her wetsuit, under her waterproofs and woolly jumper. It might be a long day. And a cold one, even if the sun was out.

A blood-orange glow seeped over the hills, promising sun. The sea was calm, with blue light and a breath of breeze. The storm had gone. Two days earlier, the sea had screamed with violence. Yesterday, it had churned with dark anger.

Today, it was just . . . still.

The same place. But different. The silence of it was haunting.

They pulled and heaved the RIB over the mustard sand and into frothy shallows. Step by step, the sea took the weight of the boat. Once heavy and static, now it became buoyant and free.

They climbed aboard. Neil captained the boat from the stern. Dan and Jo sat port, with Steve starboard. Hannah knelt at the bow, facing out, bins in hand. Ready.

The cranking whine of the engine broke the peace. They rode over the flat azure, out of the bay, then hooked left. The plan was to run parallel to the coast a quarter-mile out, transecting in zigzags. If there were orcas there, the boat would find them.

Dan, Jo and Hannah made a bet. The first to spot a fin would get a free beer when they got back. Hannah was determined it would be her.

It was surprising, this calm. A storm usually left chaos in its wake. But the south coast had taken a bigger hit, and the wind today was south. Offshore on the north, flattening the ocean. Once they'd passed Cape Kernow point, they'd see what the storm had really left.

If the whales weren't in these calm waters, they'd be there, in the wilder deep.

Or gone. That would be best. But still, Hannah wanted to see them.

Twice she thought she saw the front of a fin, carving out of the water, black and sword-like. Twice she braced herself, the shout freezing in her throat.

It was just cormorants, tricking her with their wings.

After an hour, they came round the Cape. The water here was storm-rocked. The state: 'moderate'. Choppy, Jake would say.

When the swell hit the boat side-on, they pitched and listed. When they ran into it, thick spray exploded over the bow. Hannah loved it. Her skin thrilled with it.

They ran a transect to the Pendrogeth Islands, off the Cape. 'There's no whales around, it's obvious,' said Steve.

But Neil, wordless and frowning, guided the boat steadily towards the islands.

Like orcas, these islands and the ones beyond them had fearsome reputations. And threatening names: Widow's Reef; the Giant; Devil's Horns. They stretched from the Cape to the Scillies.

The sea bed around was a maze of cruel currents and rocks like teeth.

Water that was either rocky-shallow or dark as the night. Fishing boats got caught here, like flies in a web.

They only circled the near islands. There were others, further out. It was too dangerous to go there, though. Besides, if the orcas had gone that far out, they were leaving.

They circled the furthest island they dared to. A rock lovingly named Mottle Island because it was so coated with bird poo.

Nothing there, either.

'Time to go home,' said Neil. Hannah exchanged sympathetic smiles with Jo and Dan.

'It's good they've gone,' she said. But her heart sank. She couldn't deny her disappointment.

Bins were put away, flasks and sandwiches unpacked. They slowed to a near halt, bobbing in the water.

'Not too long, please,' said Steve. 'I should be getting back.'

While the others ate, Hannah kept looking.

And saw . . .

A grey cloud on the horizon.

Was it? No, not a cloud. Something like a swarm of flies.

Birds.

No biggy. These islands were covered with them. The deep channels brought shoals of fish, easy pickings for cormorants, gannets and herring gulls.

Still, there were so many of them. Littering the sky.

Hannah held up her hand.

'Seen something?' asked Dan.

'Nine o'clock. Birds, swarming.'

'Not unusual,' said Neil.

'There's hundreds.'

Neil lifted his bins.

'I have to get back,' said Steve. 'See how they're getting on with that trench.'

'Just birds,' said Neil.

'You think there might be orcas there?' said Jo to Hannah.

'Whales and birds congregate round the same shoals. Orca

whales might too, chasing seals after fish and . . . Neil, we haven't seen a *single* seal, today.'

She didn't need to say more. The islands were a seal paradise. There were hundreds in these waters. But if orcas had been around . . . they'd have scarpered.

'Let's go have a look!' said Dan.

'No seals? That is mighty odd. We'll take a quick look,' said Neil.

'What about fuel . . .' Steve started. Neil silenced him with a scowl. Hannah smiled. You don't argue with the captain of a boat. Even a RIB.

Closer, the sky was dark with birds. Crawking and squawking, gathered round a small rock.

A rock that looked like the head of a whale.

Floating, looking to the sky.

Dead.

Coming closer, they saw a net round its tail, holding its body. A bird perched on its head, pecking at a net wound.

Behind the whale, the sharp sunlight illuminated the water fathoms deep. It wasn't just one whale down there. Black shapes were strung along a net like charms on a chain.

None of them were alive. That was certain.

The boat came to a halt. Neil tuned the engine to its lowest setting and kept it whirring, but pivoted it out of the water.

This was worse than on the beach. She had hoped – expected – to see orcas alive today, if she saw them at all. Now that hope had died.

They fell into numb silence. No one said what Hannah felt. If they'd risked the weather yesterday, they might have averted this.

'Let's get a record of this mess, shall we?' she said.

Neil unpacked the underwater camera and checked the casing. Steve took a GPS reading. It was all very practical.

'Okay, who's going to go down to get footage and stills?' said Neil.

'I am,' said Hannah. She held her hand out. Neil gave her the camera.

She wanted to see this closer, to feel. Not to turn her face from this horror, but to see it without flinching. She had to get used to it. To harden her heart. In order to do some good.

Hannah took her coat off, so she was wearing just her wetty. She donned flippers and snorkel, then fell into the water, backwards, off the side of the RIB.

The water was endless deep here.

And in it: corpses.

There were four of them, connected by the net, in a line, each one deeper than the last. Beyond them, a great trail of netting vanished in the depths.

Taking a long breath, she dived, so far down her eardrums ached with the pressure.

It was silent there. The silence not just of the ocean, but of death.

She took pictures.

The net – and the whales – shifted and rocked gently in the current. The stark curving shape of the whales was beautiful, even now. Floating ghosts.

Two had deep gashes in their flanks, where they'd struggled and the net had cut deep. The wounds were bloodless. Blubber oozed out, bloated by water.

The whales had suffocated. Held their breath. A slow death. Hannah forced herself to stay down, to use the flippers to keep going deeper, further. Till it hurt. Till she felt desperate. She did this so she would know what it was like for them. She had to feel some hurt too, some pain.

She kept down till she couldn't bear it any more. She surfaced, gasping. Hands pulled her on to the boat.

She handed the camera over, threw the snorkel down, took off the flippers. Accepted a towel and sat huddled, feeling empty like she'd left her guts and heart in the water.

Neil looked through the viewfinder at the pics and nodded.

She looked over the side and saw the fish, drawn to the flesh like iron filings to a magnet.

The whales would attract huge numbers of them, and they, in turn, would be easy pickings for the birds.

Yesterday the whales had been royalty of the sea. Now they were a feast of free and easy food.

That was nature. Cruel.

Or was it? People said nature was cruel; said orcas were cruel when they played with seals before killing them, then said they were kind when they helped drowning sailors. But, she thought, 'cruel' and 'kind' are human words. They don't have much meaning out here.

In spite of the awfulness of this, Hannah felt strangely blessed to have seen it.

Neil put the propeller back in the water, and ramped the engine throttle.

As they travelled, images ran through her mind. The rich blue of the sea. The black and white of the orcas. The nets. The white wounds and water-bloated blubber.

Hannah knew she had captured what had happened, and that it would be of some use. Evidence of pair trawl nets. Probably illegal.

The wounds haunted her the most. Deep and bloodless. Those images would stay with her.

The wounds.

The wounds!

She threw the towel down.

'Neil. Neil, wait!' She put a hand up. They slowed. 'Those wounds aren't fresh. There's no *way* they are. Steve?'

'They must be,' he said.

'No. Look at the pics. The flesh is loose and waterlogged. Those bodies aren't recently dead. Too much flesh has been picked off too.'

'Lemme see,' said Neil. Hannah handed him the camera. He riffled through the shots, his brow creased with concentration.

'Hard to say,' he said.

'These aren't the orcas that were seen yesterday,' said Hannah. 'They *can't* be.'

'We have to keep looking,' said Jo.

But Neil shook his head 'Fuel. Have to get back. We've looked all around.'

'That's right,' said Steve. 'These *aren't* the ones seen yesterday. They've gone.'

Perhaps they had.

They motored back, round the Cape, into the flat calm.

Ahead, far off, Hannah saw a black shape slip out of the water, then back in.

Just another cormorant, she told herself. *Don't play tricks with me, God*, she thought.

Then . . . what looked like a puff of smoke, shooting out of the sea.

Her heart was in her mouth now.

A stark black scimitar rose, arced and fell back into the water.

'Orca. Ten o'clock!'

The engine was killed. Heads turned . . . to see a flat ocean. Calm to the horizon.

'You sure?' said Dan.

'I saw . . .'

She focused her bins on the spot.

. . .

. . .

The water erupted. The orca full-breached out of the water.

A black bomb, freezing in the air before crashing in a white-water explosion.

'Wow!'

'Bloody hell!'

'Oh my God!'

They all shouted at once.

A fin rose up, breaking the surface. And another, and another. Black, arcing, smooth fins. *Phoosh*es of misty breath that evaporated in the sun. The orcas were heading their way.

'I knew it, I knew it,' Hannah shouted.

An orca passed them.

Phoosh. They appeared and disappeared, coal-black fins up, then sweeping down.

It became a game, guessing where they would appear, how close to the boat.

Hannah's gang were like kids, pointing and shouting. Cameras and notebooks lay on the deck, unused.

Even Neil grinned.

The whales headed past them, away from the islands and the Cape, moving up the coast.

'Why haven't they left?' asked Jo

Hannah thought of Little One.

'Because they're searching,' she said. 'For their family.'

Jake

THE PADDLE TOOK a long time.

Goofy set the pace, gliding through the water like a swan, which was annoying because Jake was huffing-tired. All his juice was gone and pure adrenaline kept him moving.

'I'm going to have words with you, you mad bastard,' Jake shouted.

Jake had a vision. Two blokes standing in the boat, looking for extremely valuable cocaine that was no longer there.

The men might have put up with 'lost goods'. 'Stolen' would get them a different kind of 'upset'.

★

The walk from Hope Cove was nervy.

Jake checked every car and van that passed. Man or woman driving? How many people in there?

But there were only pensioners, and women with kids.

Jake wanted to get in that van and get to Goofy's flat. Quick. Without seeing *anyone*.

They almost made it too. He opened the back door of the van.

'Awright, bro. Where's good, then?'

Sean was walking up the road from Whitesands. He had Rag in tow. Ned's brother. A stoner-longboarder, with short dreads and a thick gut. He was munching on a cake.

Jake weighed up how this looked. Boards. Wet hair. Sand on the wetsuits where they'd lain on the beach getting their breath back. Soaking rucksacks.

Sean walked up and stood, arms folded, head cocked, frowning.

'Where've you been?' said Sean.

Jake opened his mouth, but nothing came out.

'Secret spot?' said Rag. There were reefs that worked when the waves were small. But none were close by, and Rag knew it.

Both of the lads looked curious. Even suspicious. Or was he just being paranoid?

'What's with the rucksacks?' said Sean. Water was dripping off them, on to the tarmac.

'Er, um . . .'

'Training,' said Goofy. Jake felt his rucksack being pulled off his back. Goofy threw it in the van. 'We paddled our boards for miles, with weights on our backs.' He hoiked a thumb at

Jake. 'Getting him ready for Hawaii. Rips, big swells, giant waves. Got to get him fit, isn't it? You wouldn't want your bro hitting Pipeline unprepared, would you?'

Sean's head leant sideways, looking into the back of the van. Goofy shut the door.

'Anyhow, you worthless groms. What you up to?'

'We've been to look at the whales. There's TV cameras, a crowd, police. Everyone's down there.'

'I said not to tell anyone,' said Jake.

'I didn't . . . well, only Rag, and some girls.'

'What's the latest?'

Sean shrugged. 'Most are dead. Rest are dying. I heard they might blow up the bodies to stop them rotting. We wanna see that, right, Rag?'

Rag nodded vigorously, his mouth full of cake.

Jake shook his head. 'You grim little bastards.'

Goofy was already in the driver's seat. He started the engine, Jake got in and they drove off.

As they headed down the twisted lanes to Brook Cove, Jake thought about how Goofy had come up with a believable story. How he'd got them out of the cove on their boards. How *comfortable* he'd been, through all of it.

'You've done this before, haven't you?' he said.

'What?'

'Dangerous shit. Drugs. All that. You're a bit good at it.'

Goofy kept his gaze on the road.

'I said, haven't you?' said Jake.

Goofy's mouth twisted into a joyless smile.

'Yep.'

★

'How bad was it?' Jake sat deep in the sagging sofa, sipping a beer. Goofy sat in his armchair, skinning up a spliff on a surf mag.

'Bad.' The word fell out of Goofy's mouth like a heavy stone.

'What's your story, mate? You've always been a closed book. I've respected that. But you've got to level. Back there, on the boat, what did you mean 'for old time's sake'?'

Goofy took a long slug on his beer.

'I was into it, big time.'

'Taking or dealing?'

'Both. I got a habit, I got out my depth. Then I got clean. I hate that drug, I hate the bastards who make a business of it. It's evil.'

'It's not that bad . . . is it?'

Goofy shook his head. 'You really are innocent about all this stuff, aren't you, Jake? Where do you think it comes from? It's a trail of total destruction. From the guys who mess up rainforests to make the stuff, to the poor mugs who get forced to mule it. The only folk who benefit are scum. From the coke barons who'll kill you soon as look at you, to the types who sell it to rich kids in nightclubs. That's what we're part of now, Jake. Like I told you before, I came here to run away from that shit.'

'You ain't the kind to run from anything.'

'Oh yes, I am, Jacob. I had a proper scare . . .'

'What kind of scare?'

'What is this, man, interrogation? In my own good time, right?'

'Sure.'

'I come down here to get a new start.'

'You didn't *look* like you came for a new start. Not when I found you.'

'Right.'

They laughed at the memory. The two of them in the water at Tin Mines, a secret spot that worked a treat when the main beaches were blown out. There'd been a run of good days. Overhead waves, clean and powerful. Jake had free time, and a liking for the place, so he'd gone a lot when that swell hit.

Most days he'd seen the stranger. A wild-looking bloke, surfing Tin Mines like he owned the place. He'd seen him walk in and out the old mine entrance too, and reckoned it was a place to stash clothes and bags while the guy surfed.

Other locals came and went. They didn't like a stranger. Strangers tended to advertise secret spots. But they tolerated the wild man because he was always alone, never with a crew.

Plus his surfing talked for him. He surfed the thumping shallow shore break, and out back, dangerously close to the rocks. It wasn't just his appetite for surfing neck-breaking waves that impressed. He did solid cut-backs and spun off the lip quick. The way he took the dangerous lefts, because he was a goofy foot, with his left foot at the back of the board. The opposite of most surfers.

One day, when it was just the two of them out, they'd got talking. Jake asked a few questions, out of curiosity. The wild man didn't give proper answers, apart from one.

'What's your name, goofy footer?' Jake had said.

'That's it,' the wild man had replied. 'Goofy.'

They'd kept bumping into each other after that. They chatted between sets, waiting for waves. But this 'Goofy' clammed up whenever Jake asked him anything direct, like who he knew, where he lived and what he did.

One day, Goofy hadn't been in the water. The waves had been good too, so Jake wondered where he was. When he came out of the water, he saw the gate to the mine entrance was open. He peeked inside, and found Goofy lying in a stinking sleeping bag, sweating and shivering. And thin in the face. Nightmare-thin.

'"Come to our house for a beer." That's what I said, remember?' said Jake.

'Yeah. What you *meant* was a shower and a feed and a bed. But you knew I'd be too proud to say yes to that. Your mum took me in like I was her own. I'll never forget that, man. Never. You understand? Felt like a home it did. Still does. A family, like.'

'So why d'you come down here, with no money, no clothes? You've never told me.'

'Left in a hurry.'

'You didn't want to go home to your family?'

'No,' said Goofy firmly.

'Someone was after you?'

Goofy nodded. He lit the spliff, took a long drag, then an even longer sup of beer.

'Law or other trouble?' said Jake. 'D'you know what, don't even answer. It's both. I know it.'

Goofy nodded.

'At least we don't have the law after us now,' he said.

'Yet,' they said at the same time, and laughed.

'That was a cracking getaway,' said Goofy fondly, like he was remembering a surf, or a good piss-up. 'And they have no idea who we are . . .' he frowned. 'Or do they?'

'What?'

Goofy sat forward, looking serious, even alarmed.

'That day when you first found the stuff, you saw a surfer. You don't suppose he was one of them, do you?'

'The guy with the craggy face. Shit,' said Jake. His gut burned. This whole adventure was yo-yoing from dangerous to safe, and back again, too bloody quickly.

'The two guys, this morning,' said Jake. 'Did you get a look at their faces?'

'No. One was facing away. Saw the other one side-on. That's how I spotted the gun under his jacket. Didn't have a craggy face . . . I don't think.'

'Shit. You think the surfer I saw might be one of them? He knows what I look like.'

'Nah. He was just a surfer.' Goofy sounded too sure to Jake. Cocky. And he was getting both pissed *and* stoned. The small sack of green buds on the table would take anyone years to get through, even if you toked all day. And now Jake knew Goofy had a drugs problem . . .

'That a good idea?' said Jake, pointing at the beer cans, the weed.

'Not really. But it's not cocaine, is it?'

'You were an addict, then?'

'I *am* an addict.'

'D'you ever think of rehab?'

'I always thought rehab was for quitters. Thought I could handle it. I couldn't. I was headed for a cell or a coffin. It wasn't just coke, it was whatever I could get my hands on. The girl I was with . . . she didn't get out. She didn't want to come with me.'

'What happened to her?'

Goofy shook his head. 'I don't know, man.' He looked to the bay window, to the blue sky beyond the shadow of the valley. 'I don't know.' He sighed. 'Let's have another beer, shall we?'

'Can't. Need to go and check in with Hannah. Give us a lift?'

Goofy nodded at the spliff and the two empty cans on the table.

'Oh yeah. Right,' said Jake. 'I'll borrow your bike, then. Um, you all right, with all this?'

'Watcha mean?' said Goofy.

'Well, you have just told me you're a junky. Being straight with you, I'm not that comfortable leaving you with bags of coke.'

'You don't trust me?'

'I'd trust you with my life, mate. But can you help yourself? I mean, on the boat, you snorted some, right?'

'It was a crazy moment, that's all. Just . . . Look . . . Whatever you're going to do with this shit, do it quick, for all our sakes.'

Yes, Jake thought. *Very quick.* It had all been going all right, had seemed it would go smoothly. But in a short space of time . . . He made a list in his head:

Almost captured by guys with a gun.

Almost caught out by Sean.

And one of the men possibly knew what he looked like.

And Goofy – a certified junky – was now in charge of a lot of cocaine. Jake didn't like what Goofy had told him about the business of cocaine. He didn't like it at all.

Yeah. Sorting this out quick would make good sense.

Hannah

THERE WERE THINGS to do before she could go to the rescue. Phone calls to be made and emails to be sent, to check the progress of the rescue equipment and recruit volunteers for a cliff-top survey.

She worked in her room, sitting on her bed with her laptop. But between the pings of fresh emails arriving, she zoned out. Her eyes had been blasted by salt, sea and sun. Her bones felt as heavy as stones. She needed sleep. But she had to stay awake, to do this, to organise things.

Mum brought up thick sandwiches and steaming tea. She threatened to sit with Hannah until she'd eaten.

'I'm fine, Mum.'

'I've started running a bath. Maybe afterwards you should grab forty winks.'

'Can't.'

'Your light was still on at half two this morning. You were up before dawn. You look more tired now than you did during your A's.'

'I couldn't sleep. I was excited.' That was true. But she'd also stayed up to do research. By 3 am, she'd reckoned she'd read every paper on stranding on the internet. And watched every video too.

Mum brushed the hair from Hannah's face and stroked her cheek. 'Go and have a bath,' she insisted. 'I'll let you know if a call comes in.'

Hannah did as she was told.

Afterwards, she sat on the bed in her dressing gown, waiting for a call from Steve. Would it be okay if she put her head on the pillow? Just for a few seconds.

She keeled over. Her head sank into the linen.

'Just for . . .' She floated on an ocean of sleep. Then was swallowed into its depths.

★

The late sun beamed on to her face, waking her.

Where was her phone? Why was her computer turned off?

'Mum, how could you let me sleep?' she shouted as she yanked her jeans and jumper on.

Mum appeared at the door, with her phone. Hannah grabbed it and pushed past, racing downstairs.

'You were exhausted. I've never seen you like that, darling.'

Hannah stopped at the front door, turned and smiled. Mum was standing halfway down the stairs.

'Thank you,' Hannah said. 'For looking after me.'

'By the way, your father's had good news, about the marina.'

'That's great. Tell me later, yeah?' Hannah opened the door.

'I love you, Hannah,' Mum shouted. 'I'm proud of you.'

★

Whitesands Bay burned orange in the afternoon light. The cliffs stood sharp against a diamond sky. The sea was calm.

But at the top of the beach, in the car park . . .

It was like some alien circus had crash-landed. There was a van with the local TV's logo on its side. There were yellow floodlights on stack poles. Police in Day-Glo jackets, keeping swarms of people at bay. A small marquee. A truck. A line of people lugging equipment across the sand.

A digger was on the beach, buried half a metre deep in the sand.

Hannah ran across the car park towards the shore. She edged through crowds to the police line. Steve was on the other side, carrying an armful of floats.

'It's okay,' he said, 'she's with us.' The police let her through.

At the end of the line of people carrying floats and nets were the whales, the main attraction of this circus. As they walked towards them, Steve talked.

'There's a bigger storm on the way. The seafront at St Morwen is ruined. Shops are flooded. They're bringing in sandbags by the tonne. *All* villages at sea level are in danger. Even Penzeal. The coast is going to get hammered. We're more exposed here than anywhere. Everything you see here now will be trashed. And we're going to stage a whale rescue?

'Even if the tide gets high enough before the storm gets nasty, we'll only have a couple of hours. It's a "nine", headed our way. What happened two days ago will look like *Winnie the Pooh and the Blustery Day*. There are three live whales. Two sets of equipment. If we float two, they may come straight back in.' Steve was nervous. Gabbling. When they reached the whales, he looked at Hannah, and said: 'This isn't seals. Not even dolphins. I've never dealt with animals this big. What's the plan?'

Jesus, Hannah thought. *Don't* you *know?* She stood, hands on hips, trying to look like an authority, like she hadn't spent half last night on the phone to America and watching YouTube clips of rescues.

'We dig under a whale and place the plastic netting there,' she pointed down at the sand, next to one of the whales. 'We roll the whale on to it, till it's gone over the edge. Then we pull the netting out, so the whale is contained. We attach the pontoons and inflate the tubes.'

'Then?'

'We dig a trench . . .'

'How? The digger's stuck in the sand.'

'We . . .'

'Hannah Lancaster?' She recognised the woman with a friendly face and neat bob of blonde hair as Janet Carter, a local TV news reporter. 'You found these killer whales, didn't you? Our viewers would love to hear the story. Would you mind?'

'But the rescue . . .' Hannah looked at Steve for help.

'It will only take a few minutes.' Janet got hold of an arm and pulled her a few metres, to where a man had set up a spotlight on a pole, and was busy fixing up a second. Another man appeared in front of her, carrying a large camera on his shoulder. He pointed it at Hannah. A girl approached, armed with a metal tray covered with powders and creams. She pulled out a brush and started patting Hannah's face.

'What are you doing?' Hannah flinched.

'Don't want to look like a ghost, do you?' said the girl.

'We'll ask you a few questions,' said Janet. 'About how you found them. About the rescue efforts.'

Janet was friendly. She kept nodding as she steered Hannah to a spot between the camera and lights and the whales.

The light was blinding. Janet told Hannah to look straight at her. Hannah heard a high squeak, followed by a whistle. She turned. Little One was squirming, trying to move her head.

'The light. It's in her eye. We have to move,' said Hannah. But Janet got hold of Hannah's shoulder and kept her still. 'This is much better. Our viewers need to see the whale behind you.'

'I don't care. You can't distress her.' She stepped to the side, into the shadow, so the cameraman had to move too.

Janet was still smiling, but her eyes were hard. 'This is only a short piece. There's a merchant ship went down south of Penzeal. Five men had to be rescued. Even the lifeboats were in danger. We have to go and film them. As soon as we can. So if we could get this done quickly, I'd appreciate it.'

Hannah folded her arms.

'We'll have to move the lighting rig if you stand there,' said Janet. 'You don't want to be difficult, do you?'

'Sorry,' said Hannah. She didn't budge.

'Okay, then,' said Janet, sighing. 'Brian?'

They turned the lights off, and set to moving the lighting rig. The girl came back and started brushing Hannah's face again.

It took a few minutes to change things around. The cameraman used the time to take footage of the whales.

Then, suddenly, too quickly, the camera was on her again. A huge muffle-covered microphone was pointed at her. The light on the camera switched from red to green.

'Hannah Lancaster, whale expert. You found these whales. Now you're attempting to rescue them. What are the chances of success?' Janet's face was serious, and close. Really close.

'Um, well, er, if we can . . . get them on to the plastic netting, refloat them and get them into water, there's every chance.'

'These whales are weak. Many are already dead. We hear equipment has arrived, flown in from America at great expense. But is it too little, too late?'

Hannah's jaw dropped. She felt floored. Janet had been so friendly. Now it was like she was accusing her.

'Er . . . no. The equipment is made for pilot whales some of these orcas are not much bigger. If we can dig a big-enough trench, we have every chance.'

'I understand the digger can't get across the sand. How will you dig this trench now?'

'Is it broken, or just stuck? . . . I haven't been told yet,' she said, feeling weak and lost. These questions were being fired at her too quickly.

'We understand the sand is too soft, and the digger's tracks aren't big enough. What's your back-up plan?'

Hannah froze. Her mouth opened. But nothing came out.

Janet continued. 'The whales haven't eaten in days, and they are dehydrated. Why are you doing this, when there is little or no hope? Local rescue experts believe it would be better, perhaps kinder, to euthanise these animals, rather than prolong their suffering. Apparently the weight of their internal organs is causing them pain and distress. What do you say to that?'

'There is hope, there is a chance. Because . . . because. We have to try . . . don't we?'

But who was she trying to convince? Herself? She sounded like a spoilt child.

'We've heard there are more whales out at sea. It's possible these whales are part of the same pod, or group. What will you do if they strand too?'

Hannah looked at Janet, and at the black lens of the camera. Like an eye, accusing her.

'I don't know,' she whispered.

'I'm sorry?' said Janet. Her mouth twitched. She was smiling. She moved even closer. Going in for the kill.

'I don't . . . know.'

'Well, if that's . . . Hey!!'

A shadow appeared in front of the camera, taking a second or two to come into focus. It was Jake.

'We're doing an interview, here. Can you move, please? We'll have to run that again.'

'No, you won't,' said Jake. He kissed Hannah on the cheek, rubbed her shoulder. 'You okay, babe?'

'You've ruined the interview.' Janet was pushing at Jake, trying to get him out of the way of the camera. He turned, looking at her calmly, chewing gum.

'I don't really give a shit, Janet-off-the-telly.'

'We've got enough to edit,' said the cameraman. 'Let's just leave them to it, shall we?'

Hannah put her arms round Jake. 'Hello, stranger. Where've you been?'

Janet and the cameraman walked off. Brian began dismantling the lighting rig. Jake held her. 'You're shaking.'

'Am I?' She pulled away, looking into his steady, brown eyes. 'I don't know what I'm doing, Jake. If Little One dies a long, slow death, it'll be my fault, won't it? And everyone will know it. I made this . . . storm, this mess.'

'No. You didn't. It just happened,' said Jake. 'You're doing what you can. What you think is right. It's that simple, isn't it?'

'I don't know, Jake. I don't know.'

Hannah looked at the people outside the cordon. They'd watched her being interviewed, like it was a spectator sport. Now, some drifted off. Others got busy taking pics of the orcas with their phones. Some just stared at her, as if she was an animal at a zoo.

'It's not enough,' she said. 'Maybe Steve's right. Maybe we should put them down?' She sounded panicky, loud, to her own ears. 'It's hard, this. Too hard.'

'Hey, hey. No one knows what's going to happen, right? You're just navigating the storm. Hoping you come out the other side.'

'That's a bit deep for you.' She smiled, trying to make a joke.

'I have my moments. Look. If your mum was sick, or me, but there was a chance of recovery, you'd take that chance. Even a small one. Wouldn't you?'

'Yes, but . . . Jake, I didn't know how hard this would be, I didn't stop and think. What if it's all for nothing?'

'Then at least you tried.'

'Yeah, I suppose so.' Hannah looked to the crowd. Dan and Jo were there. They were smiling. Not gawping.

'We've talked to the guys who run the digger. They might be able to get a bigger one here by tomorrow,' said Jo.

Steve appeared at her side. 'I don't need to say this, Hannah, but time is running out.'

Hannah looked around her. At the lights and people and orcas and piles of nets and floats and buckets and spades.

'We'll dig it ourselves, then.' She spoke the words before she'd even thought them.

'We don't have anywhere near a big-enough team for that,' said Steve.

'Don't we?' She went and picked up a spade, then went and stood in front of the crowd, holding it in the air. Maybe she looked a fool, but she didn't care.

'We need to dig . . .' Her voice sounded weak. Lost in the dark. So she cleared her throat, and shouted.

'We need to dig a trench, up to and round the whales. Water will then run in and fill the pool. The water will make the whales buoyant. We need to do this before high tide.'

'By hand?' said Steve, sounding incredulous, like she'd said *with paper cups*. 'How?'

'Yes, by hand.'

The crowd – what was left of it – were leaning, cocking their heads. Listening.

'Two metres deep, to the tideline. Sloping, so it fills easily. Water, once it reaches the trench, has to go downhill. Three metres wide, enough for the whale and people on either side.' She gestured as she spoke, swinging the spade. Imagining it, painting a picture for the crowd. 'We need volunteers,' she shouted.

'Whoa, hold on!' One of the policemen turned to her with his hands up. 'There is a *major* storm headed this way. This could be dangerous.'

'Then you'll have to stay here and help, won't you?' she said. 'Make sure no one drowns.'

'We're going to be quite busy,' he said, glaring at her.

'Do you want the whales to die?' she said, loudly, making sure everyone would hear.

'Well, no, of course not. But . . .' He sounded unsure.

'Who will help?' said Hannah. 'We'll have to finish the job before the storm hits.'

'I will.' A small voice sang out from the crowd. The owner of the voice pushed and squeezed her way to the front.

'Hattie!' said Jake. April was behind her, rolling up her sleeves.

'We'll help too,' said Dan. Jo stepped up to the front.

'Us too, Hann.' It was Bess. And Phoebe.

Neil was there, with his hand up. 'I got a load of wheelbarrows and spades I can get down here.'

'I'll help,' said a man.

Hands were raised. A chorus of 'Me too!' and 'I will!' filled the air. The policeman objected, hands up, shouting. But his voice was drowned by the tide of support.

Steve shrugged. *Okay, then.*

'Jo, you're looking after the whales,' Hannah said. 'Not just keeping them wet. Talking to them, comforting them.'

'What about?'

'I don't bloody know. Anything. Sing to them if you feel like it. I need to keep out of it.' She did too. She needed to be detached emotionally. As much as she could be, at least. 'Neil. Can you organise the cliff-top survey for dawn? We need to know if those orcas come near. And if they do we have to keep them offshore.'

People left, running home to fetch warm clothes, spades and wheelbarrows. April said she would go and make sandwiches and flasks of coffee. Everyone got busy. It was a relief. She'd had enough of expectant gazes, questions and cameras.

'Bloody hell,' said Jake. 'You're a force of nature, Hannah Lancaster. You're strong.'

Was she? A part of her, deep and secret, wanted this to be over one way or another. To be on that plane. It would be a hard life with Dr Rocca, but a simple one. Then someone else would make decisions and tell her what to do.

She wanted that. She wanted someone else to be responsible for all these decisions.

But, for now, she appeared to be in charge.

Jake

FIVE THOUSAND QUID. It was a giveaway. One bag was worth tens of thousands. A stupid amount of cocaine, for very little money. But Jake wanted this over. What had happened in the cove had put the fear in him, given him a taste of just how wrong this could all go.

Now he wanted rid. But the man, Bill, had said: 'It'll take time to get that kind of cash.'

The plan was to do this deal, then more next time. Once that was done, whatever was left would go the same way as the bags in the boat. Flushed away, poured down the sink, thrown in the sea. Jake didn't care. As long as he had enough to cover the whale rescue. Enough for Ned and Tasha's cut. Enough to dig Mum out of the hole she was in. Enough for a ticket and some spends for Hawaii.

Crazy as life was, as deep in this as he was, he could almost taste the iced beer, sipped on a beach-hut deck; him and Hannah watching the sun melt into the sea. The whole dream was there, seen through a gap in the clouds. Just beyond. But close.

He kept telling himself this as he walked to the pub.

The Schooner, in Penford, was perfect. Near to home and Whitesands, so he could do it quick and not be missed, but out of the way too. Penford was a grotty little place. No one he knew ever went there.

Tasha picked him up at the top of the beach and drove him to the Schooner. It was a dark, ancient dive, with poky alcoves and a low ceiling.

He imagined he wasn't the first smuggler, or free trader, to sup a pint there while discussing 'business'.

Bill was waiting for them, with a pack of roll-ups on the table and a half-empty pint glass.

Tasha went to the bar, while Jake sat.

It took one glance at Bill's worried eyes for a bad vibe to start creeping up Jake's spine.

'I'm only going to ask you this once, son. And be *very* clear about your answer, or I'll walk out and you will never see me again. Right?'

'Um, yeah.'

'Where did you get the gear?'

'That's my business,' said Jake.

Bill smiled, shook his head. 'Fair enough. Best of luck.' He stood up to go.

'All right, all right, I'll tell you,' Jake whispered. Bill sat back down. 'Why are you asking?'

'Where did you get it? Trust me, you need to level with me.'

Was this a trick? A way to get him telling all? Bill would be asking where it was stashed next.

'Why do you need to know?'

Bill raised his eyebrows and shrugged. He grabbed the baccy pouch off the table and pocketed it. He took his beer and drank what was left, then stood up and put his hand in his pocket, jangling his car keys.

'Last time. Where and how?'

Jake sighed. 'We . . . I found it.'

Bill sat down. Tasha joined them, with drinks on a tray.

'Everything okay, fellas? You two look weird.' She glanced around, as if there was something, or some*one*, that was spooking them.

'How many people know about this?' said Bill, through his teeth.

'None of your—' Tasha started, but Jake silenced her with a shake of his head.

'Three. Us two and her boyfriend.'

'Anyone else?'

'No.' Jake thought it better not to mention Goofy.

'And where is it?'

'You are kidding?' said Tasha.

'We're not going to tell you that,' said Jake.

'All right, just tell me it's not where you found it. On the beach was it? Or some rocky cove?'

'Maybe,' said Jake.

'Listen, I put some feelers out, just to see who was interested in buying. Turns out someone was expecting a load. But the suppliers lost their cargo a few days back. A lot of it. Their boat went down not far from here. That's what you found and that's what you're selling, there's no use making out otherwise. If they suspect for a second we are offloading their goods, they will come after us. They will want every crumb of it back.' He jabbed a finger at Jake and Tasha in turn. 'They'll come after me, you, your family, your dog. They are not nice people.' Bill pushed his empty glass away, grabbed the pint of lager Tasha had bought him and drank a load of it.

The words sank into Jake's mind. *Not nice people.* Bill – if that was even his name – was a professional drug dealer. And *he* was scared. Properly scared. He wasn't even trying to hide it.

'So . . . what, Bill? The deal's off?' said Tasha.

'That crossed my mind, Tash. It really did. But no. But we keep this low-key and quick as possible. We do this now, then a bigger deal. I'll see how much cash I can get. And you give me as much as you can for that amount. I'll get the stuff out of the area. And I'm going with it. Then we never see each other again. Right?'

'Suits me,' said Jake. 'What now, then?'

'Where's today's?' said Bill. 'In the rucksack?'

'Where's the money?' said Jake. Bill looked at him, unbelieving, impatient.

'Haven't you worked this out yet, son? What good would it do me to rip you off? What do you think this is? How do you think it works? You think we go around knifing and shooting and ripping people off, for easy money? I've known a few who work that way. They always end up in prison or hospital. *Always.*

'Things only go bad when stupid people make stupid decisions and make them go bad. I do my business as smooth as it can be done. No noise, no attention, no unhappy buyers, no unhappy sellers. Get it? Doing it any other way is suicide. I don't look for trouble. It's worked out all right so far. But this? This is bad.'

'With these people. The not-nice ones?'

'It's not ideal, son. But one, they'll never find out if we are quick and discreet. And two, calling a spade what it is, this is a chance for me to make a *lot* of money, quick. But, like I say, not ideal. It's in the rucksack, right?'

Jake nodded.

'I'll go to the bogs, and leave the money behind the cistern. You go straight in after I come out. Count it if you want. Come out, let me know you're happy. I can take the bag, or you can give it to me outside when we leave. It's up to you.' Bill stood and walked to the toilet. He came out a minute later and sat down. Jake waited a few seconds then went to the toilet himself.

It was there, in a plastic wallet, stuffed behind the cistern, like Bill had said. He opened it and looked inside.

A rainbow of notes. Brown fifties and a few tenners, but mostly purple twenties. Wedged tight together. He pulled some out. They flowered open in his hands. He smelt the notes, a thick, woody scent and rubbed them together. They whispered and rustled. Then he held a couple to the light to check the thin line of metal and the watermark.

He'd never held more than a hundred quid in his hand, and he liked the feel of it. He didn't know how to check it any further, or what to check for. But he didn't need to. Stupid or not, he trusted Bill. He believed the money was all there, and that it was real.

He tried to wedge the notes in his hand back into the wallet. But they wouldn't fit. So he put them in his back pocket. He stuffed the wallet down his trousers, and covered the top with his sweatshirt. He flushed the toilet and left, to go and join Bill and Tasha.

'Happy?' said Bill.

'Yeah, happy.'

'Tomorrow. You let me know time and place, after midday, yeah?' They finished their drinks and walked out together. After a quick look around, Jake took the package out of his rucksack. It was wrapped in a Tesco bag. He gave it to Bill.

'What now?' said Tasha.

'Back to the beach.'

Jake

THIS DIDN'T LOOK good.

Bess and Phoebe were watching him get out of a shiny, blood-red Audi. A sports car. Driven by a hot girl.

'Great,' said Jake, as he got out and shut the door. 'Just great.'

Bess leant down and looked through the window. Tasha winked, revved the engine and sped off.

'Who was that?' said Phoebe.

'A friend.'

'What kind of friend?'

Jake wanted to tell her to mind her own business. But whatever he said, or did, was going to be relayed to Hannah, and they both knew it.

'Girlfriend . . . of a mate. Kind-of-a-friend. I needed a lift.' He looked at Phoebe square. His best I-got-nothing-to-hide, face. 'Where's Hannah?'

'Good that you want to know, Jake. She's gone home, to get some things. Why don't you call your friend? Perhaps she'll give you a lift to Hannah's house.'

Jake shook his head. Best to zip his mouth and head off. Which he did, quick as he could.

★

It was dark now. A clear, cool night. Stars flickered and sparkled overhead. But on the horizon, there was nothing but a black void, slowly eating the sky. It was the storm, headed for the coast. Jake looked into the blackness. It looked like nothing, right now. There was no lightning, or thunder, or strong wind. No signs of the anarchy coming their way. Just darkness.

But it was coming. Hurricane strength. That's what they said on the news. Maximum chaos and devastation.

He wished – again – for all this to be over. To be on that plane, headed into the sun.

The storm, the whales, the drugs. The lies. It was too much. Even now, bringing the money to Hannah. This was hardest of all somehow, lying to her.

He chewed all this over as he walked up the path. He didn't see the police car till he was metres from the porch. It was tucked in behind Hannah's mum's Mini.

A policeman was leaning against the bonnet.

It couldn't be real. But it was.

They had to be looking for him. Someone had told them where his girlfriend lived. And now they were here.

And he was screwed.

As he walked – in slo-mo – he saw it all. The storm eating the sky, coming to get him. The nightmare. Arrest. Court. Prison. Everything Goofy had said.

He was busted. Right in front of Pete Lancaster's house too. The icing on the shit cake.

Life and hope drained out of him with every step. By the time he got to the car, he was a shell.

'Evening,' said the policeman. He stood away from the car and smiled. 'Nice night, isn't it?'

'What?' Shouldn't he be on the floor by now, with his hands cuffed behind his back, being told that anything he said might be used in evidence?

'Big storm on the way,' said the policeman. 'That'll keep us busy. You all right, sir? You look like you've seen a ghost. Are you here to see Mr Lancaster?'

'To see Mr . . . you're asking if . . .' Relief flooded through Jake, washing the fear out and pouring the strength back in. A spasm started in his chest and he almost burst out laughing. Or crying. He wanted to hug the copper. 'Yes. No. Kind of. His daughter. My girlfriend.' He could barely string words into a sentence, but then he managed to blurt: 'Whyareyouhere?'

'My colleague's inside talking to the family. Look,' said the policeman. 'I can see you're worried. Don't be. No one's been hurt.'

'Oh. Good.' Jake stumbled away from the car, to the house, drunk with relief. He rang the bell. Hannah answered the door.

'Hello, boyfriend. Come in. Help me sort out food and flasks and stuff. It's going to be a long night.' She paused. 'You're not going to disappear again, are you . . . Are you okay?'

'Yeah, I'm fine. I've got some money.' He looked behind him, to make sure the policeman wouldn't hear. 'Five grand. Why are the police here?'

Hannah shrugged. 'They're waiting for Dad to come downstairs. Something to do with one of his boats.'

Something to do with one of his boats. The words pinged around Jake's skull like a trapped fly. There was something niggling about those words. He wanted to ask more, but Hannah was already walking to the kitchen.

Hannah and her mum, Ellie, had a factory going. Loaves of bread were lined up on the workspaces along with blocks of butter, slices of cheese and tin foil. At one end of the table, jumpers, coats, wetsuits and hats were neatly laid out. As if they were preparing for a major expedition. A policeman sat at the other end, scoffing a slice of cake. The kettle whistled.

'Hello, Jake,' said Ellie. 'Would you like some tea?'

'Yeah, sure.'

'Great about the money,' said Hannah, returning to the sandwiches.

'Yeah,' he said, forcing himself not to look at the policeman. Thinking: *Not now, Hannah, please don't ask about the bloody money now.* 'Can I help?' he said, grabbing a knife.

'So sorry to keep you, officer.' Pete Lancaster's voice filled

185

the room like smooth music. He was dressed in smart trousers and a nice shirt, but his hair was wet. He was carrying a towel. 'Just in the shower when you arrived. Please don't get up.' He put the towel on the table, shook the policeman's hand and sat down.

'I'm Sergeant Junkett,' said the policeman. 'Is there somewhere we can talk?'

'Why? Am I in trouble?' Pete Lancaster forced a laugh. Jake turned round, and looked at Hannah's dad. He was how he always was. Polite. In control. 'Is this about the whale rescue? I know it's an inconvenience to you. Especially now with this storm coming. But let me assure you, Hannah knows what she is doing.'

'No, Mr Lancaster. It's about a boat.'

Something about a boat.

No, Jake thought. *Couldn't be. Not possible.*

Pete Lancaster's grin froze on his face. Was that water running down his forehead. Or sweat? His face was ash-grey, his eyes red-rimmed.

Sergeant Junkett checked his notebook. 'A yacht, PZ 498, name of *Pandora*. It belongs to you?'

The knife clanged on the floor. Everyone stared at Jake.

'Sorry,' he whispered. He picked the knife up and wiped it with a cloth. This wasn't going into Jake's head. He wanted to sit down, to get out of there. To laugh. To shout: *What the hell?* Instead, he turned to the wall and buttered another slice of bread. Buying time while he took this in. Hannah's dad. International coke dealer.

Nope. Wasn't computing.

Sergeant Junkett carried on. 'You haven't registered it as missing, or having been involved in any incident.'

'No. She's moored up the coast,' said Lancaster.

'I'm afraid to say it's been found, sunk just offshore. In a little cove not far from here. Found by some dog-walker, apparently. The yacht's not in a good state. Got a great big hole in its side. You all right, sir?'

'Yes – no. I mean, *Pandora*? She's my favourite. I'm a little . . . slightly shocked by this news.'

Jake couldn't help but turn and stare at Lancaster in wide-eyed horror. *Yeah*, he thought, *I bet you are*. Pete Lancaster. A bloody coke runner. *And* he was about to get busted.

'She's worth a lot of money, you see,' Lancaster gabbled. 'And . . . did you say, *apparently*?'

'I don't get your drift, Mr Lancaster,' said the sergeant.

'You said *Pandora* was found by a dog-walker, *apparently*. You, the police, haven't examined her to, er, assess the damage?' Lancaster's eyes were darting, searching Sergeant Junkett's face. Jake thought of the blue crate. Of the bags Goofy had thrown away. Were they still floating about in the cove somewhere, or had all evidence been washed away by the tide?

'No, sir. It's just been reported, that's all. We don't need to look at it. It's our responsibility to inform you, and find out if any crime has been committed. However, the responsibility of salvage or reclamation is yours. There'll be a few forms of course, for your insurance. You do have insurance?'

'Yes, of course.'

The bastard was smiling. Actually smiling.

'Have you *any* idea how this happened, officer? Was she stolen?'

Lancaster had turned the tables. Now *he* was the one asking the questions. 'Perhaps she lost mooring in the storm, and was swept out to sea. I'm surprised the harbourmaster didn't report it.' Then he clicked his fingers, like all this was suddenly making sense. 'He probably assumed one of my crew had moved it to a safer harbour. That was the plan, you see. I wish we had, now.'

'My God. *Pandora*. I adore her. Pete, this is awful.' Ellie put her hands on her husband's shoulders and rubbed them. He patted her hand. 'Will you be able to rescue her?' she said.

'It's hard to say, darling, without taking a good look. We'll have to wait till the storms have passed. It might be easiest to get her to Hope Cove.'

'Pardon, sir?' said Sergeant Junkett.

'Hope Cove. There's a small harbour there, with a slipway.'

Sergeant Junkett's eyes narrowed. 'I didn't tell you where the boat was, Mr Lancaster.'

Right, thought Jake. *Let's see you worm your way out of this one.*

'Do you know this coast well, Sergeant?' said Lancaster.

'Not especially. Not more than the beaches.'

'I do. There aren't too many small, rocky coves near here. There's only one or two where it could be. They are both near Hope Cove. Thank you so much for coming and telling me this news. Now, if there's nothing else, we need to help our daughter prepare for this whale rescue.' He stood and gestured to the door.

Sergeant Junkett was shown the door by Lancaster.

Hannah and her mum set to making sandwiches, chatting away about *Pandora*. All the wonderful picnics they'd had. The fishing trips. The trips to the Scillies.

Jake stood with the butter knife in his hand, staring at the door. Lancaster returned. He clocked Jake, staring.

'Are you all right, Jake? You look a bit shell-shocked. Don't worry, man. It's only a boat. It's not that big a deal. Trust me.'

Pete Lancaster walked out of the kitchen.

Hannah

HANNAH NUDGED JAKE in the ribs.

'Let's tell Mum and Dad,' she whispered. 'About the money. About how it was you that got it. Wait till Dad hears *that*.'

Jake shook his head and indicated the ceiling with his eyes: *Let's talk upstairs.*

They left Mum to finish making the sandwiches.

★

In the bedroom, Jake carefully shut the door.

She flung her arms round him. Kissed his neck, his face. She waited for him to kiss her back. To cover her in kisses. She needed that, she needed to drown in his warmth. Just for a few minutes. Before she went back to the world, and faced everything.

He didn't kiss her. He didn't speak.

'It's really awful about *Pandora*,' she said. 'But the rescue is happening and you've got the money. It's going to be okay, isn't it? We'll get Little One safe out to sea, then we'll be off to Hawaii. You and me.' She brushed his skin with her lips, taking in the scent of him. Earth and leather. 'Tell me that's what's going to happen, Jake, I need to hear it.' She waited for his hands to gather round her.

He held her, but his hug was rigid and stiff. She pushed herself against him. Wanting to bury herself in him.

'Great about the money,' she said, kissing him again. 'Something going right, at least. I want to tell Dad. Can you imagine his—'

'No!' Jake stood back from her. 'Don't do that. Whatever you do, don't do that.'

'Oh, um, okay.' She took a breath. 'Why not?'

He shook his head. He sat on the bed and put his head in his hands.

'Jake. What's up? Why are you being like this? I thought you said you had the money?'

'I have. Some.' He reached in his jacket, and threw the plastic wallet on to the bed. 'A good chunk of it, any case.'

She picked it up, and took some out. Notes; crisp and dry. Each one was just a slip of paper, but together, they were power. The power to make a dream come true. They could pay for the rescue. Couldn't they? She wasn't sure. Jake was being weird.

'Is there a problem with the rest?' she said.

'No. I'll get it. Soon as I can. You can be sure of *that*.'

'So this is from the family? Or has Goofy lent you more?' She pushed the handful of notes at him. He glanced at the money, then at her, then out of the window.

She sat down next to him, and kissed his cheek. He didn't respond. It was like kissing a statue. When she put a hand on the back of his neck it was cold, and damp.

'Jake. What's the matter? What's going on?'

He shook his head. 'I can't tell you.'

The atmosphere between them was cold and strange. And new.

'But we tell each other everything,' she said.

'Oh God, Hannah. Oh God.' He rubbed his eyes. He looked heavy and sad, like he might cry. Jake, cry? Impossible. Worse, he looked really afraid. She ran her fingers through his hair.

'What's eating you?'

'I can't say. Not now.'

Hannah took her hand away. He turned then to look at her.

'Do you trust me?' he said.

'Of course I trust you. I love you.'

'Then trust me in this. Don't ask. Please, just don't ask.'

'If you trust *me*, then you'll tell me. Everything.'

He laughed, bitterly. 'You wouldn't believe me.'

He got up and went to stand by the window, sighing heavily, leaning on the sill.

Hannah stayed where she was. She was being kind, being patient. Perfect Hannah Lancaster. And trying to ignore the anger burning slowly inside her. Selfish as it might be, she needed Jake now. Strong Jake. Kind Jake. Who wasn't distracted like Dad or cynical like Steve.

He got his phone out of his pocket and started typing in a text.

'What are you doing? Who are you texting?' she said.

'No one.'

'Jake!' He looked up.

'All right. Okay. I'm texting Goofy, if you must know.'

'Why? Is he helping with the money?'

'Kind of. What's with all the questions? I said you have to trust me.'

She felt bad. For feeling suspicious. Then she felt bad for *feeling* bad. *Jake* was the one being shifty and strange.

Jake carried on texting.

She picked up her own phone. No text from the rescue site. But there was one from Phoebe. She read it. Three times.

'Jake.'

'Yeah.'

'Who do you know with a red sports Audi? A girl.'

He looked up. Was that why he'd looked afraid?

'It's not what you think,' he said.

'What do I think?'

'I don't know.'

'Who is she?'

'Ned's girlfriend.'

'Ned, who you've been helping make surfboards?'

'Yes.'

'But Sue's his girlfriend. She's lovely.'

'She's not his girlfriend any more.'

'Why were you in the girl's car?'

'I can't tell you. Look, I might have to go and see Goofy.'

'Don't change the subject. Jake. Why were you in her car?'

'I can't tell you.'

'You have to.'

'No. I really don't. You wouldn't thank me.'

'Jake!' Hannah stood up. 'I need you. Now. Do you understand? The TV thing. The rescue equipment . . . It's a lot. I don't know if I can cope alone. It's going to be a long night. We need to get the trench dug out by high tide. I don't know up from down. I need you here. And I need you to be honest. Why were you in the car?' She stood, folded her arms, hugging herself. 'Can you just . . .' She felt the tears rising, the choke in her voice.

He came to her and held her. He lifted her chin with his fingers, so she had to look at him. 'Listen, Hannah, it's important you get this. I am *not* messing around with another girl.'

'I didn't say you were.'

'But you *thought* it.' She tried to look away. He pushed her face back to his. 'Yeah?'

'No. I don't know. Maybe.'

'There are good reasons I can't tell you what's going on. Believe me I am protecting you. But I am *not* messing around with another girl.'

194

'Why can't you tell me, then? Are you in trouble?'

He sighed, and thought about his answer. 'No . . . look, no more questions. Just trust me.'

She didn't know what to think; what to believe. Jake seemed to be struggling with the weight of something. She wanted to know, deserved to know. But yes, she did trust him. She knew he wasn't messing around behind her back. No matter what history he had. No matter that Bess and Phoebe wouldn't believe it. They didn't know him.

'Okay.' She nodded.

'Goofy can come down. We'll get stuck into that trench. Feel that.' He took her hand and placed it on his bicep. 'Years of surfing. Good training. Reckon I can shift a lot of sand in one night. It's all going to be okay. I promise. Let's just get through the next couple of days, shall we?'

He squeezed her tight, and kissed her lips. She felt his stubble on her skin. The wetness of his tongue exploring her lips. And he was there, against her leg, wanting her.

'We have to go, Jake.'

'You're the best, you know that?'

'I love you.'

'I love you too.'

He put his arm round her waist, pulling her tight.

She wriggled away and opened the door.

'Come on,' she said, 'I have to go.' It seemed best to get back into the kitchen.

'What *have* you been up to?' said Mum. 'Everything's ready.

Let's load up the Range Rover.' She grabbed the keys off a hook on the wall and threw them to Jake.

'Is Dad coming?' said Hannah.

'No, he's expecting someone. Business.'

Jake left. Hannah and her mother began carrying the hampers and boxes.

On the second round, she saw someone standing at the door. It was Rocky. One of Dad's men. He was called Rocky because his face was carved with deep lines. He wasn't old, he just had a lined face. Craggy and weather-beaten.

'Hi, Rocky,' Hannah said. Rocky nodded. Unsmiling. He never smiled. 'You here about *Pandora*?'

'Yes. Where's your dad?'

'In his study, I think. We're doing the whale rescue,' Hannah said. 'We're taking all this down to the beach. Wanna help?'

'No, I need to talk to your father.' He entered, and walked off to Dad's study.

Jake pulled up in the Range Rover and got out. His face was white in the darkness. When he came closer, she saw he was sweating. He peered in, checking to see they were alone.

'Who was that?' said Jake.

'Rocky. He works for Dad. Why?'

'I've got to go and get my bike. I'll see you at the beach.'

'Jake, the rescue!'

The stranger-like Jake walked into the shadows, then started running.

PART FOUR

STORMS

www.Eye-Sea-Surfcheck.com

Forecast

Winds: off the scale

Conditions: horrendous

Waves: mountains

Stay out of the water. Stay indoors.

If you don't know what's coming, where have you been?

Seriously, folks, it's gonna get rough.

Jake

JAKE CYCLED SO fast, his legs sang with pain.

Goofy was down at his boathouse in Perran Cove. A lock-up where he mended engines and small fishing boats. The double doors were jammed open. Jake jumped off his bike and let it fall to the floor with the wheels still spinning.

A bare light bulb shone over the fuel cans, workbenches and tins of paint. Goofy was rummaging in the shadows, yanking at a rope.

'Loading up the van. All to help with the rescue, like. I got bags for sand, spades, shovels.'

'Did you get my text?' Jake panted.

'I know, man. I can't believe it.'

'You don't seem that surprised. Lancaster. A bloody coke dealer!'

'Yeah, well, *you* can't exactly judge him for it, can you?'

said Goofy, walking into the light, carrying the rope.

'What?'

'Er, pot and kettle? Anyways. You are sure?' He carried the rope out, and threw it in the back of the van. 'It's possible the yacht was nicked to use for a coke run. That happens.'

'No. He was crapping himself when the copper told him. And . . . Crag-face. The surfer I saw, that morning, when I found the stuff. He works for Hannah's dad. He's at their house, right now.'

'Really?' Goofy stopped still, thinking. 'Hang on, you don't mean Rocky? He's a surfer.'

'You *know* him!'

'I know *exactly* who he is. I just hadn't put two and two together, like. I'd never have guessed he was dodgy. I'm sure he wasn't one of the men we saw down the cove.'

'No, but he *was* the one who discovered the boat, and saw me the morning when I found the stuff.' Jake was breathing fast, hands on hips. He leant over, and put his hands on his knees. 'What if he saw me at Lancaster's? Shit, Goofy. Shit.'

Goofy put a hand on his shoulder. 'Even if Rocky clocked it was you that morning, Lancaster's not going to suspect you've got his cocaine, is he? He just knows it's missing. Probably shitting himself that there might still be evidence on the boat.'

'The police haven't looked the boat over. They just told him about it.' Goofy slapped Jake gently on the cheek. 'Pull yerself together, dude. Relax.'

'Okay, okay. What now?'

'I guess you haven't told Hannah her dad's the local coke baron?' Goofy laughed, going back into the lock-up and picking up a shovel.

'Nah. It would destroy her. Not sure she'd believe it, any case. Not sure I can believe it myself.'

Goofy swung the shovel around as he talked. 'What do you think a coke dealer looks like, Jakey? I don't mean fools like Ned, I mean the ones that sell to rich people. The ones that shift it from one country to another. They're at those sailing clubs, posh restaurants and hotels, you know. What's the difference between them and guys driving Jags and building marinas anyway? Sometimes they're the same people. Wass the diff, morally, between dealing coke and lending money to people who can't afford it, like banks do? Big business is big business, legal or not. The ink on banknotes is mixed with blood. That's the world.'

'Right anarchist, aren't you?'

Goofy punched the air with the shovel. 'Power to the people.'

Jake laughed. 'How do you think Lancaster got involved?'

Goofy talked as he worked. 'Let's say he's in the Caribbean for his hols keeping up the pretence, like. But really, he's total desperado for some dosh. He's had a few rum and Cokes. Who knows who he's talking to, who he meets? Someone makes him an offer. Some blokes fit his yacht out. Back this side of the ocean, their UK contacts take the stuff off. Alternatively, the *Pandora* is used to pick stuff up offshore. That's common.

It comes back in, he's known locally, so no one gets suspicious. He'd have got away with it easy too. Wasn't planning on the storm, was he?'

'Why, though? He's not exactly hard up, is he?'

'Maybe that marina is costing a bit more than he planned. Anyway, a lot of folk would do it. A one-off deal for a few hundred grand. Millions, maybe.'

'I wouldn't.'

Goofy spluttered. 'Well, I got news for you, boyo. You're doing the same thing for much less.'

'I'm doing it for Hannah. For the whales.'

'In my experience, everyone says they've got a reason. But there's no excuse, really. Not with the damage it causes. We should never have started down this road. But we have and now we need to get off it. Anyway, maybe Lancaster was doing it to pay Hannah's school fees? Just saying. Easy to judge, isn't it?' Goofy was talking faster by the second. Picking gear up and throwing it in the van. He was sniffing a lot while he talked too.

Jake had a thought. A worrying one.

'Goofy. You're not on the gear, are you?'

'I took a *bit*, like. It's gonna be a long night.' He thrust his chest out. 'I'll dig that trench myself, no problem.' He laughed, crazily. Jake took the shovel off Goofy, chucked it in the van, and shut the doors.

'Right, that settles it. Tomorrow, soon as the rescue is over I'm selling the rest of the gear. For whatever, I can get. Or some of it. Then we're ditching what's left in the sea or down the bog. Getting rid. This is getting out of hand.'

'Right you are. I'll help you. You're right, we need to get rid of it.' Goofy looked at Jake with his crazy eyes. Crazy, and afraid. It was clear what he was saying. It was clear what he was scared of.

'Where is it?' said Jake.

'Where's what?' said Goofy, pretending innocence.

'Don't piss around.'

The two of them stared at each other, nose to nose for long seconds.

Goofy sighed. 'In there. All of it.' Goofy nodded at the lock-up. 'I didn't want it in the flat, like.'

'Right. Key.' Jake held out his hand.

'Sounding like the schoolteacher, you are.'

Jake didn't flinch. He stood still as a statue, waiting.

Goofy put his hand in his pocket, then slapped the key into Jake's open palm. He hung his head, looking like a beaten dog.

'Got any on you?' said Jake.

'No, I swear. Suppose you think this is looking after me, don't you?'

'We look after each other.' Jake shut the doors, locked them and put the key safely in his pocket.

This was it now. This was final. Sell some, ditch the rest. He'd never been so sure of anything in his life.

They got in the van, and drove to Whitesands.

Hannah

IT WAS DEEP in the night when they arrived.

A full moon hung behind racing clouds. When it revealed itself, it played blue light across the bay, showing Hannah how big the waves really were. They reared like startled horses, crashing in the shallows, exploding in white clouds, swept into swathes by the wind.

The storm-sea was ferocious, and getting closer with every wave. But, Hannah reminded herself, this was a *good* thing. A storm-tide had stranded the whales and a storm-tide would take them home.

Floodlights on rigs made orange arcs, illuminating the whales and the rescue.

None were moving, making Hannah's heart beat fast with worry. Yet they *had* to be alive. The urgent efforts of the crowd told her that. If the orcas were dead, it would all have stopped.

The volunteers would be standing around, heads bowed. But they were swarming, digging, carrying. Like busy ants, next to the still, gigantic, black whales.

There were three distinct groups. The first, organised in a line leading to the shore, was passing empty buckets down and full ones back. The second group was digging the trench, leading up the beach. It was already metres deep, at least three wide, and ten or more long. Neil and Steve patrolled the length of it, keeping people away from the edges so they wouldn't crumble. Inside, twenty or so volunteers dug furiously, carving out not just a trench but a ramp. When the sea arrived, it would flood right up to the whales.

Buckets and barrows were being handed out and wheeled to the entrance of the trench, where the third group waited in a queue, taking the buckets of sand handed to them and tipping them into the barrows. All this was organised by the team wearing tabards: plastic vests, with the words **RESCUE CREW** on the front, and a large thick cross and a silhouette of a whale on the back.

Hannah scanned the scene. Saw Jo and Dan, Phoebe and Bess lugging buckets. No sign of Jake.

The digging round the whales had been left till last. To cause them as little stress as possible, she guessed. Two shallow trenches like moats had been started, so the live whales were resting on islands of sand. Islands that would dissolve, when the water rushed in.

Only two whales, though. Three had been alive before . . .

Had she arrived too late? Hannah ran to the whales. She saw the vet, patrolling, lurking like death. He was leaning over one of the whales with a huge syringe in his hand . . .

'No!' Hannah shouted.

Before she reached him, he pulled the needle out and turned to face her.

'Don't panic,' he said. 'This female's alive. I gave her a vitamin shot.'

'And . . . the young one?'

'She's alive too. One died a few hours ago. It's just these two, now . . .' He shrugged and shook his head. 'They're near the end, Miss Lancaster. I expect their internal organs are damaged from lack of water buoyancy. Moving them will make it worse. I doubt they have the strength to get to sea, let alone hunt and feed, and that is *if* they find the pod of whales that is supposed to be nearby. Even if they do find the pod, if the young one is too weak, she will re-strand, bringing yet more whales with her. Do you understand the truth of this?'

His tone and stiff body language sent a clear message. *You stupid girl. These whales will die. This is all for nothing. It's on you.*

'You may be right,' she said. 'We'll find out soon enough. In the meantime . . . You do your job, I'll do mine.'

She knew what to do. She knew what her job was. Emotional detachment be damned. She walked to Little One's side and knelt. She kissed her skin. Looked at her. And knew, immediately, fully, completely, that Little One was reduced. Somehow *less* than before. Her body was a dead weight in the sand. Her tail

206

fluke lay limp. Little One cried. A small, weak croak. Hannah saw the truth in Little One's eye. It was no longer a shining pebble in a sea-pool, but a dull, dark well.

Days out of the water had damaged Little One. She was being robbed of life, minute by minute, hour by hour.

The vet was right. Little One was near her end.

'Hold on,' Hannah whispered. 'Hold on, please.' There was nothing else to say, nothing else to hope for. She knew she was speaking to herself as much as to Little One. 'Hold on, Little One. Hold on. The sea is coming.'

★

Over the hours, the water made its way up the beach. Hannah spent the time whispering in the orca's ear, stroking her skin and pouring buckets of water over her back.

People came to try to talk to her. Mum, Phoebe, Steve. But she couldn't engage with them. Couldn't think of anyone else's needs, only of Little One. And this terrifying responsibility.

When Jake appeared, she said: 'Go. Leave this to me.'

'No.' He came and knelt by her side, trying to hug her, but she shrugged him off.

'The storms brought this on me,' she said. 'I didn't ask for it. What if this doesn't work?'

'Then at least you tried,' said Jake. 'At least *we* tried.'

But it didn't matter what pep talk Jake gave her, there was a truth, blunt and heavy and real. If Little One died, Hannah would be alone. And everyone would know she was a fool.

She didn't want to think that. She didn't want to care what others thought. She wanted this to be about Little One. But this was about her proving herself too. And she didn't like herself for caring about that as much as she did.

Hannah put her ear against Little One's head. Inside she could hear gurgling and beats. Currents of life, under the skin.

'Please don't die,' she said, and felt guilty, for needing Little One as much as the orca needed her.

★

Time melted in the dark. How long had she been at Little One's side? An hour? Three? Jake divided his time between digging and checking on her. She looked up at the sea. It was finding the high-tide bank now. It was rising fast.

A whistle blew. The volunteer diggers filed out of the trench, paddling through water.

The rescue team herded the volunteers like sheep, till they were behind a cordon, high on the shingle and well away from the water. The only ones allowed to remain were the rescue teams in their wet and dry-dive suits. The ones wearing tabards.

Hannah watched, hypnotised, as the sea trickled over the entrance of the trench. The first fingers of water sank into the sand. A wave surged more water forward, pushing into the trench. Then another, pushing more water. The rough sand, chopped by boots and hands, now softened and flattened as the water surged forward. Then, as if a floodgate opened, the water poured in, down the trench and into the moat.

Movement and noise exploded around her. Feet, arms, bodies, crowding around her and Little One.

A whistle blew again, piercing her dream-state.

More volunteers appeared, dragging the pontoons to Little One's side.

Little One cried out, panicked by the crowd around her.

'Talk to her,' said Steve.

'It's okay, Little One. It's okay. It's going to be okay.'

The whistle again. Bodies lined up against Little One's side, leaning against her. The pontoons were dragged into position on the other side of the whale. There were two tubes with scrunched-up plastic netting between them, like a giant, inflatable stretcher.

'One . . . two . . .' Steve shouted. The whistle shrieked. They pushed Little One, toppling her on to her side. 'A bit more!' Steve cried. They pushed again. Little One – as though knowing what to do – rolled slightly over till she was lying over one of the pontoons. The other was visible now, underneath her, in the crater left by her body.

Hannah dived under the shadow of the whale. Crawling in the crater, she grabbed the pontoon and dragged it till the net was stretched out.

'Gently now,' said Steve. They slowly lowered the whale back down. Little One lay on the net with one pontoon tube on either side.

Two girls appeared, with long hoses. These were quickly stuck into valves on the pontoons. The girls both gave the thumbs-up. Steve, in turn, gave his thumb-up to the guys operating the generator, up on the bank. The two pontoons inflated, quickly.

A few of the team leapt into the moat, armed with shovels, and set to digging at the sand.

Little One's tail fluke thumped. Her eye swivelled.

A series of waves crashed in, less than ten metres off.

Water came pouring, rushing, gushing, filling the man-made gulley and the moat, surrounding the whales and softening the sand. The platform began to dissolve. The rescue team hacked away at the edges, displacing more and more sand.

Little One wriggled gently, and cried out. She was trying to get free, but the weight-packed sand beneath her was stubborn.

Hannah dived to her knees. She pulled at the sand with her hands and felt the water seep through her wetsuit. Felt it rise over her hands, her waist. Little One was a giant shadow above her.

'Get out of there!' Steve shouted. 'If that whale falls on you, she'll crush you.'

Little One was wobbling above her, the water was covering her. Little One's shadow cast her in the dark. But the sand was crumbling. One last effort . . . The handfuls of sand fell apart in her grip as water raced round her. The water was at her neck . . . She was gasping.

A splash of legs in the water. Strong hands pulling her away. Jake.

She was pulled on to the bank. She saw the water doing its work. Flowing in, surrounding Little One. The pontoons were lifting her. Soon Little One was an island in a pool, with the channel ahead waiting for her.

'Get back in. Now,' said Steve. Hannah jumped into the water. It came up to her chest. 'Stay with her,' he said. 'Wait till we've floated the female.'

The whole team moved to the other whale. They would move them both into deep water at the same time.

While they worked with the larger whale, undertaking the same rapid operation, Hannah waited with Little One. Catching her breath, she whispered: 'Hold on. It's okay.'

Little One emitted a *phoosh*, then cried and croaked slowly. She was weak. Hannah sensed this weakness; a physical thing. A fading of the whale's soul. Of her consciousness.

'Don't let go, Little One. Don't let go.'

Then it was time. Dan and Jo jumped in beside her.

The larger whale was pushed first. It was amazing how the pontoons worked; how quickly and easily a many-tonne giant was pushed along to the deep. The team – twenty of them at least – got the whale to the shallows, till they were shoulder deep. The whale writhed and rolled, wanting to be free of the pontoon.

'Now,' Steve shouted, waving frantically. They pushed Little One forward. She floated easily. One push. Two.

Ahead, they were pushing the larger whale's pontoon down, opening the valves, deflating the tubes. The larger whale surged and rocked, breaking free of the equipment. It moved forward. Dipped in the water. Then swam, powerful and sure, into the waves. And was gone.

A cheer rang out from the bank. Louder than the wind and roaring waves.

Then they were pushing Little One into the sea. They pushed till they were shoulder-deep. *Dangerously* deep, if a big wave came.

Why wasn't Little One moving. Why? Why wasn't she writhing like the older female had?

The whale slapped her fluke. She rolled her fins. But didn't move forward.

'Go home, Little One. Please,' Hannah cried. She called to the sea. 'Come and take her home.'

She turned to look the whale in the eye. And saw the dying light.

'No. No.'

Hands took Hannah, pulled her away, as the water raced and grabbed, threatening to take her too. She was pulled to the bank, above the sea. Forced to sit and watch.

Little One didn't swim in the breakers like she was supposed to. She froze in front of the waves, rolling from side to side. Hannah fought the hands holding her, desperate to get to the whale. Steve's face appeared in front of her. He had her shoulders. He shook her.

'There's no point pushing her in. She has to go herself.' His fingers dug in her arm. 'She'll drown if she can't swim. Do you see?'

Hannah did see. She nodded. The awfulness of a truth that couldn't be shaken, moved or changed.

Jake came to her. He put his arm round her. They watched. And waited.

And waited.

Tears of frustration poured down her cheeks, because there was nothing she could do now. Nothing. Exhaustion and desperation began to take her, as if they were drowning her.

'Go on!' someone yelled.

'Go home, little whale!' another shouted. The crowd joined in. As though their shouts would make a difference.

But as the minutes passed these shouts got weaker. Less frequent. Till eventually there was no sound from the crowd. Just the roar of waves and wind.

The vet appeared, in a dry suit with a stethoscope round his neck. He left his bag lying on the bank, and waded in. Little One shifted in the water. But only slightly, weakly.

Hannah broke free of Jake's arm before he could stop her. She splashed back into the water.

'What are you doing?' she said to the vet.

He turned to face her. 'I'm going to see how healthy she is or if we should take action. To prevent her suffering any further.'

She stared at him. Then towards the sea.

Listening.

'Did you not hear me?' he said.

'Shut up!' she said. Listening. And hearing.

'You don't seem to understand, young lady.'

'No. *Actually* shut up! Listen. *Listen.*'

'I don't—'

'*Listen!*'

It was hardly there. A faint wailing, whooping song in the wind. It came from the water and carried in the air. Weak at first, but there. Real.

Whale song.

Little One whistled. Her tail thumped the water.

At first Hannah thought it was the rescued whale. But it was too loud, too strong. And there was another, joining the first. Then another. The calls of many orcas.

The clouds rolled away, and the moonlight shone through. Offshore, she could see fins. One, two . . . many. Whales, calling through the water. Closer now. She felt it inside her belly.

The songs lit a fire in Little One's eye. The whale called, she cried. She urged herself forward.

Others joined Hannah, undoing the valves, deflating the pontoons, letting Little One wriggle free. She slipped forward, vanished under the next wave, reappeared, metres ahead, sank into the water – and then was gone.

Cheers erupted. Claps echoed in the wind. Whistles too.

Again, hands pulled Hannah from the water, from the sand that was slipping beneath her feet and the pull of retreating waves, trying to suck her into the water. As though the sea wanted to take her too.

She collapsed on to the sand, with Jake. He covered her in kisses.

She thought of the whistles and the low songs. Remembering what she had learnt.

A unique series of clicks, whistles, low moans. Distinct for each whale.

'Her name, Jake. They were calling her name.'

The moon broke through the clouds and shone over the bay. It showed nothing but waves. The whales were gone.

'I think . . . that's why they were searching. It's why they waited offshore, Jake . . . I think one of those whales is Little One's mother.'

There was a chorus of clapping and cheering. Hannah looked up. She was surrounded by smiling, exhausted faces.

Mum, Phoebe, Bess, Jake, Goofy, April, Sean and Hattie.

The crowds disappeared, slowly, into the darkness. The show was over. There was nothing left to see. Just the aftermath of scattered equipment, piles of tabards, and heaps of shovels and buckets.

And the dead whales.

They'd be taken away and either buried or towed out to sea and sunk.

Some of the rescue team went home to get changed. Others stayed, keeping watch. Hot tea was handed out. Sandwiches too.

Many of the team stood, or sat alone, away from the rescue scene. One girl was crying.

Hannah sat with Jake on the shore, above the empty pool at high tide, watching the sea.

Mum came and sat beside her.

'Come on,' she said. 'We need to get you home.'

'Not yet. They may come back, you see.'

She couldn't go home now. It would be tempting fate. She couldn't imagine getting that call, just as she crawled into bed. It would be near impossible to get up again. Though she would, if she had to.

She waited, with Jake holding her, kissing her, telling her how proud he was.

The dawn came. Creeping, soft and grey.

Hannah scanned the metal-blue waves. The bay was chaos. Churning waves. White horses riding, right to the edge of the world.

Yet still no whales.

Hannah felt a flood pouring over her. A tidal feeling.

A feeling of peace.

Hannah

THE ORCAS WERE safe.

The pod could re-strand. But, somehow, Hannah didn't believe that would happen. She had seen Little One glide into the water, stronger than waves and tide. Carving through grey and green before vanishing into the deep.

Little One was with her family. She was home.

★

Hannah was home too. Jake had left her at the gate. She walked through the door with Bess and Phoebe, smelling the smoke from a real wood-fire, and leek and potato soup.

Mum appeared from the kitchen, wearing her apron, a wooden spoon in her hand.

'Look at you, girls. Drowned rats, the lot of you.'

Hannah and Phoebe and Bess stood in their wellies and

wetsuits and Henri Lloyds. They were coated in sand, their hair dripping water on to the flagstone floor.

Hannah stared at her friends and laughed. There was no make-up now. No fancy clothes. Just them. Sodden and ruddy-faced. Exhausted and happy.

'Food, shower, sleep, in that order!' Mum ordered. 'But first . . . well done, Hannah.' Mum's lip wobbled. She fell forward on to Hannah, wrapping her in her arms. 'I'm so, so proud of you, my love. You did it.'

'We *all* did it, Mum.'

'No,' said Bess. 'You did it.'

'Okay. Emoshy-moment warning!' Phoebe shouted. '*You* did it, Hann. You saved them. Group hug, group hug! Come on, Bess, get involved.'

Hannah was surrounded and squeezed and kissed. She closed her eyes against the stinging daylight and tears of joy.

They stood, hugging and crying for a while, then went to the kitchen and had soup. It burned Hannah's mouth. But she felt a need for it, even greater than the desire to shower and – finally – get dry. Afterwards, she stumbled up the stairs, using the bannister to pull herself up.

Phoebe and Bess came too, the plan being that they would all shower and rest. Phoebe went first. Hannah stripped off her wetsuit, peeling and pulling, the rubber sticking to her. She barely had the strength she needed, and had to get Bess to help her.

Once in the shower she leant against the wall, the water

blasting her head and neck. She felt grateful for it. The force and heat washed the salt water away.

It was a release and relief.

But still . . . the questions about Jake niggled away in her mind. She couldn't feel the joy she should; couldn't let the promise of dry sheets feel as final and warm as it should. She was like a boat in the storm that hadn't quite made it to harbour.

There were too many questions. Why had Jake been distant and strange before the rescue, and how had he got some of the money? The rescue had blocked out all those thoughts. Only now, here, alone, the doubts were there again. Refusing to be pushed away.

She turned the shower off and put on her dressing gown.

When she came out of the bathroom, Phoebe was crashed on the bed, wearing Hannah's old-man pyjamas, spread out like a starfish.

'Get some zeds, babe,' said Phoebe, patting the bed.

'He's lying to me, Phoebes.'

Phoebe sat up and rolled her eyes. The look on her face said: *Do we have to do this now?*

'He's paying for the rescue, isn't he?' said Phoebe.

'How? This whole story about him inheriting money – it doesn't feel right.'

'You want my advice? When men offer lots of money, don't ask questions about how they got it.'

'I'm not like that.'

'I know. You're perfect Hannah Lancaster. Now lie down, sleep.'

'I can't.' Hannah stood frozen to the rug, hugging herself, though she wasn't cold.

Phoebe lay back down, sighing dramatically.

'I need to go to the Cape,' said Hannah. 'To the house.'

'What house? D'you know what? Doesn't matter, tell me later. For now: Bess is in your spare, I'm here with you. Lie down. Get some kip. I'll help sort this out. Later, Hann. *Okay?*'

'Okay,' she said. She lay down.

Her mind whirled. Images of whales. Of Jake. The money. A house on the Cape, where his grandmother had lived. The wind and rain outside, whirling and crashing.

But soon the images and sounds were drifting away from her, becoming distant and vague, no matter how hard she tried to focus on them.

Sleep swallowed her. Sent her to dreamless depths.

Hannah

LATER, AFTER A few hours' sleep, Phoebe took her to the Cape.

Phoebe parked in the car park, just before the headland. It was as far as you could drive unless you lived in one of the houses on the Cape.

'I'll come,' said Phoebe.

'No, please don't. Just wait here.' Hannah got out, with Beano at her heel. The rain was stinging and the wind chilly, but she hardly felt them. She headed down the path, to the headland. To the Cape.

It stuck out into the Atlantic like a bulging thumb of granite. Almost an island.

She knew it from summer days, looking for dolphins. It was a wilder place now, the sea and storm raging on all sides.

There were a few houses here. Some small cottages, and a

few larger ones. It could be any of those. But most of them, she guessed, were holiday homes. Their windows were dark. No smoke rolled out of their chimneys. Apart from one – the house furthest out on the Cape. It was big and square, white and bright, somehow shining, even in the grey rain.

Hannah leant into the squall, and huddled her coat against her body with her arms. She felt that if the wind got hold of her, she might take off.

Down in the bay was a huddle of upturned boats, sheds and lobster pots. The boats had been hauled up and tethered. The roofs of the sheds tied with rope and weighed with rocks. But these efforts were no match for the storm. One fishing boat had already been ripped off the slipway, picked up and smashed on the rocks. It was half a boat now. The rocks had eaten it. You could see the teeth marks, the splintered wood.

She watched – hypnotised – as the wind tore at the corrugated iron roofs of the huts. One flapped violently, like a giant hand was pulling at it. It came loose, flipped and spun high in the air, then crashed down, hammering against the rocks.

A wave rolled up the rocks, surging, rising like a one-wave tide, exploding in white water on the shore, sending a sheet of spray up in the air. Water smashed into her.

It seemed there was no tideline now, no line where the sea ended, and no safe place it could not reach. She walked high above the track, on a sheep and rabbit path. The road was too exposed to the waves. Not safe.

The house – when she got there – was high on the rocks. The waves couldn't reach it. Not yet at least.

An orange glow shone from the windows. She walked to the door and paused, her hand a fist in the air, not-yet knocking.

What was inside? Did she really want to know? She took a step back, feeling nosy, feeling wrong. Like none of this was her business. Like she should run back to Phoebe. But a dog barked, behind the door. Beano's ears pricked up.

The door opened.

The boy looking at her was a bit younger than she was. He had black curly hair, green eyes, and the brown, weathered skin of a surfer.

He looked a bit like Jake.

The boy screwed his face up at the weather. Wind and rain rushed in through the open door. He questioned her with his gaze.

'Hi,' she shouted. 'You don't know me. I'm sorry to bother you. I've come about . . .' She hesitated. What to say? *Your house? My possibly lying boyfriend?*

Blinding lightning exploded above. Thunder followed a second later. Breaking the sky and deafening them.

'You'd better come in,' the boy shouted. Hannah and Beano entered, and the boy shut the door behind her. A sheepdog, just like Beano, sniffed at Hannah's leg. The dog and Beano set to play-wrestling on the floor.

'My mum's not here,' said the boy. 'Can I help?'

'I've come about . . .' Why was she hesitating? All she had to do was say his name. The boy would know. *Ah yes, Jake, about the house*, he would say. Hannah took a deep breath.

'Jake Hawkins. He's my boyfriend. You actually look like him.'

The boy's face didn't light up. It didn't change at all. It remained stubbornly, worryingly, the same.

He shrugged. 'Do I know him?'

Hannah held on to hope. A lit match in the wind.

'Oh, right. Perhaps this is the wrong house. I'm looking for a house that an older woman lived in. She passed away recently.'

'That was my gran.'

'Oh, sorry. That must have been awful.' It sounded stupid. But she didn't know what else to say. 'She um, left you this house?'

'Yes.' He looked quizzical now. She guessed what he was thinking: *What business is that of yours?*

'Jake. He's a relative of yours. Distant, but a relative?' She gazed into the boy's face for recognition. She took a deep breath, steeling herself to get to the point, then she blurted the words out: 'He gets some money when you sell the house. Is that right?'

'Ah. Right. Okay.' The boy smiled, his eyes widening; knowing. 'Yeah, ah, this makes sense now. You've come about *that*. Wow. You'd better come into the lounge. I'm Sam, by the way.' The boy held out his hand. Hannah sighed, feeling relieved and pleased. She wiped the rain off her face, dried her palm on her jeans as best she could and shook his hand. She squeezed hard. Too keen, too eager, but feeling some connection. As if this Sam wasn't a stranger, simply one of Jake's family like April, Sean and Hattie. She followed him into the lounge, where a fire was roaring. She sat in a leather chair, but right on the edge, not wanting to soak it.

'Tea?' said Sam.

'No. Thanks. I'd rather just . . . talk, if that's okay?'

'What do you want to talk about?' said Sam, sitting on the sofa. The dogs lay by the fire, squeezing together on the rug like old chums.

'Well, Jake, he's my boyfriend and . . . this is so stupid, I *feel* so stupid. It's hard to explain why I'm here, really. You see, I knew about the will. Jake told me. But I didn't know . . .'

'Yes. It's in the will. Someone who gets some money if we ever sell.'

'Right, well that somebody. *That's* Jake.'

Sam shrugged. 'If you say so. We've been wondering. The will says we have to pass on a chunk of money to executors. They give it to some relative of Gran's.'

Hannah felt confused. Something wasn't right; wasn't connecting 'But he's . . . Jake's *been* here. He's talked to you.'

'No,' said Sam. 'We don't know who it is. A condition of the will. We've been wondering.'

'Or maybe he hasn't talked to you. I must have misunderstood. The lawyers – he must have talked to them.

You have to give him a portion of the value, if and when you ever sell. But you're giving him his share now. Buying him out.'

Sam shook his head. 'No. I'd know about that. And we ain't planning to sell. Ever.' Sam looked above the fireplace, at a large, framed photo of a surfer on a giant wave, in a storm. He smiled. 'This Jake – you said I looked like him. I wonder what kind of relative he is.'

Hannah felt the world shift. The story about the house and the will was true. But clearly Jake had never met Sam. And he wasn't getting any money now or soon. So where had he got it?

'Um, why are you here?' said Sam. Not rudely, but wondering. He looked at the window, where the rain was drumming loudly. 'It's a strange time to come knocking.'

No words came. She thought she might cry, but no tears came either. She felt empty.

'Who is Jake?' said Sam.

'That's a good question,' she whispered. 'I'm so sorry to have troubled you. I think I'd better go. Come on, Beano.'

She stood, and walked to the door, followed by Sam.

'What's going on?' he said. 'I don't understand.' She turned. This poor guy deserved some explanation, some truth. Just like she did.

'I don't understand either, Sam. I'm so sorry.' She opened the door herself.

'Wait! We'd like to meet him, if he's a relative,' Sam shouted.

Hannah didn't answer. She ran with Beano back into the storm.

As she ran, she thought of Jake. Of his rough hands and brown skin. Of his eyes and voice, deep and soft. And she cursed herself for being fooled by these things. Because they weren't him. They were just like a mask. Underneath he was someone else. Someone she didn't know.

She thought about the girl in the red Audi. And words Dad had spoken so often – Bess and Phoebe too.

'He's never made much of himself, has he?'

'He's got no ambition.'

'He's an easy charmer, Hann, but he's not boyf material.'

'He's not Simon, is he?'

'He's using you. You're just a passport for him.'

She climbed into the car.

'Well?' said Phoebe. Hannah shook her head.

'Let's go find Jake,' she said. Phoebe started the engine. The headlights cut through the gloom.

Jake

THE AUDI RACED through the lanes, Tasha driving, Jake riding shotgun and Goofy in the back.

Jake watched the storm through the window.

In some places clouds rolled and thundered; in others there was nothing but thick darkness. Nearer, curtains of rain swept sideways, blown by the wind.

The storm was a bonus. No one would be walking dogs today. No one would be driving past, including the police. They'd all be down the seafront, piling up sandbags and helping folk evacuate. There was even a rumour some cliff-top houses were going to fall in the sea.

Jake tried to watch the storm, tried to focus on it — or on anything but the massive drugs deal they were about to pull off.

They weren't going anywhere public this time. Bill had

texted the location of a lay-by, off the coast road, near some woods. Goofy reckoned this made sense. The whole public-place thing was about establishing trust. Once that was done, it was best to be away from people to carry out the main deal. This wasn't a Tesco bag wrapped round a package, swapped for a thick envelope of notes. This was a mountain of the stuff. A rucksack-full. Swapped for twenty grand, and worth God knew how much more. Hundreds of thousands, Goofy reckoned, maybe a million plus. This was bigger in every way.

They'd do the deal for that. They'd already chucked the rest.

They found the lay-by and parked. There was no sign of Bill's Range Rover.

Fields leading to the sea were on the other side of the road. On the side of the lay-by, a path led into a small wood. Jake knew it. He and Hannah had walked Beano there in June, when the buds were out and the sun shone through the branches. Now the trees and bushes were dense after summer growth, swaying in the wind, dripping rain.

'Go down the path,' said Goofy. 'That's what yer man's text said. I'll stay in the car. If he parks here, I'll make sure he turns up alone, or at least that he goes to meet you alone. As his car's not here, he's probably parked somewhere else, any case. Probably waiting for you already.'

'How long to do the swap?' said Jake.

'Enough time for him to check he isn't getting bags of milk powder. Enough for you to count the money.'

'All of it?' said Tasha.

'The money will be in sections, in elastic bands or envelopes. Grab one, at random. Make sure you choose, don't let him give you one. Take out a few notes and check them. The metal strip and the watermark. This is the only bit you don't do quick, like. Do a calculation of one part of the money, then multiply it. If it looks roughly the right amount, give him the stuff and head back here.'

'If it doesn't?'

'Hold him there, keep him talking, till I get there.'

'This is all unnecessary,' said Tasha. 'I know Bill. He's all right.'

'Yeah,' said Jake. 'He is all right. We . . . Tasha knows him. Why don't we just do a super-quick swap and get back soon as we can. '

'You *think* you know him. This is a different level to what he or you are used to. And you have no idea who he is dealing with up the chain. Do what I tell you. You should be fine. Everything you said about this Bill does sound like he's straight. Still, you never know. I don't see why you can't just do it in his car. Maybe he just wants to be private as possible.' Goofy checked all the mirrors, looked up and down the road.

'Maybe you should come with us?' Jake croaked. His mouth was dry.

Goofy shook his head. 'You don't introduce new folk now. It would upset the balance, like. Set off alarm bells. I'll keep the window open. Anything wrong, you shout, bloody loud, right?'

Goofy got his phone out and looked at it.

'If he's not there, come straight back. I'll wait five minutes. More than enough time.' He pointed at Tasha. 'You count the money. You, Jake, keep looking up the path, behind a tree, anywhere someone might be hiding. When you leave you are easy pickings, so move quick. Give me the keys, Tasha. I'll get in the driving seat. Soon as I see you, I'll start the engine. I'll also let you know if anyone else turns up. Okay?'

'Who put you in charge?' said Tasha.

'Done this before, have you?' Goofy glared at her.

'No, not like this.'

'Exactly. Well, I have. Do like I say, and you'll be fine.'

Jake saw the fear in Tasha's face. He could see his own in the wing mirror too. Of the three of them, Goofy was the only one who had a clue.

'Are you paying him from your cut?' Tasha said to Jake.

'I ain't doing this for cash,' said Goofy, sounding angry. 'I'm doing it to make sure he gets out of this in one piece, right? You too. Okay?'

'Okay . . . I suppose,' said Tasha.

'All right, let's do this,' said Jake. They got out of the car. The rain had stopped. Jake didn't feel the wind. He felt like he was in a bubble. He wasn't even walking. He glided to the path, as if on a magic carpet or a conveyor belt. Dreamlike.

Five minutes. That's all, he thought. Five minutes and it would be done. Over. Forever.

They walked twenty metres, round a corner, down the path.

It was quiet here. Sheltered. They waited. Jake checked over the trees and bushes. He kept his ears alert for the Range Rover. Why wasn't Bill already here? It was time now. Had to be.

'We'll wait a minute then go back to the car,' he said.

Then Bill was walking quickly towards them, down the path.

In seconds he stood in front of them. He nodded. Jake nodded back.

'Got the gear?' said Bill.

'Yes, got the money?'

Bill reached into his jacket pocket and took out a thick envelope. Then another from his other pocket. Then one from the back of his jeans.

Jake took the rucksack off his back. They swapped.

Jake handed the envelopes to Tasha. Bill stood there, staring at Jake.

'Aren't you going to check it?' said Jake. Bill just carried on staring at him. His eyes.

Alert.

A warning.

'Whatever you do, son,' said Bill. 'Whatever happens now, *don't* run. Or shout.' His eyes flickered, over Jake's shoulder. Jake spun round.

A man was walking down the path behind them. A man with a gun in his hand.

'Shit,' said Tasha. Coming from the other end of the path

was another man. He also had a gun, and he was moving fast. There was nowhere to run. And no time. The men had them sandwiched in seconds.

One look at Bill's face told Jake the truth. Bill wasn't ripping them off. These guys – whoever they were – weren't his friends.

'Sorry,' said Bill. 'I didn't have a choice. Do what they say and we'll get out of this all right. He laid the rucksack on the ground, and put his arms up and his hands behind his head.

The two men were in their twenties. One wore a Harrington jacket, the other a cheap leather. Both had cropped hair and hard faces.

'You do the same as him,' the man barked in a gruff Essex accent. He gestured with his gun. 'You, girl, put the money down.'

Tasha put the envelopes of cash on the ground.

'Do what I say,' he said. 'Don't speak.'

Like Bill, Tasha and Jake put their hands up and behind their heads. Jake saw the guns had silencers on. There was a cold, hard truth in those guns. A truth that put a sick, stony feeling in his gut. There was no choice other than to do *exactly* what the men said.

Jake had no doubt that the men would use the guns if they didn't get their way.

The one in the leather, the one doing the talking, put his gun up to Jake's nose. His friend picked up the money and rucksack, and headed a few metres down the path.

'Look at me,' said the man, pushing the end of the silencer

against Jake's nostril. 'Your mate in the car – how much time did he give you? Don't lie.' He pushed the end of the gun up, forcing Jake's head back.

'Five minutes.'

The man took a step back. He waved his gun, slowly, pointing it at Bill, then Jake, then Tasha. He nodded to his friend. Jake heard clunking and rustling. The other man was checking the money and the drugs.

'We're taking the money and the coke.' he said. 'How much is there?' he said to his mate.

'This bag's packed full. But it ain't all of it. Not even half.'

'You can't do that,' said Bill. 'That's my money.'

The man cracked a sick smile. He snorted. 'Maybe you'll get it back when we get the rest. Where is it?' he said to Jake.

'What do you mean?' said Jake. He thought of the rest of what had been in the crate, which they'd already poured into the sea. And of the bags Goofy had chucked into the ocean.

'Step forward, girl.'

Tasha did as she was told.

'The girl's coming with us while you try and remember.' He pointed the gun at Tasha's head. She yelped with fear. 'You get her back when we get our gear.'

'No way,' said Jake.

'Don't, Jake,' said Bill.

'Please,' said Tasha. 'No.'

'Where's the rest, then?' The man nodded at his friend. The other man pointed his gun at Bill's leg.

'One kneecap, Bill. Fair punishment. Yeah?'

'You got my money, didn't you? You're getting the gear,' said Bill.

The man's smile dropped.

'This isn't just about the dosh, Bill. We need to make an example. ' He waved the gun in Bill's face.

'I'll get you the rest,' Jake blurted, desperate to buy time with a lie. Because how could he tell them the truth? 'Just let us go, all right?'

'I don't think you understand,' said the man. 'I'm going to blow his kneecap off to teach you fucking idiots a lesson. *And* the girl is coming with us till we have what's ours.'

'All right, all right,' said Bill. 'But let them go, okay. Keep me – they'll come back. I trust them. And don't make them watch this. Do what you have to do if you have to. The kid will come back with the gear.'

Jake couldn't believe what he was hearing. How Bill was accepting all this. But what choice did he have?

The man laughed, and shook his head. 'I like how you're trying to call the shots here, Bill. But you really don't have a leg to stand on. Not for much longer, anyway. You see . . . I'd actually *like* them to watch. Then this guy will really, *really* believe he has to fetch us the rest of the gear. It's a good lesson, Bill.' He tapped his head. 'Teach him not to do anything stupid.'

'No, you don't need to do that.' Jake's voice cracked with fear. If he just got them talking he could buy time. Where the hell was Goofy? He didn't care about money or drugs. But he didn't want Bill getting his knee shot off. Or Tasha being carted off.

'Maybe I'll reconsider,' said the man. 'Start talking.'

'My mate's got it in a lock-up. We'll go straight there, come back with the rest. Right now. We can meet you here, or anywhere you like. No police. I've got as much to lose as you have.' Jake's mind raced. He was buying time. Maybe convincing them not to shoot Bill. But what then? The police. There was no other choice.

Jake needed more time. He needed Goofy.

The man laughed. Smiled again. Not worried any more. It looked as if he'd reconsidered, like his threat was just that. A threat. A way to scare them.

Then . . .

'Anyway, just so you get the message.' He nodded. The other man took a step forward and pointed his gun down towards Bill's kneecap. Bill looked at the sky, gritting his teeth.

'Not with them watching, please,' he said.

'Shit,' said Jake. 'Oh, shit.'

No more choices now. No more time. No more words.

This was happening.

Jake looked. Then closed his eyes.

'Lay off him!' The shout filled the air.

Jake opened his eyes. It was Goofy, running, waving his phone in the air. 'The police will be here in a minute. I've got them on the phone right now. I'm filming you.' He pointed the camera at them like a weapon.

The second man moved quickly, backing down the path, carrying the money and rucksack, turning his face away. The first man stayed rooted, his eyes filling with panic.

'Smithy, let's go!' said the second man. Smithy looked at Jake, hard. Put a finger to his lips. He shielded his face with one hand, but pointed the gun – at Jake.

Thoot. A dull sound.

Both men ran.

Jake turned to see Goofy. There was horror in his face and his mouth was moving, shouting something. But Jake couldn't hear.

Tasha was staring down at Jake's leg. Bill's arms reached out to stop him.

Falling.

Because . . .

Jake looked down. The ground was shooting towards him. He saw the blood.

Hannah

SHE SAT BY the hospital bed, watching him sleep.

The operation had taken an hour or more.

Plenty of time for the call to run through her head on constant replay.

★

She was in the car with Phoebe, looking for Jake. Her phone rang.

'It's me, Goofy.'

'Have you seen Jake? I need to talk to him.'

'It's him I'm calling about. Hannah, Jake's in hospital.'

'What! Why?'

'He got hurt. He'll be all right, but right now his leg is hurt bad.'

'Phoebe, head for the hospital. Now. Goofy, how is he hurt. How?'

'His leg. Look . . . he's going to have to talk to you. He's been in trouble. He's been a fool. We both have. We've done foolish things. But it's over now.'

'What trouble?'

'I can't say.'

'Goofy, *tell* me.'

'Not my place. Jake has to tell you.'

'Goofy—' The line cut dead.

★

They raced, crazy fast, to the hospital.

Waiting. And waiting.

Goofy wasn't answering his phone.

April arrived just as the doctor came to talk to Hannah, in the corridor outside Jake's room.

She checked his face for signs and clues.

She stood there, listening.

'He's going to be okay,' said the doctor. 'He's lost a lot of blood, but he'll be fine. Before he went under, he said he'd fallen on a spike. Is that true?'

Hannah looked at April's face, seeing the fear there. She was looking at Hannah, for answers that she didn't have.

'I . . . I don't know,' Hannah said. 'I wasn't there. Yes, I . . . maybe.'

'Hmm,' the doctor's eyes screwed up, examining her. 'Well, whatever it was went straight through the outer side of his thigh. He's lucky. No arteries punctured. It missed the bone. If it had been an inch or two lower and further in, it would have shattered his knee.'

'Will he . . .' April swallowed. 'Will he be *okay*?'

'Yes. Like I said, he'll be fine. Before he lost consciousness, he asked if he'd still be able to surf.' The doctor smiled. 'Well, not for a while. He'll be on a crutch for a day or two. Nothing's broken, but we need to keep the pressure off while it heals. He'll have quite a scar. This, er, spike.' He paused. 'Or . . . whatever it was. It took out a chunk of flesh, about this big.' The doctor looked meaningfully at Hannah, holding up his hand and showing a gap between his finger and thumb, a few centimetres long. 'And half an inch deep. He lost a lot of blood. A lot.'

April had to leave, to pick up Hattie. Phoebe left too, because Hannah insisted. She wanted to be alone with Jake when he woke.

They let her into the room he was in. She sat by the bed. Watching him. Waiting.

*

First of all, his eyes opened, his long lashes stirring on his cheeks. His strong brown hands twitched.

He looked at her. And smiled.

Don't, she thought. *Don't try to smile your way out of this one.*

240

She laid her hand in his when he reached out to her. He squeezed, but she didn't squeeze back.

'Are you okay?' she said.

He nodded. 'Been better, but yeah ... My leg ...' He looked down at the heavily wrapped bandages.

'Don't worry. Doc says you'll still be able to surf,' she tried to joke, but her words sounded flat. 'What happened to your leg?'

He smiled at her. In pain, but *making* himself smile. Rubbing his thumb on the back of her hand. She dropped his hand and put her own in her lap.

'What happened, Jake? Goofy said you've been in trouble.'

'What's he told you?' said Jake.

'Just tell me.'

He looked at her with his big brown eyes full of shame and apologies.

'I never meant for you to ... I never meant to ... I'm sorry, Hannah.'

He reached out his hand again. It hung in the air. She looked at it, but didn't touch it. The hand was familiar, but it belonged to a stranger.

'I went to the house,' she said.

'The house?'

'On the Cape. The house of the old woman who died. The people there have never met you.' She felt the slow, gentle warmth of a tear sliding down her cheek. She wiped it away, sniffed and swallowed.

'Where's Goofy?' asked Jake, looking around her at the door.

'Your mate hasn't told me anything.' She spat the words out. 'Just that you're in trouble. Involved in something bad. Jake? The truth. Please?' She paused, her voice slowly finding its strength. 'The truth.'

He sighed, pulled himself up on the pillows and winced.

He used the moment, to get kind-of comfortable, looking at her, then at the bed, then back to her.

'What did Goofy get you into?' she said, urging, *needing* him to tell her.

She waited.

But he said nothing.

She stood up as though to leave, staring and disbelieving as tears filled her eyes.

'Okay, okay,' he said, panicking. She sat back down.

'It's nothing to do with Goofy. I got him involved. This is me, Hannah. *I* messed up.'

'Involved in what?'

He coughed and looked away, at the window. His voice cracked as he spoke. 'It was a drug deal. To get money. A lot of it. For the rescue, for Hawaii . . . It went tits up, and I got shot.'

She gasped, put a hand to her mouth.

'Oh my God, Jake. Who shot you?'

'Someone called Smithy, if you must know. It's all right. I'm going to be okay.'

She felt sick. Scared.

She tried to talk, as slowly and deliberately as she could, but her voice wobbled with hurt and anger.

'You tried to help me by doing a *drugs* deal. Jake?'

'It wasn't like that. It wasn't planned. Not really.'

'Don't treat me like an idiot, Jake. How can you *not* plan a drug deal? What kind of drugs?'

'Cocaine.'

'What?' The word sank slowly into her mind. Had he said 'cocaine'? Was this Jake in front of her, speaking these words? Or a total stranger?

'That stuff is evil, Jake. How the hell did you get involved in *that*?'

'I . . . found the stuff in a cove . . . well, er, on a beach actually. Washed up by the storm.'

'How?'

'A wrecked yacht . . . boat.'

'What boat?'

'I don't know,' he blustered. '. . . I'm just guessing it was a boat. I found a crate. Look, I didn't plan this – it just happened. I knew someone who could help get rid of it. I thought I could make quick money. To help you. Mum too. We got involved with some bad characters. We didn't manage to do the deal. It all went wrong. The bad characters have the stuff now.' He sighed. His head bowed down. Shame came off him in waves. Hannah tried to understand, to feel some pity. But she felt cold and hard. She felt sick.

'I'm sorry. I'm so sorry,' he said, shaking his head.

'Jake, you could have got yourself killed. Thrown in prison. What were you thinking? These bad characters, do you know them? This "Smithy" who shot you.'

'Not him but, oddly, I know who the drugs belonged to and who has them now . . .' Jake stopped, bit his lip, like he'd said too much.

'You have to tell the police who it is.' She was speaking simple logic. But she felt disbelief, seeing his face. He wasn't taking this in. 'You *have* to. They shot you.'

'No, I can't.'

'You idiot. You stupid, stupid idiot.' She put her face in her hands. The tears flowed through her fingers.

'I want to make this good,' he said.

'Make it good? I've got to find over ten thousand pounds now, Jake. And that's your fault. And you've been involved in something terrible and wrong. If you know who has this stuff, you have to tell the police everything you know. Don't you?'

She lifted her head and stared straight at him, looking for some reaction, some sign that what she was saying was going in, making sense.

The storm was inside her now. Dragged out of the sky and the sea and raging inside. Disbelief. Anger. At him, for being so stupid. For putting himself in danger too. That thought was stronger than anything. She might have lost him. And it would have been *his* fault. She hated him, for making her feel this way. And for wanting to stand up and walk away, without being able to.

'You might never have walked again, Jake. You could have died.'

Simple facts.

'I want to make this right,' he said.

'I don't know if you can.'

She stood up.

'Where you going?' he said.

'I don't know,' she said.

'What about us?' he said.

'I don't know if there is an us,' she said.

She turned, and walked out.

'Hannah!' Jake called out, after her. 'Hannah.' Him calling her name was a pull on her, slowing her down, until she felt she was wading through deep water. But she carried on, till the slow pull of his voice was replaced by cold numbness.

★

Phoebe was outside. They got in the car.

Phoebe started the engine, but Hannah held a hand up and she turned the engine off.

'You okay, Hann?'

'I just need a . . . a mo . . .' Hannah shook her head. Her face crumpled. Her shoulders juddered. She felt the seatbelt loosen. Phoebe's arm was round her, pulling her, till her head lay on her friend's shoulder.

She sobbed, for long minutes. Phoebe didn't speak, but kissed the top of Hannah's head and rubbed her shoulder.

Eventually Hannah sat up, sighing deeply, gathering herself.

'It was drugs, Phoebes.' She told her friend what she knew, running through everything she and Jake had said to each other.

Phoebe spoke with gentle kindness. 'Hann, how long have we been friends? Forever, right?'

Hannah nodded.

'You know I love you. That's why I'm going to tell you what you need to hear, not what you want to hear.'

Hannah knew what came next. She could have guessed it word for word.

Phoebe undid her own seatbelt and turned to face Hannah, square.

'You have to finish it, babe. You have to get on that plane to Hawaii and leave him behind.'

'But . . .'

'Don't say it, Hann. Just don't say it.'

'. . . I love him.'

'You said it.' Phoebe sighed.

'I didn't know how much till this happened. Seeing him lying there. I know it's stupid. I know that. But it's true. I know all of you are right about him. And I should end it. But I love him. Jake is part of who I am. I need him, just like I need to see the sea every day. It's not about whether it's right or wrong, it's about belonging.'

Phoebe shook her head. 'Christ, Hannah Lancaster.' The

corners of her mouth pulled down. She knew Phoebe was being kind, and hiding how sickened she really was. 'Right,' Phoebe said, starting the engine. 'I'm taking you home.'

'No! No . . . just wait here. Please, Phoebe. Five minutes. That's all I need.'

Phoebe frowned. 'Five minutes for what? You going back to see him?'

'Wait here. Please.'

Hannah got out of the car and marched back to Jake's room. A nurse was talking to him.

Jake's face lit up, then dimmed. Maybe she looked fierce. She felt it.

'Can you leave us, please?' she said to the nurse.

'You can't just—'

'Now. Please.' The look she gave sent the nurse scurrying.

'Hannah . . .' That hand reached out to her again. A trick he kept trying. She didn't take it. She didn't sit down either.

'Jake.'

'Yes?'

'You know who did this.' She pointed at his bandaged leg. 'So, you go to the police. You tell them everything.'

'But—'

'Shut up and listen. You tell them *everything*. You haven't actually sold any drugs, have you? You said the deal went bad. And if you give them the criminals, you can do a deal and they won't prosecute you. I'll get Dad to help you, with a lawyer. You'll have to fess up. Come clean. Give the police these people. The ones that shot you. Who they work for. You know who that is, right? Do this. And maybe, just *maybe,* you and me – we'll be okay.'

'You don't understand, Hannah. You don't know what you're asking.'

She was shaking now. 'I do. I bloody do. Don't fucking patronise me. You, Dad, Steve. All of you, telling me I don't know what I'm doing. All of you telling me what I *should* be doing. I'm sick of it! You're going to tell me we don't know who we're dealing with. That they are – what was that expression you used? – "bad characters". But I'm not afraid of them. If you are, you're a coward. Are you afraid of them, Jake?' she said, spitting sarcasm.

'No,' he said. 'I ain't.'

'And do you love me?'

'You know I do.'

'Well, right now, I don't even know you.' She pointed at him. 'These men are evil, Jake. You tell the police. Everything.'

He looked deep into her eyes. 'You don't want me to do that. Trust me.'

'Last chance. It's time to grow up, Jake. Well?'

Sadness filled his eyes. The light in them was dying.

'I can't. I couldn't do that to . . . I can't say why.'

She tried to force the words to her lips. *Goodbye, Jake.* But she couldn't speak them. And he didn't deserve them. Not even that.

She turned and left. Jake didn't call after her.

Jake

JAKE WAS WOKEN by the rattle of curtains being pulled round his bed.

The pain in his leg was dull. The painkillers were doing their job. But the memory of Hannah, walking away forever, pierced through the fog.

'Shiiiit,' he slurred. He looked up, expecting to see a nurse ready with questions and pills.

No nurse. Just Goofy, sitting in the bedside chair. The lights were on. It was evening.

'Oh, it's you,' Jake said.

'Expecting Hannah?'

'I got binned. No thanks to you.'

'What?'

'Hannah. I told her the truth, most of it at least.'

'Good.'

'But she said I had to go to the police and fess up, or else me and her . . . we're over . . . So we're over.'

Goofy's brow was creased.

'Well, she's making sense. But right now you got bigger things to worry about, my friend.' Goofy got up, peeked outside the curtains and sat back down. 'You've had visitors. And they weren't here to wish you well.' Goofy shot Jake a knowing look. It took him a second to twig. He sat up, tried to force his head into alertness, but he was woozy with painkillers.

'They here now?' he said. 'They see you?' Jake strained his ears for voices or footsteps.

'No. But they'll be back.'

'How do they know I'm here?'

Goofy talked fast and low. 'They shot you. Not rocket science, is it? Where else you gonna go? Probably why they did it. So they can find you. They wait a day or two in case there's cops about, then they come and "visit" you.' Goofy made rabbit-ear air quotes with his fingers.

'Not a lot they can do here,' said Jake.

'You reckon? They can threaten you, and your family. They think we've still got the rest of their gear, don't they?'

Jake winced, remembering Goofy throwing the stuff into the water.

'Told you that was stupid.'

'Mebbe. Any case, they're never going to believe we haven't got it, are they? Not that I'd give it them if we had. Scumbags.'

'What can we do?'

'Tell the law, of course. Face the music. Come clean. With everyone. You're out of your depth, man. Me too.'

'Can't do that. Think what it'd do to Hannah. And you can't be involved, can you?'

'I can disappear. Done it before.'

'No, Goof. No way. You've got a life down here. This is your home.'

Goofy leant closer.

'Then we've only got one option,' he said.

'We have?' said Jake, pleased there was even one.

'Yeah. Avoid them. Get out and lie low. When you due to leave?'

'Tomorrow.'

Goofy reached out and pushed the large red button on the panel by the bed.

The nurse came running. When she saw them, she sighed and folded her arms.

'That's for emergencies,' she said.

'This is one,' said Goofy. 'Jake is discharging himself.' He stood up, opened the bedside cupboard, found Jake's bag and began filling it. Clothes, book, wallet, phone. Boxes of pills he'd been given to take home.

'You can't just go,' said the nurse. 'There's paperwork.'

Goofy dropped the bag on to the bed. He stood close to the nurse, holding her gaze.

'Have men come looking for him?' he said.

She looked to Jake, confused. 'Two guys came asking, yes. London types. Said they'd seen the accident and wanted to know if you were all right. But they didn't even know your name. I was suspicious, truth be told.' She looked from Goofy to Jake and back.

'Did you give them his name?'

'No.'

'Listen carefully.' Goofy held a finger to her face. 'I don't know you, but I'm going to trust you. Those men are dangerous . . .'

The nurse bit her lip, held her breath and gazed at Goofy with badly hidden excitement.

'Then the police—' she started.

Goofy shook his head and wagged his finger 'Can't help, believe me. Anyone you love ever been in danger? Your boyfriend, your mum?'

'No . . . but—'

'He is. So we're leaving. Now, if they come back, make sure they don't know *who* he is, or *where* he is. Threaten to call the law. Those guys won't hang around if you do that, trust me. Can you do that?'

The nurse held her breath. Then nodded.

'Come on, Jake.' Goofy filled the bag with the last of his stuff. Jake pulled the sheets back, grabbed the crutch by the side of the bed, and slowly, painfully, got to his feet. Goofy put the bag over one shoulder and took Jake's arm on the other.

The nurse watched them, wide-eyed and open-mouthed. Goofy winked at her. She smiled.

They limped slowly along, a monster with four legs, puffing and groaning. They hobbled and wobbled down one corridor, then another. When they got near the hospital entrance Goofy leant Jake against the wall.

'I'm going to scout the car park,' he said, and left.

Fear and strain pumped through Jake's head along with blood and adrenalin. Pain sang through the thick numbness of the pills. Cold sweat tickled his back.

In the distance at a crossroad of corridors, a man with a leather jacket and short hair walked across Jake's field of vision. He was visible for a second or two at most, but there was no mistaking him. It was the one who'd done the talking and the shooting: Smithy.

Jake pushed himself away from the wall and panted, lurched, step by step round the corner – and into Goofy.

'Coast is clear,' said Goofy.

'No, it isn't. They're here.'

Jake hadn't known he could move that fast. Adrenalin pushed and Goofy pulled him. They moved fluidly, suddenly able.

As they rushed out of the entrance, a voice cried: 'Hey!' They carried on, faster. To the van.

They got in and drove off, Jake panting heavily and sinking into the seat.

'This is bad, man,' he said. 'This is messed-up bad.'

Goofy didn't speak. He fixed his eyes on the road and drove.

It had all been so close, Jake thought. The money. Hawaii. Hannah. A future.

It had been ripped away with a piece of his leg. Just so he got the message, felt the agony and knew what he'd done.

Jake

HE WAS GLAD to be out of hospital, and not just because it was a whole lot safer. Before Goofy had come and got him, spending long days in that soulless place had left him dying inside.

He was reeling as if he'd been thumped, the same way Hannah had delivered him a killing blow when they first met. A different kind of punch now. Worse than a bullet to the leg: one straight to the heart.

He had needed her to come and see him. But she hadn't. She hadn't answered texts or calls, either.

So now, instead, he needed the sea. He needed air. He needed beer.

Something, *anything*, that might bring him back to life.

Walking was painful. He hobbled on crutches out of Goofy's flat.

'Where we going? Let me help,' said Goofy, trying to get an arm round him.

'You want to help? Take me somewhere to get good and drunk.'

'Few pints, is it? Drown your sorrows, like.'

'A few pints? Licking-the-carpet shit-faced, more like.'

'That a good idea, in your condition?'

'Yeah, it's a *very* good idea. Long as we're nowhere those bastards will find us. What else am I going to do? Can't go see Hannah, can I? Can't surf, neither.'

Goofy shrugged. 'All right, then.' Good idea or not, Goofy never needed much persuading when it came to necking ale.

Jake let Goofy help him into the van. He didn't have a choice. And he hated himself for it.

'Totally over, is it?' said Goofy, starting the engine.

Jake looked out of the window. The weather had cleared a bit since the storms. There were patches of blue in the sky, a sunny day in the offing. He thought it might do some good, seeing sea and sky instead of walls and screens.

'Yeah, man,' he said. 'It's over.' Saying it out loud made it real. Not just him and Hannah being over, but the drug deal. The weight of it was lifted. And that, at least, was something good.

'Pub?' said Goofy.

'Nah. Let's go to a beach, the sea.'

'There's sea here.'

'Too much shadow. I need light.'

'Let's go to my lock-up. We can sit outside. Enjoy the autumn sun.'

★

They picked up beer, then drove to Perran Cove. It was a small, natural harbour, a deep gulley in the cliffs with fishing boats and a couple of yachts. A quiet place.

Goofy went into the old boathouse and came out with ancient deck chairs. He wiped dust and cobwebs off them, then went and found a table. Jake waited, sitting on the harbour wall.

Jake looked along the bay, down the track at the cottages and other boathouses. He felt the breeze, and the sun's rays on his face, listened to the ropes on the masts chiming and clanking, and looked at the rowboats, upturned and tethered.

Sights like this usually did his heart good, but not today. In the distance, he could see one of Lancaster's boathouses, a massive thing, blue and white and shining, where Lancaster kept a speedboat. He looked at Goofy's lock-up with its engines and oil, then at the filthy deck chairs and wonky wooden table with beers on it.

He finished one beer quickly and opened another.

'Should you drink like that, with the painkillers?' said Goofy.

'Gonna judge me, are you?'

'No need to lose it, man. Course I'm not going to judge you. Do whatever you like. Just saying, take it easy. Thass all.'

'Yeah. Sorry. It's just . . . all so screwed up, Goofy. It all went so bad, so quick. And it's my fault.'

'Well, it's over now.'

'Yes. It's over now.'

Goofy sat down in a chair. Jake thought it might be hard for him to get into one. And he might struggle to get out after some beers. So he stayed sitting on the wall.

'Still,' said Goofy, leaning forward, pointing. 'I will give you one bit of advice.'

'Oh, Christ. Here we go.'

'You *should* tell Hannah the truth.'

'I can't.'

'Because of Lancaster?'

'No. I don't give a toss about him. But if the police get involved, you get dragged in and that's not good.'

A shadow of worry darkened Goofy's face. 'You don't have to tell *them,* man. You just need to tell Hannah *why* you can't tell the law. In other words, that it's her dad. Then she'll understand.'

Jake shook his head. 'You reckon she'll thank me? For her whole life falling apart in front of her, right before she's meant to go to Hawaii? No, Goof. No. She adores her dad. It would break her heart. I can't do that.'

Goofy set to rolling a fag. 'So let me get this crystal. You won't tell her because you love her and don't want to hurt her. You'd rather lose her than hurt her, and meanwhile that smug bastard Lancaster gets away with everything? Hannah thinks Daddy's a guardian angel. One that's full of purity and virtue. And she thinks you're a coward for not going to the police. She believes these lies. You've lost the best thing that ever happened to you and that bastard Lancaster comes out the sewer smelling of roses and lavender.'

'Yeah,' said Jake. 'That's the size of it.'

Goofy lit his rolly. 'Making a martyr of yourself, you are. I dunno which smells worse, man, your burning flesh or your bullshit.'

'You said you wouldn't judge.'

Goofy shrugged, staring into the distant sea. 'All right, then. I'll tell her. Fuck Lancaster. He ain't getting away with this shit. And you deserve to have a chance with that girl.'

'No!' Jake picked up his crutch off the wall and hurled it, sending the small wooden table and beers flying.

He had Goofy's attention.

'You think she'd thank me? You think she'd run into my arms? I'm still a screw-up. Finding out her dad's a drug dealer would mess with her head big time. And anyway, what good would it do? I don't have money for Hawaii. She doesn't have money to pay for the rescue. Even if I could go to Hawaii now, I wouldn't. What about Mum? I was going to help out, wasn't I? No. It wouldn't do any good, Goof. I couldn't do it to Hannah. Why aren't you getting that?'

'All right, then,' said Goofy. He stood, picked up the table and handed Jake his crutch back. 'Might as well have a little fun.'

'Fun?'

'See Lancaster's boathouse?' Goofy walked into the lock-up

and came out with an old pair of binocs, which he handed to Jake. Jake's gut burned with worry. Goofy had that old crazed look, and twisted smile on his face. That *always* meant trouble.

'What you going to do?' said Jake. Goofy put a finger up, like saying, *Wait a minute.* He went back into the lock-up and came back with a tin of white paint and a paintbrush taped to a long stick. Jake had seen Goofy use it to paint parts of boats that were hard to reach.

'This'll cheer you up,' said Goofy. He marched off down the track and along the harbour.

'Stop, Goofy,' Jake shouted.

Goofy waved the paintbrush in the air, without looking back.

Jake necked more beer then looked down the track again. Goofy had disappeared. Jake used the binocs, searching: the track, the boathouses, the hill behind them, the rocks below the harbour wall. Nothing. Goofy had vanished.

Then he spotted movement. Goofy's head appeared on the roof of Lancaster's boathouse.

'Shit!' Jake looked around, frantically. There was an old guy down at the shore, scraping seaweed off some lobster pots. But there was no one else around.

He looked through the binocs again. The side of the boathouse was painted a deep ocean blue, behind the logo for Lancaster Holdings, a huge silver anchor. Goofy was leaning over the edge of the roof, so far that Jake couldn't believe he didn't fall off. To the left of the anchor logo, Goofy painted a vertical line, about a metre long. Then he pulled the stick-brush back, reloading it with paint. He painted another long line, about a metre from the other one.

What was Goofy doing?

The stick-brush disappeared again; came into view again. Goofy painted a giant upturned V between the two lines.

Jake put a can of beer to his mouth, tried to drink, but . . . realised what Goofy had done. He snorted beer out, spluttering. Shock-laughing. Seeing . . .

A massive 'W', followed by a pic of an anchor.

'Oh shit. Oh shit!' Jake shook his head, laughing. He imagined Lancaster's face when he saw it. Jake got a fit of the giggles. Bad.

Two minutes later, Goofy appeared from behind the nearest boathouse. He looked around. 'Sneaked back like a cat, I did. Anyone see me?'

Jake shook his head, laughing.

'Whatcha think?' said Goofy, grinning, stick-brush in hand, looking up the track at his handiwork.

'I think you're mental,' said Jake. 'You know, he'll know me and Hannah are finished. I think he'll guess it's us.'

'Who gives a toss? Put a smile back on your face, didn't it?'

It had too. Jake felt human again, a bit like his old self. Getting out of that hospital, seeing the sea, drinking beer, watching Goofy behave like an idiot. It was a good mix. What he needed.

He looked out to sea. The storms had gone, for a while at least. The horizon was lined with wind-ruffled water. Shafts of sunlight were poking through the clouds.

He laughed some more. Told himself life could be better again.

But as soon as he stopped laughing he felt that small, brief joy leak out of him.

It was funny, what Goofy had done. Childish, stupid-arsed fun. And it had made a difference. But only for a minute.

He tried to laugh. Forced himself. As if, if he didn't, he might cry. He'd heard that before: *If I don't laugh, I'll cry.* He'd never thought it might be a real thing.

'Christ,' he sighed, and opened another beer. 'This isn't doing the job. Get us some vodka, will you?'

'Seriously?'

'Yes. You don't know what it's like, man. I never felt this. I never . . .' He felt himself choking and tearing up, but pushed it away and breathed deeply. 'I had it sussed, Goof, I had it all ready. I was going to help Mum. Now what? Losing the house? And Hannah? I loved the bones of her. Her skin, the smell of her. Her laugh. Now my guts have been torn out. My heart too. Get me some vodka.'

'No.'

'She's like the sun, man. All the rest of it, my shitty life. I didn't know anything about anything. She put sunlight on everything. And it was straight off with her, Goof. I swear. The second I saw her, I knew. D'you get it? I knew, man. She's the

261

one. She's it. And I . . .' He choked again. 'Get me some bloody vodka.'

'You're not making much sense, dude. And still no.'

'Bastard.' Jake necked his beer, finishing it in seconds. Now the ground was spinning; it was working, he was getting drunk. Booze on top of painkillers. He was coming away from the earth. It was somewhere else. Or he was. Like a spaceman. He looked down at his leg, at the bandage below the shorts. It was someone else's leg. Distant.

'Time to get lost,' he said, and put his hand out for another beer. Hoping it would be filled.

He saw, from the corner of his eye, Goofy walk towards him. Jake kept his hand in the air, waiting.

The ground was moving, slowly circling. And the deadness inside too. Moving away. He wanted more booze. He put his hand inside his jacket pocket and found the painkillers. He put them on the harbour wall, laid them there till he could get a beer to wash them down.

He looked up. Goofy was looming over him like a giant vibrating shadow – moving sideways – staying still – moving again. Jake put a hand on the wall, to steady himself.

How many beers had he had, and how quick? It didn't matter.

'Come on, Goof, gissanother . . .'

The slap hit him hard and clean. His face sang with smart pain. He took a few seconds to get his breath, to speak.

'What was that for?'

Then another. Bam! Stinging.

He swung an arm out. Goofy stepped neatly back. Jake lost his balance, and had to steady himself.

'Grow up, Jakey.'

'What you doing?' He glared at Goofy.

'Judging you.'

'But you said—'

'I know what I said.'

'You do know Hannah chucked me? That she's in debt now? That I ain't going to Hawaii. What can I . . .' He was losing it now. The tears were running. 'I lost her, Goof!'

'Sort it out, then. Get her back.'

'How?'

Goofy sighed and shook his head, like he was dealing with an idiot, or a child. 'That's the growing-up bit. I don't *know* how. *You* don't know how. You promise yourself you are going to do it and you work it out. You stop feeling sorry for yourself.' They stared at each other for long seconds. 'Grow up, man. Stop whining like a kid. Have a few drinks, sure. Pity yourself . . . for a bit. But you're taking the piss. Now man up. Sort this shit out.'

Hannah

'HANNAH, THEY'LL BE here soon.' It was Mum's voice, muffled by the bedroom door. Some sharp raps followed. 'You will come down soon . . . Hannah . . . ? Hannah?'

Hannah. Hannah. Knock. Knock. Knock. Hannah. Hannah. Like an alarm clock, breaking the silence of early evening. 'Hannah!' The door opened. 'You're still in bed!'

She wasn't. She was lying *on* it, in her PJs. With her dress next to her. And make-up on the dresser, lined up ready to use. She just hadn't had the energy to put on either. Those tasks seemed like oceans that couldn't be crossed. She just wanted to lie there. Forever.

'Really, sweetheart.' Mum came and sat on the side of her bed. She held Hannah's face in her hands and rubbed at her cheeks with her thumbs. 'You've been crying again. Your face is puffy.'

Hannah tried to smile. 'Yeah, sorry.'

Mum sighed. 'I know it's hard. But we're here for you. We love you. In a few days you'll be on that plane. You can put all this behind you.'

'I don't know if I want to put it behind me.' She sat up and drank some water. Her mother's face was wide-eyed with panic. 'Don't fret, Mum. I just mean the memories. Not . . . Jake. He *is* behind me, now.'

'Oh. Right. Well . . .'

It was awkward. Mum and Dad had been trying to disguise their relief; trying not to look actually *pleased*. Trying.

'You'd better get dressed. And, Hannah, dear, I'm not sure that's the right dress.'

She had picked one at random, not caring what she wore for Simon and his parents. Only now did she see she'd picked out her Roxy summer dress. The one she'd worn for Jake the night they'd first made love.

Mum walked to the wardrobe, riffled through Hannah's clothes and picked out two dresses, both of them black, simple and smart. She put them down on the bed, picked up the green Roxy, folded it and put it in a drawer.

'Do put on a brave face, Hannah. We're celebrating tonight. Please don't spoil it for your father.' Mum left.

Hannah was annoyed by this bossiness, this pick-yourself-up attitude, but she knew she had no right to be. She had moped for long days. And Mum had been so kind: running her baths and bringing her thick sandwiches and steaming soup. She'd held her as she cried, as if she was a child again. Mum had indulged her, covering her with a blanket of care and kindness, trying not to ask *too* many questions, but unable to help herself.

What went wrong, Hannah? I don't want to talk about it.

What did he do? Nothing, Mum. I just don't want to talk about it.

Is it final? Have you finished for good? Is it over? Yes. Yes. Yes.

She picked up one of the dresses, got out of her PJs and put it on. Some make-up too. Enough to hide behind.

She heard the doorbell. The cooing, the 'welcome's, and 'darling's.

'Hannah, they're *here.*' Dad's voice. Not messing: *Come down. Now.*

She duly walked down the stairs and found the visitors in the kitchen. She forced a quick, brave smile at Mum. *Don't worry. I won't let you down.*

There were hugs and kisses from Simon's mum and dad, Lottie and Richard. There was warmth in it. Real affection. The families were old friends. She did feel better, a bit. Simon just stood there, smiling awkwardly.

'Hann, sweetheart,' said Lottie. 'You're a hero. The whales! I saw it on the news. They talked about you. Said you organised the whole thing. How come they didn't interview you afterwards?'

'They wanted to. I said no.' They were examining her. Like Mum with her questions, expecting more from her than she could give. Hannah tightened her lips. A voice inside her begged: *Stop asking me these things. Talk about something else. Question someone else. Please.*

Silence.

Dad clapped his hands together, getting their attention. He opened the fridge. There were multiple bottles of champagne in there. He got busy with one, unscrewing the wire and peeling off the foil.

'Well, our families have *much* to celebrate.' Dad was being good-natured, theatrical.

She looked at the table in the connecting dining room, laid for six and perfectly decorated with blue glass plates and marine-blue napkins. There were different glasses for different wines, and dusted bottles of red on the table. One had the same label as the bottle she and Jake had stolen. No, *Jake* had stolen. These were Dad's best.

Dad stood with everyone around him in a semicircle. He coughed to get their attention. 'Hannah, has, in spite of everyone's doubts, yes, including mine, pulled off an *amazing* rescue of stranded whales. Simon has got into Oxford. And the marina project is finally on its way.'

Pop. The froth exploded. Lottie and Mum whooped, as if a firework had gone off.

Dad looked different now. The lines of worry were still there, the greyness in the skin. But he looked lighter, somehow. His eyes were lit by a brightness that Hannah hadn't seen in months.

'Yes, the marina,' said Mum. 'Your father said we shouldn't make a fuss, but I absolutely insist.' Her voice was high-pitched, excited.

'Why, what's happened?' said Hannah. Dad looked sheepish. Almost embarrassed.

'Go on, Pete. Tell her,' said Mum.

'Well . . . I didn't want to worry you, nor did your mother. But for a while it really looked like the marina might not happen. Money. Investments not coming through. That kind of thing. Very dull. And if it hadn't . . . well, it would have landed me . . . er, us, in *very* hot water.'

'But now the money has come through,' said Hannah.

'Yes. Well . . . not as much as we were expecting, but enough to keep things moving in the right direction.'

'That's great, Dad. You said you would do it. You said you'd get there.'

She needed to feel good about something. It was hard, but she was pleased. For Dad. And to be here, with family and friends, drinking champagne.

'Look,' Dad said. 'I don't want to be American about the whole thing, but, well, in a few months we're all going to be raaaaather well off.' Dad and Richard laughed, like this was the biggest, funniest understatement ever. 'And, Hannah, I'm going to help you. With the money for the whales.'

Don't say it, she thought. *Don't say 'because that ex-boyfriend let you down'*.

Dad didn't say it. He didn't need to. He smiled. He was

being playful and bright. Very unlike Dad. The Dad of the past few months, anyway.

And that was good too.

He poured the champagne. Mum raised her glass.

'To Hannah. To Simon. To the marina.' They clinked, and drank.

The parents started chatting. Glasses were quickly topped up.

The older folk gathered in a tight group, leaving Hannah and Simon together.

This same show had been played out a hundred times. The 'grown-ups' leaving them together. It was how she and Simon had ended up an item in the first place.

They stood, glasses in their hands.

'Hi, Hann.'

'Hi, Simon.'

'Great about the whales, well done.'

'Thanks. Great about Oxford.'

They clinked glasses.

'And the money,' he said. 'Your Dad helping. That's great too. I would have helped, you know, if . . . well, sorry to hear about things not working out with . . . him.'

'No, you're not.'

He smiled. 'All right. Truth be told, I'm not.'

Hannah laughed. At least Simon was honest.

'How's it going with Bess?' she said. Simon's smile dropped off his face. 'Oh, come on, Si. It was obvious. And I don't mind. I don't mind at all.'

'Okay. But . . . it wasn't . . . *isn't* serious. It was just a brief summer thing. I'm off to Oxford, so we couldn't carry on anyway.'

Hannah thought of Jake, how he'd once said he'd wait for her while she was in Hawaii. 'Anyway,' she said, wanting to *not*-think about Jake. 'Good news about the marina.'

'Weren't you worried?'

She shrugged. 'I didn't know how big an issue it was till you told me in town that day. And I thought Dad would sort it, to be honest. He always does.'

'*Really?*' Simon scrutinised her face. He looked sideways at the 'grown-ups'. He closed in, talking quietly.

'They were screwed, Hann. Mum levelled with me. They were up to their necks in debt. There was no money to carry on with it and huge contracts to pay. They were going bust.'

'Come on, Si. This is the dads we're talking about. Pete and Richard. They'd have sold a cottage or two, maybe a yacht. Some shares.'

'No. You don't understand. They were in for millions. *Millions.* Over their heads. They'd have gone bankrupt.'

'And it all just magically got better, did it? The money just turned up?'

'Yes. Something happened. But I don't know what.'

'What are you two whispering about?' Dad came over and filled their glasses.

'The marina, Dad. We're just pleased it's all come good.'

'So am I, so am I.' He put the bottle down, wrapped his arm round Hannah, squeezed her and kissed her cheek.

★

The table was set beautifully. And she hadn't eaten properly in days, in spite of Mum's efforts.

Tuna carpaccio. Lobster and salad. Amazing wines. Hannah settled into the evening. She promised herself to make an effort, to put the last few days behind her. Because maybe that was what you had to do with a broken heart: decide you would put it behind you, then work hard at doing just that.

The memories of the storms – of Jake, of the whales – all those hard realities seemed a little more distant now. So different from the life she now had in front of her, perfectly laid out like the dinner table.

She had needed those days, though. Without make-up, lying in bed, or walking Beano on the beach. Thinking. Being alone. She had been through so much.

But maybe it was okay to enjoy this now. The simple, elegant, fresh seafood. The cool lemon and vanilla wines. Gold and apple-coloured liquids that made her taste buds sing and her skin tingle.

Dad had lit a fire in the hearth, to keep them warm when the sun went down.

Old family friends brought a different kind of happiness to the one she'd had with Jake, but it was happiness all the same.

A feast. Of all the good things in her life. Things she had

taken for granted, even forgotten, while she and Jake were chasing Beano on the beach. Sand between your toes was a delicious thing. But it wasn't real. It was holidays, not life. And it couldn't have lasted.

Meeting Jake. Whales. Jake getting shot. Danger. Storms. All that was an adventure all right. But you had to have somewhere to come back to. Somewhere safe. A home.

And that was this, now.

She even enjoyed Simon's company: his attention, and the familiar, clumsy flirting. Occasionally he touched her arm, or his leg brushed against hers. She pulled away from these small intimacies, but always slowly and carefully, wanting neither to lead him on, nor to hurt him.

Everyone was in a good mood.

She told herself it was good, this life.

She had once told Jake it was a prison. How foolish had she been?

'Being a bit quiet, Hannah,' said Dad. 'More wine?' She pulled her gaze away from the fire. She had been lost in its flames, thinking.

'Sorry, Dad. Just stuffed.' She patted her stomach, which was tight as a drum. 'No more just now, thanks. I'm fine.' She covered her glass before he could top it up.

Dad and Richard carried on talking about the marina. The oyster bar they'd open. The regatta they'd run every year. They were buzzing with booze and plans – their old selves.

'Shall we leave them to it?' said Simon.

'Sure,' said Hannah. 'Fancy a cup of tea? Then maybe take Beano out. Get some air?'

Hannah half listened to the boisterous chatter as they walked to the kitchen:

'. . . Caribbean connection.'

'. . . Offshore stocks . . .'

'Charlie came through for us in the end.' A clink of glasses at that comment. Sniggers and guffaws. The mums politely clinking too. 'You two leaving us?' Dad shouted.

'Yeah. Too much food and vino. We need tea and air. Delicious, though, thanks so much, Mum. And Dad, thanks for the amazing wines. Who's Charlie?'

A look passed between Dad and Richard. Richard raised his eyebrows. He muffled a snigger.

'What's so funny?' said Hannah. 'Who's Charlie?'

They didn't answer. Neither Dad, nor Richard. The only sound was the crackle of the fire.

'Well, go on,' said Mum. 'Who is this Charlie? You've never mentioned him before?'

'Someone from Peru we invested in heavily,' said Richard, his words slurring slightly. 'Looked like he was going to let us down for a bit. The stormy waters of offshore investments, and all that. But he delivered in the end. Here's to Charlie.' He raised his voice. He raised his glass. Too loud, too boisterous. When no one joined the toast, he drank the whole glass, in one go. 'The thing about our chum Charlie is—'

'Shut up, Richard,' said Dad. Quietly.

Mum and Lottie looked confused. The atmosphere had changed. Hannah didn't know why. She stepped forward.

'Who is Charlie, Dad? Someone who lent you the money?'

'Why are you asking, Hannah?' said Dad.

'Just curious.'

She was confused. She never asked Dad about business. She wasn't usually interested. But this seemed so strange. Two days ago, he had – apparently – been going bust. For millions. Now they were drinking champagne. All because of someone called Charlie. From *Peru*?

Dad sighed. 'An investment, if you're really interested. Long-held offshore stocks. Tied up. Didn't think we could sell them yet. But we did, and at the right price.' His smile was back now; he'd regained his composure. Just like when the policeman had told him about *Pandora*. 'Of course if you're *really* interested we can go through the paperwork. Do you want to see the accounts, Hannah?'

'I was only asking,' she said, and turned to go . . . except she'd had a thought. An *insane* thought. Odd connections were forming in her head, words and events weaving together into an impossible thread.

Pandora. The marina, and their miraculous turn of fortune. Jake and his drug deal. The word 'Charlie'. A nickname for cocaine. How Dad and Richard had reacted to it. Jake in hospital. Jake saying he'd found the drugs in a cove, then changing his mind and saying it was on a beach. Saying the drugs came from a yacht, then saying that was just a guess. A yacht like *Pandora*? No. Not possible. Questions piled up in her head. She felt her face flush red. A moment of panic. Did she really want to know the answers to these questions? Yes, she did. And she knew her father. She would know, now, if he was lying.

'Do you know anyone called Smithy?' she said. 'A friend of Charlie's, perhaps? Someone who had something to do with *Pandora* sinking?'

'Pete,' said Mum. 'What's going on?' Dad looked at her, then back at Hannah.

'*Nothing,* darling. Hannah,' he said, in his kindest, softest voice. 'I've never heard of this Smithy. Okay?'

He smiled. The way he said 'okay' was final. A conversation-ender, telling her to trust him – and to shut up. He smiled. 'Now go and have your tea, Hannah.' It sounded like a threat.

And she knew. She *knew.*

She put a hand over her mouth.

'Are you okay, darling?' said Mum.

Hannah felt the world move. She heard it in the soft howl of the wind outside. And in the silence in the house. She saw it in the puzzled gaze of her mother and in the stifling air, thick as water. Everything was suddenly, overwhelmingly, a nightmare.

'I feel sick,' she whispered. She took a step back, shaking her head. 'It can't be. You . . .'

'What, darling? Me what?' Dad put his glass down, stood up and stepped towards her, as though to hold her.

'No! Don't touch me. Don't you *dare* touch me.'

'Hannah?' said Mum, looking from Dad to Hannah and back again.

She knew what Jake hadn't told her – and why.

'Dad,' she said, 'who are you? Who the hell are you?'

'Hannah, don't speak to your father like that.'

'You don't know him, Mum.'

The horror of realisation spread over his face. Because she knew the truth of him now. And he saw it.

Hannah left the room with Simon. They walked through to the kitchen. Simon went to the kettle, but Hannah grabbed Beano's lead and her coat, and charged out of the door. Simon and Beano followed.

'Hey, what about the tea?' said Simon.

Hannah ran to the bushes, into the dark, bent over and threw up. Then ran . . .

She ran into the night, ignoring Simon when he called her name. Away from houses and streetlights.

She ran till the wind drowned Simon's shouts, the village was behind her and she was in darkness.

She stumbled and tripped. Blind, but still running. Beano at her heel. She ran and ran and ran, till she found herself at the cliffs. The moon was half hidden by cloud, but she could see the old tin mines, the ruins that clung to the cliffs near Penford Cove.

She gasped. The mines were *miles* from home. How long had she been running? How had she even got here? She had no idea. The time between leaving the house and now was a blur. All she could remember was darkness and running.

She fell to the ground, dripping sweat and tears. When she had caught her breath, she sat up and looked around.

Most of the mine's walls and towers had crashed down on to the rocks long ago. Chunks lay broken on the ground, grown over with moss and lichen.

But the main chimney still half stood, jagged and black against the sky.

Inside it was a stone stairwell with a dark space beneath. Perhaps an old furnace. She stood for a moment, walked over and crawled into the hollow.

The ground was dry there, and the walls a protection from the wind. She took her coat off and sat beneath it, with her knees hunched under her chin, looking to the sea.

Beano nuzzled into her. She clung to his fur. And thought: *What now?*

Her life had been safe and secure. Certain, unmoving. Her family, her home, her boyfriend. The future too: her career.

Were any of these things real, now? Had they *ever* been? Or had it been an illusion: one massive, fantastic lie? The ground beneath her had just been a flimsy raft. Her life had tipped over. She'd fallen into a dark sea.

If there had been no storms, there would have been no stranded whales, no need for Jake to find money to help her. None of this would have happened. She'd still be living in blissful ignorance about Dad.

Was it better to know the truth, however awful?

She didn't know.

Beano sat up and licked the tears off her cheek with a hot, sandpaper tongue.

'Gerroff, you disgusting beast.' She laughed, in spite of everything. Breathed deep, felt a little calmer. Tried to think.

She couldn't stay there. Maybe she should go to Phoebe or Bess's.

She would. Soon. But drops of rain were falling outside. And the wind was blowing stronger.

So for now . . .

She lay down and pulled the coat over her shoulder. Beano lay down too. She put her head on his tum.

'Makes a change, eh, mutt? Me using you as a pillow.'

She would go soon. But the longer she lay there, the less she wanted to move.

What was that thing Mum said when Grandpa died? The news had 'knocked the stuffing' out of her. That was about right. That was how Hannah felt now. She'd had the stuffing knocked out of her, and now she was hollow.

Jake

HE HAD WOKEN in the night, in pain, taken more pills, and then slept.

The rest had done him some good. The ache in his thigh wasn't so sharp. The storm in his head was less violent than it had been in the middle of the night.

But he still felt like crap. A hangover weighed on him like a blanket. His leg was messed up, Hannah was gone, and now Goofy had smacked him round the chops.

That still stung.

He reached out for the bottle of pills by the bed. Paused.

The doc had said to take them *before* the pain got too much. Every few hours.

Yeah, they killed pain. But they made him dizzy-sick too. And he didn't like the fog they wrapped round everything.

He'd needed that fog yesterday. Not today.

★

Tackling the stairs was tricky. He put both feet on a step, then moved his good leg down to the next one before hopping the bad leg down, using one crutch.

Mum and Hattie came running from the kitchen. Sean followed, gawping.

'Oh, Jake. Let me help you,' said Mum.

'No. I'm fine. It just takes time.' Jake reached the bottom of the stairs, panting. Somehow, all this was harder with them watching.

'You have to let us help you, Jake,' Hattie said, as he made his way to the kitchen. 'We want to.'

Maybe he would let Hattie play nurse. She was clearly into the idea. Sean came in behind and leant against the fridge, arms folded, grinning as Jake struggled with sitting.

'If you need help going for a dump, I'm not doing it.'

'Thanks, bro.'

'Shouldn't you have a parrot on your shoulder, Long John?'

'Your jokes aren't funny, Sean,' said Mum.

Sean grabbed the crutch, and hopped around the kitchen. 'Oh, yes they . . . aaaarrrrrrr,' he groaned, in his best pirate voice.

Hattie laughed. Sean playing the fool, Mum setting to making breakfast, the Saturday smell of bacon and coffee, the sound of eggs being cracked – it all meant normality. Normality was good. Normality was what Jake needed.

Hattie and Sean sat opposite.

'Go on, then,' said Sean. 'Tell us how you fell on this spike.'

The little git was stirring. Mum might buy whatever story he cooked up. Sean already didn't.

'I was working with Goofy, down the docks. Storm-damaged boat. Lost my balance trying to get the thing out the water. There was a spike off an old iron harbour fence, in the water. Storms must've uncovered it. Could be worse. People have lost homes in the storms. Folk have died on the roads.'

'Ned's new bird almost died.'

Jake froze, lifting a glass of juice to his lips.

'What . . . um . . . about Ned's girlfriend?'

'Rag told me. She hit a deer on the road. Came home covered in blood, apparently. Same day as you fell on your "spike". Rag says her fancy car's fine. You'd reckon it'd be a write-off.' Sean raised a cheeky eyebrow. The little bastard knew something. Not the whole story, but *something*.

Jake didn't want Sean to know *that*. Not ever. He glanced at Mum, but she wasn't paying attention. Too busy with breakfast.

'Are you all right to fly?' said Mum. 'With that leg.'

Jake took a deep breath. 'I ain't going to Hawaii, Mum.'

Mum turned. 'Not . . . going?' She looked at Jake, frowning and puzzled. She wiped her hands on her jeans.

'I can't afford it, Mum.'

'Oh. I thought . . . you were coming into some money?'

Jake shot a look at Sean. Sean shrugged.

A cloud had fallen on Mum. She was suddenly hunched, and sad. What had Sean told her, what had she been led to hope for?

'And Hannah? You . . . and Hannah?' Her voice was high-pitched, clinging to hope.

He shook his head. 'Over.'

'Oh, Jake, no! Sweetheart, it's only a few months. You can—'

'It's over.'

'But I love Hannah!' Hattie shrieked, her face a *the-world-just-ended* mask of horror. 'I really love her!'

'Yeah,' said Jake. 'Me too.'

Even Sean looked beaten by this news. 'Bro. That's a bad deal,' he said.

'Yeah.'

Mum went back to cooking, picking up the frying pan and moving the bacon around. 'I loved Hannah too. But if that girl isn't prepared to wait for you. Well . . . I'm not sure I can say.'

'It weren't her fault, Mum.'

'Well, she finished it, didn't she? I can't believe it was you.'

'It was my fault. In a way.'

Mum looked round again. 'What did you do?'

'Something so massively stupid, I'm not going to tell you. So there's no point asking. Okay?' He pointed at Sean.

'Okay,' said Sean.

'Never mind, Jake,' said Hattie. 'You can spend more time

with us now. And . . . it's bad you're not going away, but it's good too.' She came and hugged him.

'Yeah, little sis.' He kissed her cheek.

'How come you're suddenly so broke, then?' said Mum, routing in cupboards and drawers for a plate, a knife and fork. 'Hattie, get your brother a slice of bread, and butter it for him, will you? You can serve.'

Nurse Hattie got to work. Mum sat down. 'Well, it is good you'll be around. I'm going to need help . . . I was going to ask you for a bit of help with the rent, with the money you're getting.'

Jake glared at Sean, and Mum saw. 'It's not Sean's fault, Jake. He was just trying to help.'

He didn't like to see Mum like this. Embarrassed, her words breaking up with shame. 'I was only . . . talking about . . . *borrowing*, for a bit. This money you're getting. It's your money, love. It'll help set you up. I just meant for a bit, you know.'

'It's *our* money, Mum. But I ain't getting it. Not for a while. Sean told you wrong. Sorry.'

'Oh.' She sighed, deflating like a balloon, until she looked more crippled than he was. Like she might find it hard to stand again. Knocked out.

'We'll find a way to sort the rent,' he said. 'Don't worry.'

Mum's gaze dropped on to the wood of the table. She put her hands on its surface, like if she didn't hold herself there, she'd slip to the floor. 'Don't worry? That's easy to say, Jake, my son.' The words were barely whispered.

'We'll sort it out, Mum.' He leant across the table, wincing with the pain of doing it. He took her hand. 'Okay, Mum. Okay?'

'How? You're not even going to be able to do bar work for some time.'

'I don't know yet. But we will. I promise. Sometimes you have to decide you're going to do something, then you work out how.'

She looked up, smiling through the worry. He winked at her.

Hattie plonked a plate of eggs and bacon in front of him. The bacon was burnt. One of the egg yolks had burst, leaking on to sloppily buttered bread.

'Deeeelicious!' he said, and tucked in.

Hattie beamed. 'Yay! Mum, it's time to take me to Suzie's.'

Mum looked up at the clock. 'Oh yeah. Come on, then.'

They went to get their coats and shoes. Sean sloped off too.

Jake waited for the door to click shut then counted to twenty, to give Mum and Hattie time to get out of earshot.

'Sean! Get here now.'

Sean didn't answer. Jake stood up, which hurt. Balancing a hand on the chair, he lifted the crutch, and used it to stab at the ceiling, so hard it shook.

Boom, boom, boom, boom. 'Now, Sean!'

Sean padded down the stairs.

'Sit down.'

'I'm just going out.'

'Sit. Down.'

Sean did as he was told.

'You little shit. Why'd you tell her I was getting the money? I *said* not to.'

'She was desperate.' He wasn't grinning now. He wasn't taking the mick, either. 'I found her crying. You said you were going to sort it, give her some money. I had to tell her, bro. I had to. You said you were going to help. But now you're not.'

'No. I can't.'

'What's going on, Jake?'

'What d'you mean?'

'The money. Ned's girlfriend. What are you involved in? Rag said your name was mentioned. The girl was going mental. Ned couldn't calm her down.'

Jake felt sweat on his brow. Pain was singing out in his leg, begging for attention.

'None of your beeswax,' he said.

'Bro. That blood, on Tasha. It was yours, wasn't it? I don't know what you're involved in, but be careful.'

Jake shook his head. This was his *younger* bro, telling him what *he* should do.

'Don't worry. There's no more trouble I can get myself in. It's got as bad as it can. I'm going to make it right with Mum too.'

'How?' Sean was a low kind of angry. Not fierce, or piss-taking. A scared kind of angry.

Jake sighed. 'I don't know.'

'Oh, that's all right, then!' Sean sat back. For all the sarky banter, he wanted Jake to come good. He was looking at Jake, *to* him, *up* to him. And Jake could hardly look Sean in the face. He couldn't face the hope he saw there.

'You going to make it right with Hannah too?' said Sean.

'I'd like to, mate. But I'm not sure if I can.'

Sean stood, making a 'tchuuuh' sound of disgust. He made to walk out of the kitchen then stopped at the door.

'Are you okay?' said Sean.

'Yeah. Go on, you'd best be off.'

Sean left. Jake crunched on the bacon and mopped the egg up with his bread.

His phone rang. He didn't want to speak to anyone, but he checked the caller ID anyway. It was Goofy. He cursed himself for hoping it might be Hannah, and put the phone down on the table.

Seconds later, a text arrived.

Answer yr phone, u muppet!

The next time it rang, he answered.

'How's the head?' said Goofy.

'Sore.'

'How's the leg?'

'That's sore too.'

'You heard about the whales?'

'No, what?'

'I might have a way for you to get back in Hannah's good books. I'm going to mail you a short vid, taken this morning. Fishermen mates of mine took some footage, on their way out to the banks. No time to waste, mind, you need to get this to Hannah.'

'What is it?'

'I'll forward it, and come round. Then I can drop you round hers, if you like.'

'What, Goofy, what footage?'

'See you in five.' The phone went dead.

He heard Sean at the door, putting on boots.

'Oy, don't go anywhere,' he shouted. 'Go get the laptop.'

Sean's head appeared round the kitchen door. 'Please tell me you ain't going to watch porn at the kitchen table while we're all out?'

'Funny. It's important – get it now.'

Sean did as he was asked. He set up the laptop in front of Jake, and sat back down.

'You can go now,' said Jake. Sean sat still, not going anywhere. Jake found his email account and opened the attachment from Goofy. Sean dragged his chair round, so he could watch too.

It was grainy, shaky footage, taken from a boat that was riding a rocky swell.

Jake could only see the sea at first, grey and green, then blasts of blue-grey sky and white clouds. The only sound was the whistling wind, making the phone mic crackle.

Then . . . a black fin, cutting out of the water. And another. Whales.

They were weirdly terrifying. They weren't the black and white blobs they'd been on the beach but great beasts, strong and supple. *Phoosh.* Their breaths sprayed into the air.

The footage was seasick, shaking and rolling in the waves. In the background, islands and rocks appeared and disappeared.

Jake knew where it was. Dangerous waters. Him and Goofy had been there, spear-fishing. But that was summer, when the water was calm.

The footage showed the whales circling something. The boat got closer. The whales didn't move away. They just kept circling, surrounding whatever it was, as the boat got closer still.

'It's caught, look.' A voice was shouting above the wind, and a hand was pointing.

Jake saw nets at the surface – and under the nets, a whale. Smaller than the rest.

'Little One,' Jake gasped.

'What?' said Sean.

'The whale. The young one. Shit, is she dead?' But she breathed a spume of spray and mist. Her mouth was opening. Yawning wide and clamping down, trying in vain to bite the net.

She was alive, all right. But pushing up, against the net.

'Hold up, there's rocks!' a voice shouted. There came the sound of the throaty groan of an engine's throttle.

'They can't get the boat nearer,' said Jake.

Yet whoever took the footage was close enough, to see . . . to film . . .

Below, in the deep, a whale was pressing against Little One's body underneath her. Another great black shadow swam into view. It did the same thing, on the other side. Siding up against Little One. The first whale then fell away, swam off, surfaced and breathed. Another whale appeared out of the depths, replacing the first.

Jake and Sean watched this happen, three times. One of the whales took over from another every minute or so.

'The whales are taking turns to keep Little One afloat,' said Jake. 'She must be so knackered . . . they're keeping her alive.' The film stopped on a blurred, frozen screen shot of the young whale's head. Its black marble eye was staring up at the men.

The door opened and Goofy bounced in. 'Seen it? Right, you gotta tell Hannah.'

'But the boat – didn't they do anything?'

'No. They couldn't get near. Besides, they want to get out and catch fish before the next storm comes. It wasn't till half an hour after that they even got a signal and sent me the clip. They know I know you and Hannah. They seen it all on the news, like.'

Jake looked at Goofy, then at Sean. Both of them stared back at him, expectant.

'We can sort this out,' he said.

Sean and Goofy looked at each other. 'Sort this out?' they said, together.

'Yeah. We can get out there, with wetties and snorkels. Get in the sea and cut the net.'

Goofy pointed at the crutch, leaning against the table. 'You probably can't go for a piss without help. Now you're Bear Grylls? Don't be soft, man. Tell Hannah and her whale-hugging mates. She'll be grateful you told her.'

'Tell her what?'

Goofy put his hands up in disbelief. 'What's going on! Where the whales are!'

'You got coordinates?'

'No.'

'What then? We gonna give her directions?'

Goofy opened his mouth to answer, then shut it again. Opened. Shut. Jake had a killer point. Those rocks and islands would all look the same to anyone who didn't know them. There were dozens of them too, spread over a lot of sea. Jake and Goofy knew *exactly* where the whales were, but they'd struggle to explain how to get there, even if they spent a while poring over a chart. And Goofy knew it.

'All right, well, I'll go with them,' Goofy said. 'You can't.'

'You know exactly where? You need me.'

'You're wasting time. Call her.'

'She's not answering my calls.'

'Send her a text.'

'I reckon she's blocked my number. And I dunno how long it'll be before she can get hold of a RIB. Goof, we need to get a boat.'

'Your leg, man!'

Jake looked down. Blood had seeped through the bandage. He would need a new dressing soon. They'd shown him how to do it at the hospital. The doc's words rang in his head: *Time and rest will heal it.*

He didn't have time. He couldn't rest. And this was a chance for him to come good. A little at least.

'It's a quick dive with a knife. We gotta move quick. You got any boats in?'

'Yeah, I got work lined up for weeks. All storm-damaged.'

'Any seaworthy?'

'There's one still on the water. Old thing. Got a high crack where it smashed against the harbour. It floats, though.'

'Good enough to go out in?'

'Spear-fishing, sure. But not in these conditions.'

'We have to go.'

'You do know there's another storm on the way?'

'How long have we got?'

'Hours. At the most.'

Hannah

HANNAH WOKE TO hear Beano grumbling. It was morning. Hard sunlight and fresh wind invaded the hollow.

'Hannah? Hannah!' It was Dad's voice, some way off but getting closer.

'Shut up, Beano,' she whispered, grabbing his muzzle. She put a finger to her lips. 'Shhh. I don't want to see him. Not now.'

'Beano!' Dad called, and Beano whimpered. Then: 'Hannah!' Closer. She held her breath. 'Beanoooo! Hannaaaah!' The dog wriggled, wanting to get up, to go and see.

Hannah turned to face the wall, and the darkness. Hiding.

'Hannah!' His voice croaked with desperation. How far had he walked? How many times had he called her name? Had he searched all night?

A shadow fell over her. She looked up. His silhouette blocked the light.

'Hannah. Thank God.' He crumpled down to kneel in the dirt. 'Thank God.'

She had a strong urge to hit him, followed by an equally strong urge to hug him. To cry on his shoulder.

She sat up and saw a bottle of water in the pocket of his coat. She leant over, took it, flipped the top, and drank.

'We've been worried sick,' he said.

She opened her mouth to speak, but nothing came out.

'We've looked all night. We've called all your friends. I even tried to get hold of Jake.' He looked to her for a reaction, like he always did. The old routine: father asks, daughter responds. Apologises. Explains.

Not this time.

'Well?' he said, glaring. Hannah kept her silence.

Dad's frown softened: 'I know this is . . . difficult, and we need to talk about it. But you at least owe me an explanation as to why you ran off and spent the night away.' He looked at her, unblinking, like he always did. Waiting.

Me? she thought. *I owe* you *an explanation?* It was almost funny. She kept her silence, still. It was the only weapon she had.

They looked at each other for a long while.

Dad took his phone out and made a call.

'I've found her. Yes . . . yes . . . she's fine. A little dishevelled, but fine.' He offered the phone to her. 'Your mother wants to talk to you.'

'Does she know?'

'Can you just speak to her?' He waved the phone in Hannah's face.

'*Does* she know?'

He shook his lowered head. 'No.'

She grabbed the phone. 'Hi, Mum,' she said, then held it away from her ear, so as not to be deafened by the stream of high-pitched cries.

She caught the odd word between choked tears and wails. 'Worry . . . sweetheart . . . home . . . Why?'

'I'm fine, Mum. I'm perfectly okay. Dad will explain. Later.'

He scowled.

'Dad will explain *everything*.' Hannah pressed the button ending the call.

His face was crumbling with shock.

'I can't do that, Hann. What would I say?'

'You could try the truth? Or just work out some bullshit lie. You're clearly good at it.'

He smarted at this. Pained by the words, as if she'd slapped him.

'Look, Hannah. We'll work it out, somehow. The important thing is, you're okay.'

'I'm not okay. I've never been less okay.'

'I mean . . . you're safe. We've spent all night searching. We've been worried.'

'You could have called the police. But you wouldn't do that, would you?' Her every word felt like a dart, dipped in poison and thrown hard.

He slumped against the wall. 'I know you hate me right now. I just wish you'd called, if only for your mother's sake. You owe me that at least.'

'I don't owe you *anything*,' she said. 'I don't even know who you are.'

'Perhaps . . . we should go for coffee. So we can talk.'

Hannah put her arm round Beano and squeezed him to her. 'No. I'm happy to talk right here.'

She was too. Comfortable on the dry earth, in the old mine. Crusty and unwashed as she was.

Dad sighed. 'How did you find out?'

'That doesn't matter, Dad. You're not turning this round. I know, okay? It doesn't matter how. You need to answer the questions. One at least. Why, Dad?'

He sighed and shook his head, burying his gaze in the ground.

'Rich and I got in deep with the marina. Things started going wrong. Promised investments not turning up, costs spiralling, delays. The usual stuff. We've been there with projects, a hundred times. But this was different. It was bigger. Much bigger. We were headed south, Hannah. I . . . was on my way to being bankrupt. It was all going to end . . . All of it . . .' His voice tapered into nothing. His head sagged lower.

'You've never said that before, have you? Not to anyone.'

'No.'

She wondered if he'd even admitted it to himself before now. She tried to feel pity. *Wanted* to feel it.

'So you thought you'd make it right by dealing drugs?' It sounded strange, saying it out loud. It seemed impossible. Ridiculous.

He sighed, as if a weight was falling off him, a great rucksack full of rocks dropping to the ground. But he still didn't look at her – maybe he couldn't – while he gathered the strength to talk.

'We'd have had to take you out of college, sell everything, and we'd still be in debt. We'd have lost the house. The cottages. The marina. The boats. We'd have had to move into a rented cottage.'

'Right. Unthinkable.'

'Quite . . . Oh, you were being sarcastic.' He coughed. 'I couldn't have got a decent job. Ever again. We'd have been ruined. I couldn't do that to you.'

'Oh, right. You did this for me. Christ, Dad.'

'How did you know?'

'I told you. It doesn't matter. So, you did this to avoid going bust? Like there were no other options. *We'll get there*, that's what you always say. You always do, so not this time?'

He put his hands up as if surrendering. 'All right. It was an easy way out. I admit it. At least that's how it seemed. But a one-off, I *swear*. They just wanted to use the boat, and I had to put in some investment. My last throw of the dice. It's nearly done now. We don't ever have to talk about it again. I am so sorry. I promise you, I will never, ever, ever do anything like this again. I know I've let you down. Please.'

He looked up at her with glistening eyes. He was pleading, looking for forgiveness. Dad, who could never be weak, was begging.

She couldn't forgive him. But she did begin to feel a kind of pity.

Beano's ears pricked up. He'd heard something, probably a bird or a rabbit. He got up and raced outside.

It was worse somehow, without Beano there. More awkward.

Hannah stood up and walked outside into the day. Dad followed. He put his hands in his pockets and walked a few feet away, to the top of the cliff. Right to the top.

'I'm sorry, Hannah. I'm so sorry.'

And she had the thought, the crazy thought . . .

'No! Dad!' And ran to him.

He turned, shocked. 'What, Hannah?'

'Oh, nothing.' Her heart hammered through her whole body. 'Nothing, I just thought, for one second.'

He looked down at the sea, and realised. 'Oh no,' he said. 'No. Things aren't quite that bad.'

Hannah reached out and hugged him. A voice inside her told her not to be so stupid, not to have pity. But this was Dad, and for one second she had thought the worst.

She held him tight, as if the world was spinning and he was a rock. She couldn't hate him. Nor could she stop loving him, even if she wanted to.

'I know this is awful, Hannah. I know. But at least the

marina's back on track. And we can pay your debt. You can go to Hawaii.'

She let go of him, stood back.

'What did you say?'

'I mean . . . It's over. Everything's going to be all right now. I know how stupid I've been. But it will never happen again. Never.' He was almost spelling out the words, wanting her to get the message loud and clear.

She felt her gut churning as if she might be sick. She took a step back, reeling. 'Dad? Don't you *get* it? You think I want your cocaine money? You think we can just pretend this never happened and move on?' She waited, searching his face for some sign, some flicker of regret, of penance. 'You have to get out of this, you have to wash your hands of all of it.'

'It's too late for that, Hannah. I can't go back on it now. It's almost done. These people, I've been . . . working with, they wouldn't let me,' he blustered. His hands flailed, imploring her.

'Don't you get it? I'd rather live in these ruins than live a life paid for with that money.'

'But you owe that Rocca chap. If I go bankrupt, you'd be in debt. Not just me!'

Hannah stamped a foot, folded her arms and shouted.

'If I have to do nothing but wash up in a pub for twenty years to pay Dr Rocca off, that's what I'll do! If we lose the house, we lose it. None of that matters, Dad. Not really. Don't you get that? We can start again.'

'No,' he said, shaking his head. '*You* can start again.'

The truth of it smacked into her. That was what it came down to. *She* was young. *She* had her whole life ahead. But not Dad.

'Jesus,' she said. 'You're worse than Jake.'

'Why, what's he done?'

'This isn't okay, Dad. This isn't you saying sorry for what you did, and me forgiving you. This is about you undoing this mess. You can do anything you want, you always have. You have to undo this. And Jake? Ha!' Another dart. The biggest one yet. '*He's* the one that found your cocaine, okay? He confessed everything to me and I ended it between us, because he wouldn't tell me who was involved, that it was your drugs he'd found and stolen. He ended it between us because he'd rather lose me than hurt me. Do you get that? Are you capable of even understanding that?'

'How much does he know?'

She shrugged, feeling braver now. 'Everything, as far as I know. Where it was, how much, who's got it now. That fact that it was *your* boat, *your* drugs. Everything!'

'Has he gone to the police?'

She wasn't hollow now. She was filled with iron. 'Not yet. But he will. I was the only thing stopping him. He will now. Or I will, if you don't end this.'

Dad walked backwards, staring at her. His phone rang. He answered, still keeping a careful, fearful eye on her, then strode quickly away, talking and listening. When he put the phone away, he came back.

'Who was that?' said Hannah. 'Was it Mum?'

'He can't go to the police, Hannah. Neither can you. You do understand that?'

'Who were you on the phone to?'

'No one.'

'Was it them? The people you're involved with? What were you saying?'

'They're going to *talk* to Jake. And I'm talking to you. No one is going to the police.'

'Oh my God, Jake!'

Dad put his hands up, then waved down, trying to calm her. 'They're just going to talk to him. He'll be fine, as long as he doesn't do anything stupid. They're just talking. That's all. Everything will be fine, but you *don't* go to the police.'

Was Dad threatening her? Using the threat of those people hurting Jake?

'They shot him in the leg, Dad. Did you even know that?'

'Just *talking*.' He was getting louder. Not shouting, but showing his teeth.

'The more you say *just talking*, the less I believe it, Dad. You're trying to be in control. Like always. But you're not. Are you?'

He looked at and through her, but didn't answer. Hannah knew he wouldn't. He couldn't hear those words. He couldn't acknowledge not being in control.

He backed away from her and turned, half running. Leaving her alone.

'Jake,' she said. 'Oh God, Jake. What have I done?'

Hannah

HANNAH RAN. HER breath and heart beat loudly in her head. Adrenalin pushed her over rocks and down paths.

It had felt good, facing up to Dad. Letting him know the truth. But what had she done with that truth? What damage had she caused?

Jake wasn't going to the police. But Dad didn't know that.

Would the people he was working with threaten Jake? Buy his silence? Beat him up?

Worse?

Just how far would these men go to protect themselves?

She didn't want to think about it, yet she couldn't think about anything else.

★

It took at least half an hour to get there. She didn't stop running, flat out, till she reached the end of the terrace. She hammered on the door. April answered.

Hattie was standing behind her mum. 'Hannah!' she shouted, squeezing past April. She threw her arms round Hannah and buried her head in her chest.

'How lovely to see you,' said April. 'Are you all right? You seem a bit out of breath.'

'Where's Jake?' said Hannah.

'He's not here, love. Gosh, everyone's looking for him today. And there was a message from your dad on the answer machine this morning, asking if you were here. All very confusing.'

'Who was looking for Jake?' Her voice cracked. Her heart pounded with panic. 'Tell me who, April.'

'A man. Said he has a contract for Jake. Some boat work. He didn't know about Jake's leg. Good money too and—'

'April, did Jake go with the man?'

April frowned. 'No. Jake had already left for the harbour.'

'When was this?'

'Not long ago. Is everything all right, love?'

Hannah gently unlocked herself from Hattie's embrace. 'Yes, everything's fine.' She forced lightness into her voice. 'I just need to see Jake, that's all. As soon as I can.'

She saw the secret smiles. The hope on Hattie and April's faces.

'Ah, you need to *see* him. He left a note. He's gone fishing with Sean and Goofy. But the man may have got to him before they set off. You might catch him if you're quick.'

'I need to use your phone. Now.'

'Um, sure,' said April, standing aside to let Hannah through. Hannah kept smiling. She didn't want to worry them. She *forced* cheerfulness. A cap on the fear inside her.

She picked up the phone. 'Oh God, oh God . . . What's Jake's number?' She had never called him on a landline before, only on her phone, which was sitting on the table by her bed. 'His number, April, what's his number?' she gabbled.

April gave it to her. Then: 'You *sure* everything's okay, love?'

Hannah turned away, focusing on listening to the rings. One. Two. Three. Too many. *Pick up, Jake, pick up.*

'Hi, Mum,' said Jake.

'It's not April, Jake. It's me.'

'Oh . . . Hannah.'

There was silence for a second or two. The heavy gap between lightning and thunder. Her heart burned just hearing his voice.

'Um, how are you?' he said.

'Listen to me! Where are you?'

'Down the harbour. We're about to set off. We can do this, Hannah. Get your people out here soon, but we can do this.'

'Do what? Never mind. Listen. Has my dad's man found you?'

'Your dad's man? What do you mean?'

Hannah turned. April and Hattie were standing there, following every word. Eager for clues indicating the Great

303

Reunion. 'He's been round here. Your house. He's got a contract for you.'

'Your dad's . . . man . . . contract.'

Her words were like cogs falling into place.

'Don't speak to him, Jake. The deal he's offering is bad. Very bad.'

'We're about to set off to sea.'

'Don't do that. Come home. Now.' Hannah didn't want to scare Hattie, but her voice was shaking. So was the phone in her hand. Jake's mum saw it.

'What's going on?' said April.

'The offer of work isn't a good one, Jake,' said Hannah. He had to understand.

'We'll deal with that later,' Jake said. 'We're out to sea. We've got a whale to rescue.'

'What?'

'There's a whale caught in a net.'

The words made no sense. *Whale. Net. Rescue.* Impossible.

Then she realised. 'It's dead, I told you. Days ago. Just get here, now. Away from the harbour.'

'*You* don't understand. This is new, it happened this morning. A whale is caught in nets. I thought that was why you were ringing? We can do this. Just get your people out here. They'll see our boat. We'll shoot flares if we can get them.'

'You need to come home . . . Jake, please.'

'Okay, okay. I hear what you've said. I get it. I know Mum's listening. Don't worry, we'll deal with your dad and his crew later. But we have to get out to sea now. It's probably the safest place. Yeah?'

She bit her lip. There was no time to talk. No way to reason with him. She had to act.

'Jake, let us know where the whales are, soon as you can. I'll tell Steve and Neil and we'll head out. And I'm going to call help. *Proper* help.'

Another pause, as he realised.

'No, Hannah. You can't do that.'

She put the phone down.

'What's going on, Hannah?' said April.

She couldn't find a lie to tell. She had to speak the truth, even if it meant scaring them.

'April. I'm calling the police. To get them to the harbour, to Jake, soon as they can get there.'

April put a hand over her heart.

'The police? Hattie, go to your room. Me and Hannah need to talk.'

'No!' said Hattie. 'Is Jake in trouble?'

Hannah took Hattie by the shoulders and held her gaze. 'Jake's going to sea to help with a whale rescue. He's safe out there. Do you understand? He's safe. But when he gets back in he's going to need the help of the police. We all are.'

'Why, Hannah, why?'

It was a burning question. It would have to be answered. But not now.

'Honey, there's no time to explain.'

'April, get the car started. We're going to the harbour.' A plan was forming in her head. She'd ring Neil on the way. She'd make sure Jake was okay, or, if he'd left, follow him out to rescue the whale from the nets.

Hopefully the police would find Jake, or the men. If not before, if Jake was already out to sea, then after the rescue.

Then he would be safe.

And after that?

There was no 'after' in her head.

Jake

JAKE PUT THE phone in his pocket and looked out to sea.

Hannah. He'd spoken to Hannah. Just hearing her voice had set him spinning. It made the ground shift like sand in the tide, made him sick with missing her.

'Oy, daydreamer,' Goofy shouted. 'Thought we was in a hurry.' Goofy had laid a pile of gear by the skiff. He was picking the last items up and chucking them in. Flippers, wetsuits, surfboards in bags. Goofy tapped his nose. 'Useful for shallow water, see. Go places a boat can't.'

'That was Hannah, Goofy. Bad news.'

Goofy froze, a pair of flippers in his hand. 'Go on.'

'Lancaster's men know who I am. They're coming here. Now.'

Goofy chucked the flippers in the hull and spat on the

ground. He grinned. 'We'll be ready for the bastards. We owe them for your leg.' He put a fist in the palm of his other hand and crunched his knuckles.

'We've got Sean with us. And . . .' Jake took a deep breath. 'Hannah's telling the cops.'

The grin fell off Goofy's face. 'Oh.'

Jake walked up to Goofy and put a hand on his shoulder. 'They'll be waiting when we get back. The men or the police. Maybe both. This isn't your mess. You should get away. Me and Sean can deal with the whale.'

Goofy's eyes darted to the road, to the cliffs. Searching for Sean, or the men, or the police. 'I can't be got by the law, Jake. I can't.'

'It's all right. Go.'

Goofy dry-swallowed. He looked at the skiff, then at Jake. 'Sod it!' He booted the side of the boat.

'I mean it,' said Jake. 'Scarper.'

'You're going to take care of stuff, are you? Like that? And what if the men come and Sean's involved?' Goofy pointed at Jake's leg. 'I think we'd better crack on, don't you? And leave Sean here.'

'I got cans and cakes and everything!' Sean ran up, waving a loaded plastic bag. Goofy grabbed the bag and hurled it into the boat. He grabbed Sean too, by his jacket, and pushed him towards the boat. 'Help get the skiff afloat. Quick.'

Goofy and Sean put their shoulders to the fore, either side of the long boat, and heaved it down the slipway.

Jake stood by, feeling useless, still reeling from speaking to Hannah.

Goofy helped Jake get in, then climbed aboard himself. Sean waded in up to his knees. He put a hand out. Goofy ignored him, grabbed an oar, and pushed the boat away from the slip, into deeper water.

'Hey,' said Sean. 'I'm coming.'

'No, you aren't,' said Goofy. He knelt by the outboard motor, and lowered the propeller into the water. 'Stand clear, Sean. Unless you want to lose a hand.'

'Bastards!' cried Sean. He waded deeper, to the port side. He clung to the boat, tipping it. 'You said I could come!'

'Things have changed,' said Jake. 'It's dangerous.'

'I don't care!' Sean got an arm over the side and tried to haul himself up. Jake pushed his brother back into the sea.

'Listen. I was shot, all right? Bloody shot. There are men after us. The police are coming. Go back to the shop till they arrive. You'll see their car go by. Tell them where we are.'

Sean was shoulder-deep, now. His grip on the gunnel was stopping them leaving.

'I'm coming with you.' Sean's eyes stabbed into Jake. With hope, disappointment, pleading.

'Shit!' said Goofy. He was staring at the harbour. A Range Rover was racing up to the boathouse. Goofy leapt up, grabbed the back of the boy's jeans and pulled him over the gunnels like he was a sack of spuds.

'Sit there!' he ordered, pointing to the starboard side.

Goofy squatted at the aft. He sparked the engine and released the throttle. The boat lurched up. They raced out of the harbour.

Jake's gut heaved, with the acceleration and with fear. He half expected a *BAM* of gunshot to break the air.

'Stay low,' he shouted at Sean.

The boat screamed through the chop, batting through waves, sending sheets of spray over the bow, charging up bigger waves and thumping down the other side.

Jake looked behind Goofy. The Range Rover stopped outside Lancaster's boathouse. The painted 'W' was still there, next to the anchor. The doors opened, showing a gleaming motorboat on rollers.

'Shit,' said Jake.

'What?' Goofy shouted.

'Lancaster's speedboat,' Jake shouted back. 'They'll wheel it down and launch in a minute.'

Sean lay hunched in the side of the boat, clinging to the gunnel with one hand, grasping his bag of food with the other, his eyes shot with excitement and fear.

'What they going to do?' he whimpered.

'They aren't joining us for a picnic, are they?' said Goofy. 'Hold on. This is going to get sick.' The engine sounded a throaty, desperate whine. The aft sank and the bow lurched high as they picked up speed. They headed for the Cape.

Jake's stomach melted as the skiff swerved a portside arc. Goofy was dodging waves. But he couldn't dodge them all.

They charged into a hefty one. It dragged at the skiff like a heavy hand.

He looked at Sean, cowering there, and cursed himself for being a fool and putting Sean in danger.

'Boat's not made for these conditions,' Goofy shouted. 'We'll need to be careful.'

'And lucky,' Jake said to himself.

They charged past the edge of the Cape and out to open sea. Straight ahead were the Pendrogeth Islands, stark, sharp and dark in the thick sea. A lighthouse shone on the largest rock. Normally they'd go round it, because these rocks had teeth. One crack, one savage denting, and they'd sink.

Jake looked back. The land was distant already. The men, stick figures, were climbing aboard the boat. How many? Two, at least.

Jake tried to imagine what would happen if the men caught them.

What weapons did they have against guns? Knives. A spear gun in the locker. He pictured them throwing the cans of fizz Sean had in the bag.

Laughable.

If they were caught, they were screwed.

If.

Goofy's plan was clear enough. Take the skiff where the motorboat couldn't go and run quick out the other side. Make distance, buy time. The rocks were deadly, the swell mean, and the skiff too small for the conditions. But right now these things weren't a disadvantage, and might even give them an edge. They could get through. The motorboat would struggle.

And they knew the place. Lancaster's men didn't.

After the Pendrogeths there was a long stretch of water past Mottle Island, then the Gunner Isles where the whales were. A maze of reef and rock.

If they made it there, they had a chance of losing the men altogether. A good chance too.

Jake looked back. The motorboat was in the water now, racing towards them, a steady 'V' of white water in its wake. Jake calculated how soon it would catch them; how soon they would reach—

His body slammed into the side of the skiff. The boat made a gut-churning turn.

'Jesus!' A stack of hard granite loomed ahead.

'Look out!!' Jake braced. He put one arm over his head, exactly as he did when he got thrown off a big wave. The skiff carved round the rock, missing it by a foot.

A cloud of gulls and gannets filled the air. Goofy slowed the throttle as they swooped another tight bend.

'You almost killed us,' said Sean. He sat up, his head bobbing about like a panicked meerkat.

Goofy didn't seem to hear. His hand gripped the tiller and his gaze stayed dead-ahead steady.

'Watch out!' Sean screamed as they skimmed another rock.

The boat slowed. 'Get over the bow,' said Goofy.

Jake pulled himself to the front of the skiff. It hurt. His leg shrieked with pain.

'You're bleeding,' said Sean. A small trickle had escaped the bandage, run down his leg and smeared into the water at the bottom of the boat. He must have torn the wound when he was thrown. He leant over the bow, as far as he dared.

They were in the shallows. Smack in the heart of the Pendrogeths. A risky place for a bigger boat, but it was easy to see the rocks: patches of light stone and banks of seaweed. In between were thin, curving paths of deep water to follow.

Jake shouted instructions: 'Left. Sharp right. Dead ahead.' Slowly they weaved and dodged, till they saw a gap between small islands, showing the open sea.

The sight of it teased them. But they could hear the motorboat getting closer.

Goofy released the throttle. The skiff charged forward – and a sickening crunch sounded. The skiff croaked as it scraped across rocks. They were stuck.

'She'll tear if I force it,' said Goofy.

'Shit,' said Jake. 'We got to get out of here!' The engine was *phutt*ing quietly now. They could hear Lancaster's boat getting closer every second.

Jake felt sweat drip down his brow and heard his own noisy breath. Gulls cried sharply above, a cloud of them, like they were singing out: *Here they are, here they are.*

'Sean, take the tiller,' said Goofy, then launched himself off the side, landing on the rocks, thigh-deep in water. The boat lifted a few inches.

Goofy pushed the boat forward. It stuck again.

'Steady. Kill the engine. Lift the propeller.' Sean did as he was told.

The swell was sweeping over the rock, lifting the skiff a foot only for it to drop again when the water retreated.

'Quick!' said Sean.

'I can't force it,' snapped Goofy.

With every wave that came through, Goofy pushed the boat onwards a couple of feet.

They did this to a rhythm.

Strand, lift, push.

Strand, lift, push.

'Shit . . . oh shit,' Jake mumbled to himself. What had he done? What had he got Sean into? He wasn't religious, not a bit, but in his head Jake spoke to someone, to something: *Please, please let us get out of this*. Back to land. To safety. To the world they knew. Not this alien world, where men with guns were slowly, steadily making their way towards them.

Lancaster's boat throbbed and whined nearby. But . . .

'It's not getting closer,' said Jake. 'Sounds like they're looking for a way into the rocks.'

'Good,' said Goofy. 'Because they won't find one.' A surge of swell lifted the skiff, and they were free. The boat wobbled, like she was surprised to find herself in deeper water.

Sean helped Goofy in.

The waters ahead were clear. A channel, as wide as a road, led between the rocks and out to open sea.

Goofy lowered the propeller and started the engine. The boat shot between the rocks, hit the deep and headed out in a straight line.

Jake looked back. The men must have heard them: the motorboat was racing for the outskirts of the rocks, away from the Pendrogeths. It was a long distance, a large semicircle tract, but the boat was fast. And as soon as they rounded the outer rocks they'd be headed their way. Straight at them like a shot arrow.

The skiff covered the open sea quickly. They made the distance to the Gunners before the motorboat was even halfway across, then headed round the islands, in a long arc. It would look like they were going further, to the Outer Gunners. Maybe even headed to the Scillies.

But as soon as they'd gone far enough to lose sight of Lancaster's boat, Goofy swerved the skiff in a U-turn and headed into the heart of the islands.

The skiff carved and weaved. Its wake vanished quickly in the choppy sea. There was no trail for the men to follow. No way for them to see where the skiff had gone. And there were plenty of channels: pathways between the islands.

Jake was lost too. Only the sun, sneaking behind fast-racing clouds, gave him any clue as to which direction they were headed in.

They broke free of the bulk of the islands, and made a line to the smaller Gunners.

When they were near, Goofy made a sharp starboard turn and raced to the largest of the Outer Gunners, then round it. They hugged the steep granite shore. They had the Gunners island, and the main Gunners Islands, between them and the men.

There was no way they'd be found now. No way at all.

Goofy grinned. Sean too, like idiots.

Goofy toned the engine right down.

Lancaster's boat was a far-off whine.

Then all Jake could hear was the wind whistling and the swell whooshing up and over the shallow rocks, lapping against the steeper ones. Their breath came in long and heavy puffs. Jake saw the sweat trickling down Goofy's forehead. He felt it on his own brow too.

'That was insane,' said Sean, his eyes bulging, his skin white.

Goofy laughed. Jake and Sean joined in.

They were high and mad with what they'd done.

It felt like victory.

He'd been more scared than he had ever been in his life. He thought back to that moment in the cove − finding the stuff − then later deciding to sell it. Pound signs in his eyes had blinded him to what could happen. It was supposed to be a couple of meetings in a pub, not this.

They came round the rocks into open sea and saw the black fins. There was Little One, covered by orange netting. The other whales swam round her. Up and down, in and out, along and under. One disappeared under the young whale, holding her up, taking over from another. Round and round like a dance.

Little One breathed: *Phwooooosh!* The spray from her blowhole misted in the morning sunlight.

Goofy killed the engine. He set the oars, and rowed. The skiff bobbed gently towards the whales.

When they were twenty or so metres away, Goofy grabbed a wetsuit and snorkel, flippers and a knife, and piled them in front of him. He took his jacket off.

'No,' said Jake. 'We need you steering. In case those bastards show up. And the whale knows me, from the beach. It'll trust me, when I get near. I'll do this. I need to do this.'

'But your leg?' said Goofy.

The stain was seeping up his jeans. His thigh looked like a bottle of red wine had been poured over it.

'It's nothing,' he said.

Jake

JAKE TOOK OFF his jumper, T-shirt and jeans and sat naked but for his pants and the bandage round his thigh. It was soaked red and leaking. He grabbed the T-shirt and wiped his leg down to make the blood go away; to make it look better than it probably was. Immediately, a crimson pool welled through the bandage.

'Shit,' he said, and wiped it again.

'You can't go in like that, man,' said Goofy. 'We have to get you to hospital.'

Jake ignored Goofy. He tore at the bloodied T-shirt till it was a long strip, then held one end in his teeth and twisted the other. When it was as taut as a rope, he tied it round his leg.

'That'll stem it,' he said. 'And before you try and stop me – I'm doing this! D'you understand?' he shouted at Goofy and Sean, glaring. He picked up his wetsuit and squeezed a leg inside. The rubber was tight. The tourniquet and suit would keep the wound as bound as it could be. But—

Jesus, it hurt. He tried not to wince, not to show that every time he moved, a thrill of pain shot up his body.

Should he take pills? No, he needed to be sharp.

While Jake changed, Goofy picked up the mesh diving bag he'd brought. He put in a knife, the spear gun and a snorkel. Jake slung it over his shoulder and round his back, then put the flippers on.

'What's the spear gun for?' said Jake.

'Well, you never know,' said Goofy, nodding at the whales.

'They're just giant dolphins,' said Jake. 'They don't attack people.'

Hannah had told him that. But as he put his arms in the wetsuit, he thought: *Do I believe it?* Any animal would fight to protect its young. And what would he look like to the whale's mother? Help? Attacker? *Food?*

A memory crept into his head from a programme he'd seen about whales – *killer* whales. One had been holding a seal in its jaw and thrashing its head from side to side to tear the animal apart.

Would the whales think *he* was a seal?

Would the blood in the water make them hungry?

Best to get in before he thought about it too much. He zipped up the wetty, then took the board Sean handed him and gently leant over and laid it in the water.

He sat down on the edge of the boat, breathed and paused, getting ready to slip in. Instead he stuck there, looking.

The boat had floated, inch by inch, towards the circle of whales. They were *massive*. Bigger in the water, somehow, than they had been on land. And moving. All the time, moving. Muscle and black skin.

Killer whales.

And he was getting in the water with them.

But there was Little One, under all that netting. And if he didn't do this, she would die.

He steeled himself, just like he did before paddling for a big wave. Feeling the cold fear in his gut. Owning it. Controlling it. Turning it into energy he could use.

DO IT, he told himself.

He was about to go in, to force himself. But . . .

One of the whales, its dorsal fin as tall as a man, broke away from the circle. It dived and disappeared into the deep.

Then bubbles rose from below, popping and frothing right next to the boat.

A shadow was rising in the deep.

'Shit!' cried Jake. He grabbed the gunnel. Sean sank low in the boat. Goofy picked up an oar.

The shadow became a shape, the white of its underbelly showing like a light. Jake could see the patches above its eyes, its open mouth, its teeth.

It shot from the gloom.

Just in time, it turned.

Its head broke the surface, mouth open like it was showing them its teeth, just so they knew what it could do. It turned again, looking at them one by one, then fixed its gaze on Jake alone. Like it was talking to him with its eye.

Who are you? What are you doing here?

Electricity ran up Jake's neck. His skin sang, not with fear but with awe. Sheer, mind-blowing wonder.

The whale lingered a moment, its gaze steady as it turned over and headed back to the deep. Seconds later it reappeared, back with the other whales.

Jake's legs wobbled as he stood. This had nothing to do with pain. The pain had vanished. He moved to the side and put a leg over, dipping his flippers in the water. He had the mesh bag on his back. And before he could think – because thinking might stop him – he turned and slid backwards into . . .

Their world.

He climbed on to the board, and started paddling, as slowly and gently as he could, though adrenalin was coursing through him. He could hardly feel his body, or his hands dipping in the water. They looked mechanical as he paddled, like his arms were out of his control. He was numb but trembling as he forced long, deep breaths.

He watched their backs; the fins, the rhythm of their circle dance. He was looking for movement, for change. Some sign that they'd seen him.

Soon he was almost at the edge of the circle.

He sat up on the board, took the snorkel out of the mesh bag and put it on, then dropped off the board and put his head under the water.

He could see clearly that Little One was pinned under a great bulk of orange net. On the near side it was knotted and bunched, rising straight out of the deep.

On the other side of her, it stretched out endlessly, floating into open water.

The whales were still circling, but they saw him now. He was close enough to watch their eyes swivelling as they swam.

He looked into the huge blue deep. There were two whales under the surface, swimming low, beneath the others. They left the pod and swam underneath him.

He turned and twisted, to see where they went. What now? Would they attack? One of the whales passed him, and rose up. He felt sick. But it was only interested in the board. It nudged it: nosing, testing it to see if it was alive. Then the whale left it, to focus on the other thing in the water: Jake.

It watched him as it swam softly by. It let out a series of booms and clicks and whistles.

He felt the boom vibrating in his gut, being absorbed into his body.

And what could he do? Swimming back to the boat would be pointless. It wouldn't make the whale less likely to attack. Maybe more so.

He had an idea.

He put his head out of the water, took a long breath, turned over and swam down. And down. Till he was level with the whales, so deep that his ears were throbbing with pressure.

He faced them, and put his arms out, so they could see him square. Then let his body rise steadily upwards.

He did this so they could see him. How small and useless he was. That he was nothing. No threat. He felt naked.

Because if they attacked him there was nothing he could do anyway. The spear gun was pointless.

Whatever happened to him now, happened.

When he surfaced, he used his flippers to reach the net. The whales didn't follow.

What now? Drag it off? No. Too heavy. If he could get near Little One, but not so near as to panic her, he could cut the net. Enough to make a big tear that she could swim through. Up close to the net, though, he saw that the job was enormous. He'd have to cut through dozens of links.

He took the knife out of the mesh bag, grabbed one of the links of the net, and brought the blade to it. The knife was sharp, but the fibres tough. He sawed, watching the fibres break. One cut. A start.

The net was wide and he was weak. He'd be at it for hours.

All right, he said to himself. *If that's what it takes.*

Moving the flippers slowly, enough to keep him upright, he took another chain link, and cut it.

'All right, man?' Goofy shouted out.

Jake nodded. 'Bring her over. Slowly. Really slowly. We'll have to do this in stages, and . . .

Bham

Gunfire cracked through the air.

Hannah

BHAM.

The sound was distant, but loud and sharp. Hannah felt a shock in her gut. That was the sound of a gun firing.

'Jake!' She scanned the water, seeing only rocks and sea. A small group of islands was ahead to the right. Two o'clock. The sound had come from there. A long way distant.

She looked back at Neil and pointed to the islands. He nodded, swerved the RIB, and headed where she was pointing.

The RIB strained, crashing through the waves. Great sheets of water and foam banged over them.

Dan and Jo were with her. The police were behind, launching their boat at the harbour. The coastguard were on their way too.

But they were too slow. Too late. She wanted to race there. To *be* there. The desperation in her heart was tight and painful.

Minutes passed.

'Faster,' Hannah shouted.

'She's going hard as she can,' Neil shouted back.

Then more shots.

Her heart did somersaults.

'Jake. Jake.'

'Look,' said Jo, pointing.

A dark red flare fell out of the sky like a burning star.

Jake

A MAN STOOD high on the rocks, pointing a gun at the skiff. He was short-haired and wore dark clothes. It was the man who had shot Jake. Smithy.

'That was a warning,' he said. 'Next time, I shoot *you*.' He smiled, madly, like it was a great joke.

Smithy had his gun and gaze focused on the skiff. He hadn't seen Jake.

Jake dived, praying the man wouldn't see him, that he would be lost, among the rocks, seaweed and . . .

The board. It was directly above. A giveaway.

He braced himself for shots, expecting to see bullets whizzing through the water and feel them explode into his flesh. But they didn't come.

His only hope was to go deep. But the flippers moved slowly, like dead weights on his feet. He forced his legs to move, feeling his thigh throb sharply with the effort. As he swam down, water rammed painfully against his eardrums.

When he'd gone as deep as he could, he swam to the submerged cliff off the island and followed it towards the skiff, below where Smithy stood. There was a ledge of rock and seaweed jutting from the cliff. Breaking the surface, he breathed deep and tried to calm his thumping heart. If he raised his head even an inch, the man would see him. So he floated, his nose and ears just above the water.

'Where's your mate Jake?' said Smithy. He sounded relaxed, almost jolly. It was surreal, hearing the man speak his name. The man who might kill him, out here in this other world. This, here, was real. His whole life and everything he had ever known was so far over the horizon it no longer existed.

'It was a trick,' said Goofy. 'We left him on shore. We scarpered. Throw you off the scent, like.'

'Bullshit.'

Goofy kept his gaze on Smithy. But Sean glanced sideways and round towards the whales. Looking for Jake.

'Why the surfboard? What's with the whales?' Smithy's voice was hammer-hard now. Impatient.

'We're rescuing the whale that's trapped in the net.' Goofy pointed at Little One. The whales still circled, keeping up the rhythm, keeping Little One afloat. They didn't seem to have been disturbed by the gunshot.

'Crap. You said you came here like a decoy. What's the truth?

Perhaps you came here to hide the gear? Pass it on to a boat, maybe?'

'We're not smugglers,' said Goofy. It was the truth, but it sounded lame. Like a lie.

The motorboat chugged slowly round the cliff and into view. There were two men inside it. They must have dropped Smithy on the other side of the island, and waited for him to climb over. Clever. If they'd all come round in the boat, Jake, Goofy and Sean would have escaped. The motorboat stayed in the open sea, moving in an arc till it had trapped the skiff between itself and the island. When the boat stopped, it was behind the skiff. Jake couldn't see it, so the men couldn't see him. It was a small bit of luck, but it made Jake high with hope. If he could stay hidden, they might – just – get out of this.

Sean looked from the man to the boat.

'The police are coming,' he blurted. Smithy laughed. His men did too. It was the sick laughter of men who might kill. Not even for money or drugs, but because they could.

'Course they are. Where are the drugs?' said Smithy.

'Jake gave them to you,' said Goofy. 'You took them off him.' Jake couldn't see Smithy, but he could see and hear Goofy.

'You think I'm stupid. What we got back was part of it. There's more. Off the boat.' He said it as a fact. He was certain.

'No,' said Goofy. 'We didn't take the rest, we . . .' He paused, gulped. 'We . . .' He gasped, struggling to get his words out.

'What? Speak.'

Jake saw the danger now; the fear in Goofy's eyes.

'I cut up the bags and poured it all into the sea.' Goofy hung his head. His hands, still in the air, began to tremble.

No laughing from the men now. No sound at all, but the whistle of the wind, the distant gulls and the sea gently lapping against the skiff.

What Goofy had said was true, but Jake knew the truth wasn't enough. Not this time. Not here.

Jake's arm slowly, gently shifted the mesh bag off his back and round to his side. His hands searched for the spear gun. Jake's heart felt cold as his fingers found the shaft and lifted it out. His head was light, as if all his blood was draining into the water.

'I did it,' said Goofy. 'If you're going to punish someone, this is on me. Let the kid go.'

Smithy laughed again. His men joined in, like Goofy had told them the most stupid lie.

'Yeah, right. You steal the drugs then throw them in the sea,' said Smithy. 'Makes really good sense, that.' He snorted, coughed, spat. The globule spattered in the water near Jake's head. Maybe it was a good job the man didn't believe Goofy. He was more valuable that way. They thought he could still lead them to their cocaine.

'Where are my fucking drugs? You either have them here, or you can take us to them,' said Smithy. Goofy lifted his arms a little higher. Sean collapsed in the boat with his hands over his head. He cried, a series of soft, desperate whimpers.

Goofy lifted his head, showing a tear on his cheek. 'I told you the truth. I swear.'

Jake lifted the spear gun as quickly as he dared. It was their only chance. But Goofy had to gain time. Jake needed seconds to prepare the shot.

Jake looked at Goofy, willing him to do something, to say something.

Bham. A gunshot exploded above Jake's head.

His eyes shut. His ears rang. His heart froze.

But when he opened his eyes, Goofy was still standing. Sean was still cowering, with his arms over his head.

Smithy must have shot another warning. Their last chance. Goofy turned his head. Jake followed Goofy's gaze.

As the ringing in his ears subsided, he heard the whale's shriek. A raw cry of pain, both animal and human.

Below the net, just under the water, he could see a hole in the white skin under Little One's eye and jaw. Blood flowed out like water from a tap.

Jake's heart filled with cold hate. He would kill Smithy, if he could. He would kill him. Jake unclipped the safety, and pushed himself away from the ledge before edging slightly further out. From under the man's chin he saw the spittle flying and heard the screaming: 'Where are the drugs? Next time I'll shoot the boy!'

'Okay, okay.' Goofy put his arms down, then turned and crouched to go into the locker. 'In here, right? I've got the bags here.' As Goofy turned and leant over, he glanced at Jake and nodded so slightly and quickly that Smithy didn't see. Goofy's back was turned to Smithy, and as Goofy stood up Jake saw a flare gun in his hand. He was lifting it, pointing it at the motorboat.

Jake raised his good leg and pushed himself out. Smithy looked down. *Pointed* down.

Bham.

Smithy looked up, startled by the flare gun.

Thwup.

Smithy looked down again, surprised to see the spear buried in his gut at an upward slant. Jake reached up to the cord connecting the gun with the spear, and yanked.

'Yaaargh!' Smithy screamed, trying to point his gun. But Jake pulled again and Smithy lurched, jerking like a giant fish on a hook. His gun clattered on to the rock.

Smithy grabbed the end of the long spear with both hands. Jake pulled, as hard as he could, and Smithy toppled over him, crashing into the water.

There was a tangle of arms and cord. Smithy was thrashing, the two of them were tied together and tumbling. A storm.

Then the light was eaten by shadows as the world became a mess of blue and black, and white bodies, and red blood.

Smithy's hand grabbed the flesh of Jake's neck.

Smithy let go as the whale rammed his body, smashing him against the rock. Jake rose in the water, turned, and reached out his hands to stop the nose of the next whale ramming *him*. Below, the head of the first whale was pushing Smithy against the rock. Jake saw his face: his bulging eyes, his mouth open in a water-silenced scream. The whale covered Smithy with its body. He disappeared.

The second whale turned now, pointing at Jake. The whales knew they were in danger. They would kill anyone in their way. Jake grabbed the ledge and with an almighty effort tried to lift his body.

His leg stuck. He looked below and saw white teeth gripping the flipper, pulling at him. One yank, and it slipped off his foot. Jake crawled free. On to the rock.

A thudding shot rang through the air. Another flare.

Jake sat up and looked over to the motorboat. One man was trying to get a burning flare out of the chest of the other. Using his gun to knock it out. But it stuck there, burning. The man was screaming.

Goofy stood in the boat, reloading the flare gun.

Below in the water was chaos. Blood, bubbles. Two whales, thrashing.

He saw Sean, looking stunned, and Goofy, using the oar to paddle the skiff towards him. Goofy was shouting, but Jake could hear nothing.

The light was shifting and moving like the sea. The rocks and the boats were becoming a dream, Sean and Goofy becoming ghosts. Jake couldn't see them. Just haze.

He lay back and looked into the sky.

Goofy was above him, his mouth moving.

A red star. Falling, burning, fading.

Part FIVE

AFTER THE STORMS

www.Eye-Sea-Surfcheck.com

Forecast

Winds: --------------

Conditions: --------------

Waves: --------------

Storms over. A lot of air and water moving around in the aftermath. Sorry, folks, but all systems are down. No data. Forecast unknowable.

Hannah

HER HEART WILLED the boat forward, urging it to get round the headland, to see what was on the other side.

She saw, and her hand rose to her mouth.

A storm of things.

Orcas circling Little One, who was trapped under a net.

A motorboat – *Dad's* motorboat – with two men in it, wrestling with a fire. Only, the fire seemed to be in the chest of one of the men. The other was pouring water over his burning jacket.

A skiff, rocked by a commotion of thrashing, rolling orcas, fins and black skin. Blood and froth in the water.

Beyond the whales, Goofy and Sean leaning over something.

Some . . . *one*.

'Jake!'

Neil turned the RIB straight towards the island. He killed

the engine and they floated past the whales, thumping into the side of the skiff. Hannah launched herself, climbing and bouncing over the boat, slipping on seaweed, falling on rock, crawling, to where Jake lay cradled in Goofy's arms.

'Jake.' She put a hand to his face. His eyes were closed, his skin cold-white and clammy. She leant down, and whispered in his ear: 'Jake,' believing – for a second – a tiny, precious sliver of time – that her voice might wake him.

'Jake,' she whispered again. 'Jake.'

But he didn't wake up. He lay there, still and limp.

'He's lost blood,' said Goofy. 'Loads. We've got to get him to hospital. Quick, like.'

She leant down and put her ear to Jake's mouth. She felt his soft, seashell breath in her ear, as she had a hundred times. Only now, the breath was weak. Only just there.

She put her hand to his neck. Searching, till the slow drum of his pulse beat through her fingertips.

It was as weak as his breath. Erratic.

She sat up and noticed the trickle of blood seeping between Jake's wetsuit and his ankle.

'Get a knife,' she cried. Goofy found one somewhere and handed it to her. She put the end of the heavy blade into the wetsuit at the top of Jake's leg, and made a nick. Then again, picking till she'd made a hole. Next, she slid the top of the blade under the rubber, being careful not to touch Jake's skin, and moved it round his leg, above the wound, cutting the rubber away.

Tattered stitches and open flesh lay revealed. The wound was gaping and streaming. The torn-cloth tourniquet was soaked, loose and useless.

Sean squatted next to her, crying. Hannah pushed him away. 'Give me space,' she shouted, and carried on cutting. She was getting into a zone. A focused trance. Pushing emotions deep down inside her. His life depended on her doing that.

'Lift his leg,' she said to Goofy and Sean. They did what she told them to. 'Higher,' she ordered. 'Hold him there.' She turned, searching frantically for something to use as a tourniquet. 'Sean. Your belt,' she said, her hand out, clicking her fingers. 'Give it to me.'

Sean took it off and handed it to her. She cut away more of the wetsuit, then the ragged cloth. She replaced it with the belt, did the buckle up and pulled, as tight as she dared. The yawning wound stopped running: the tap of blood had turned off.

'Okay, let's get him in the RIB,' she said. Mercifully, the whales had stopped their thrashing and moved away.

They carried Jake: Neil and Goofy taking his arms, Hannah and Sean with his legs. It was hard. Dan brought the RIB over. It rocked violently as they lugged him on, a dead weight. It was quick, and clumsy, and they almost capsized. But they got Jake on and laid him near the bow. Neil squatted by the engine.

Hannah looked around. Where was Goofy? He had gone back on to the rock and was standing there with a gun in his hand. It seemed surreal, cartoonish. He was pointing the gun at the men in the motorboat.

'Take Jake,' he said. 'I'll stay here till the law come.'

'Wait,' she said to Neil. She looked over at the whales. Little One's nose was barely above the water. And in the water . . . was that . . . ?

'Blood!' she said.

'The man shot the whale,' said Sean. Hannah watched with horror in her heart, waiting for the blow, the plume of breath and life.

But seconds passed. And there was no plume. Little One sank lower in the water.

'Nooooo!' she cried.

A red cloud grew in the water around Little One's body. The young orca rolled, showing the harsh gape in her underside. A bullet hole.

'We have to . . .' Hannah started, but the words died in her mouth. She looked at Jake, and knew the truth.

Steve was beside her, grabbing her shoulder. 'She's dead already,' he said. 'Or dying. If we don't get Jake to hospital soon, he'll die too. Do you understand?'

She looked at Little One, lolling on her side.

'Not this,' said Hannah. 'Not this.'

The whales had stopped circling now. One by one, they were swimming away, leaving Little One.

Leaving her.

'I can't . . . we can't leave her,' said Hannah.

'You must. Just like they must. You see those whales now?' Steve pointed, forcefully. 'At least one is alive because of you. That has to be enough.'

He left her and sat by the engine, waiting.

'Go,' said Goofy. 'Go.'

She looked at the whales. At Jake's bloodless face. She nodded. The engine choked into life.

Hannah sat with Jake. She watched the sea, and the far-off land on the horizon, not back — she couldn't look at that hard, cold, wild place. She pictured the whales swimming away, in her mind. Was this how it was? Animals didn't have burials and ceremonies. One minute they were there, the next they weren't, and their family left them, moving on. She wondered, numbly, if they grieved.

She looked down at Jake. His breathing was slow, and under his tan his face was bloodless. Lifeless.

'I've lost everything, Jake,' she said. 'I'm not losing you.'

★

The ambulance was waiting at the slip. Police cars too.

'Go home,' said Steve, after they'd put Jake in the ambulance. 'I'll call you with any news.'

'No,' she said. 'I'm coming to the hospital. I don't have a home.'

Hannah

STEVE DROPPED HANNAH at A&E, where she stood watching them take Jake off the ambulance. There was a mask on his face, and a drip in his arm.

A nurse came out of the hospital. She had a thin, serious face. She talked with the ambulance man, nodding and taking notes on a clipboard.

'What's happening?' asked Hannah. They wheeled Jake through the doors of A&E, past the desk, down the corridor. The nurse walked beside them.

The ambulance. The stretcher-on-a-trolley. The nurses. A routine. Smooth and practised. Quick, but not rushed.

Hannah sped up her pace, catching up with them.

'What's happening?' she said again. But no one paid attention. She was an invisible ghost, watching people in the real world.

Then they sped up, racing Jake down the hall. Another nurse appeared, from nowhere, and doctors too. They surrounded Jake, talking in numbers and strange words: *five mil* of this; *get supplies* of that; *rate lower than sixty*.

'What's *happening*?' Still no one noticed her. The doctors were in their zone. Doing their job.

They turned sharp left through swing doors. The nurse stopped, turned and put out the palm of her hand.

'I'm sorry. You can't come in.' She vanished through the doors, leaving Hannah alone.

She stood in a huge, clean hall like a desert. The air hummed and vibrated around her and she gasped, struggling to breathe.

She went to the door and tried to open it. But the nurse came out.

'What's happening?' said Hannah.

'He's lost a lot of blood. His heartbeat is weak.'

'I know that,' Hannah snapped. 'Talk to me, please. Tell me something.'

'And you are?' The nurse put her hands on her hips.

Hannah was thrown by this question, which sounded like an accusation.

'What did you say? I'm his ex-girlfriend. I have a right to know and . . .' She caught her anger before it exploded. 'Sorry, I . . . I know you're doing what you can. I just . . .' Her mouth went dry. The walls closed in on her.

The nurse sighed. Her eyes softened. 'I don't honestly know. He's in a bad way. Perhaps you could tell me what happened, how long he was bleeding. Anything you know that might help.'

Hannah nodded.

'We can sit,' said the nurse, pointing down the hall to a row of orange plastic chairs.

'Is it okay if we talk here? I want to be near . . . That sounds stupid . . .' Her voice cracked in her throat. 'Oh God. Oh God.'

The nurse reached out and held Hannah's shoulders, as though to stop her falling. The desert was transforming into a hole in the universe that was slowly widening. A silent earthquake had made a rent in time and space. And she was being sucked into it.

'It's fine,' said the nurse. 'In your own time.'

Hannah breathed deeply and fought to come back, to be in this world. She told the nurse what she knew, which wasn't much. Where was Goofy? He had been there. He would know.

'Will he be okay?' said Hannah.

'As soon as there's news we'll tell you. I'll come and find you. Why don't you go and wait?' The nurse gestured, to the chairs.

Hannah shook her head and folded her arms.

She was left alone, again.

She noticed, after a while, that she was shaking. She had the vague, abstract thought that she might be in shock.

Then April came running towards her.

'He's in there,' said Hannah. 'We can't go in. He's having blood. They'll let us know.'

April reached up and round her, hugging her rigid body

342

till her flesh melted. The shaking grew, taking her over. She began trembling violently.

Then she was weeping in April's arms.

★

An hour later, a doctor, a young man, summoned them to a side room with charts and a desk.

Was it a place for delivering bad news? So they could break down in private?

Hannah had imagined a moment like this, but she had thought it would come later in life. A parent or grandparent in hospital. Speaking to a doctor who delivered news of death, or life.

She'd imagined she'd know what was happening, just from the face. An expression of careful hope, or the unblinking gaze of someone steeling themselves for an awful task.

But she couldn't tell anything from this man's face. Nothing. April clung to Hannah, who clung back.

'He lost a lot of blood,' said the doctor.

Hannah sank into the hole. Air became water and enveloped her.

'His heart stopped,' the doctor said.

'Is he alive?' she whispered.

'I'm afraid he's . . .'

'*Is he alive?*'

'Yes. But . . .' The doctor looked to April. Her eyes were bright with fear.

'Tell us,' said Hannah.

'He's in a critical condition. He's had new blood, but his body isn't responding as well as we'd expect. I'm afraid he has a bad infection, possibly contracted in the water. It's in his blood. It's gone to his brain. His body has shut down. He's unconscious.'

'Unconscious,' said April. 'For how long?'

'We don't know.'

'Is he going to be okay?' said April.

'In cases like this, there is often cause for—'

'Please. Yes or no,' said Hannah. 'Just tell us.'

The doctor sighed. 'I don't know.'

'What are his chances?' said April.

'This is serious. But he's young. He's fit and healthy. All of that's in his favour.'

The doctor left them.

'You'd better go home,' said April. 'To your family.'

'I can't do that,' said Hannah, wishing people would stop saying she should. She hugged herself.

'Why?' said April.

'My home isn't my home. My family isn't my family.'

'Come to ours. Me, Sean and Hattie. We love you. Jake loves you. And Beano too. We'll look after you, love. We're in this together.'

Hannah

PHOEBE TOOK HANNAH to the hospital.

'Please try not to worry too much, Hann,' said Phoebe, as she parked in the drop-off zone. She looked at Hannah, concern etched into her face.

'How can I not worry?' said Hannah. 'He's lifeless. Half dead. He can't even hear me.'

'I'm sure just the sound of your voice makes a difference,' said Phoebe, trying to smile.

'I hope so,' said Hannah. She repeated the words in her mind. *I hope so.* It seemed a lame thing to say, or even think. But what else did she have?

'Come on, Hann,' said Phoebe, placing her fingers under Hannah's chin and lifting her face up. 'Put a brave face on, eh?'

She got out of the car, breathed deep, and walked in to see Jake.

She talked to him, a little. In stilted chunks of one-way conversation.

'Oh, Jake, if only you knew the trouble you've caused.'

'There's a storm happening. You're sleeping through all of it. Bloody skiver.'

'I dunno why I'm saying these things, it's not like you can hear me.'

'I love you.'

She sat holding his hand for long periods of time, not speaking at all.

Part of her didn't want to be at the hospital. She wanted to walk the cliffs with Beano. Part of her knew she couldn't be anywhere else. It was the only place for her *to* be. Like the hollow, that night at the mines, when she had run away from home. A refuge.

Part of her believed that her voice might wake him.

'I love you. We miss you. Please come back to us.'

But that was a wish from a fairy tale. And life wasn't like that.

★

Phoebe was outside, ready to pick her up. Hannah slumped into the passenger seat.

A minute passed. Phoebe didn't start the engine.

'Aren't we going?' said Hannah.

'Are you okay?' said Phoebe, gazing at her. What did she look like? Broken, probably. Hannah didn't check the mirror. She didn't want to see. The look on Phoebe's face told her enough.

Hannah leant over and put her head on Phoebe's shoulder. Neither of them spoke for a while.

She was lost. Zombified. In her own waking coma.

'Thanks,' said Hannah, eventually.

'What for?'

'Just being here.'

'I don't have a choice, Hann. I'm your friend.'

'You do have a choice. You'd be surprised. The people who haven't called. The ones who don't know us, all of a sudden, now this is all out.'

'Yeah, well. Screw 'em,' said Phoebe.

Hannah pulled her head off Phoebe's shoulder and folded her arms.

'It means something, Phoebes. A lot, actually. I know you think I'm foolish. That he's not worth it. But thanks for not saying it.'

'I'm not here to judge you, Hann. Just to look after you.'

'Like after that party.' A memory shot through Hannah's mind. Of the one and only time she had been drunk before she met Jake. Lying on the sofa, dying, while Phoebe collected bottles off the floor, and brought her cups of tea.

'Yeah,' said Phoebe. 'Something like that.'

'You probably think he deserves all this. Dad too . . .' She sighed, then thumped the door. Phoebe jumped. It surprised Hannah too. She hadn't known she was going to do it. 'Why didn't he tell me?' she said. 'Why didn't he tell me about Dad?'

'He was trying to protect you. Even if it meant losing you.

347

He didn't want to hurt you. I can't believe I'm saying this, but . . . he was doing the right thing. At least he thought he was.'

'Bloody hell, you're standing up for him,' Hannah said, sniffling through tears.

'Well,' Phoebe shrugged. 'That *is* what he was doing. And once he's out and you're together, I think he'll do right by you.'

'You think we should . . . make a go of things? If . . . when he comes out.'

'Well, look at the state of you, Hann. If this isn't love, I don't know what is.' Phoebe reached into her pocket and handed Hannah a clean handkerchief. 'I know he'll have your back, always. He'll take care of you just as you'll take care of him. Means I don't have to all the time. Frankly that would be a relief.'

Hannah laughed, and Phoebe grinned at getting the reaction she wanted. She clicked her fingers, waved one in the air and turned to face Hannah.

'Hey! Maybe you can go out as a four: you and Jake, Bess and Si. What do you think?'

Hannah laughed again. 'I think you're an idiot, that's what I think. Start the engine.'

Hannah

THE NEXT TIME Hannah visited, April came too.

April looked at Jake, watched him and examined him.

'I . . . don't know what to say,' she said. 'Do you think he can hear us, at all?'

'I don't know.' Hannah held April's limp, cold hand. Hannah squeezed, and April squeezed back.

It was good, April being there. It forced Hannah to put on a brave face, like Phoebe told her to.

'Hi, Jake,' said Hannah. 'I'm back. Your mum too.'

'Hello . . . Jake,' said April.

'I've left home,' said Hannah. 'Dad is there, you see. And he blames me for a lot of this. For calling the police. I've been there and picked up some stuff. Beano's stuff too. So . . . I'm living at yours. For now.' She paused, half expecting a reaction. A flicker of eyelids. A murmur. But Jake was a frozen statue.

'She's in your room, Jake,' said April. 'She won't let me wash the sheets.'

'Because they smell of you,' said Hannah. And felt embarrassed for saying that in front of Jake's mum.

'She wears that stupid T-shirt of yours, son. The torn one I'm always trying to throw out.'

'It feels odd being there,' said Hannah. 'Without you, I mean. Familiar and strange at the same time. But it's like I've got a new family. Your family . . .'

'Hattie's loving it,' said April. They both smiled at the memory of that morning: Hattie following Hannah from room to room.

'Can I come in?' she'd pleaded, when Hannah was in the loo.

'No.'

'Can we do a makeover?'

'Another one? I'm a bit busy. Got to get ready to visit Jake.' But when she'd come out, Hattie was waiting there, clutching her teddy, looking up at Hannah with wide brown eyes.

'He'd want you to look pretty . . . I mean you *are* pretty, but . . .'

'Go on, then,' said Hannah.

'Yay!'

She'd sat, patiently, while Hattie got busy, knowing she could scrape it off in the car.

Beano lay on the bed.

'He's not really allowed on beds,' said Hannah.

'He is here – Jake wouldn't mind.' Hattie ran off and came back with two biscuits.

'He'll get fat,' said Hannah. 'Collies aren't really meant to be fat.'

'It's okay. We'll walk him when you get back.'

Hannah and April smiled at each other.

'So I've got the little sister I never had. Seems I've gained a brother too,' said Hannah. 'His name is Sean. Christ, he's annoying. Not sure he likes me. Takes the piss out of my "posh" accent. My clothes. The amount of time I spend in the bathroom. My pesky-tarian diet. I think he's not liking being in an all-girl household. I think he wants you back.'

'He plays tough, doesn't he?' said April. 'But he's scared, Jake. He doesn't want to come and see you. Keeps saying there's no point. But every time me or Hannah come in the door, he looks at us hard. He can't hide the hope.'

'So all in all, it's great being at your house, Jake.'

'It's not what you're used to,' said April. 'We haven't even got a dishwasher.'

'You have now,' said Hannah.

★

Hannah visited daily after that. She talked about different things.

'The whales vanished. The police said there was no trace when they arrived. Honestly? I think they're dubious about whales being out there at all, like it was just a cover story. I don't know what happened to Little One. I think she might be dead . . . but I don't know.

'It's strange, how I feel about it. Sad, of course. But I accept it. Because we did what we could, didn't we? We saved some of them. We stopped a lot of them from stranding. That has to be enough, right?

'I know that's what you'd tell me, Jake. And I'd cry, and say how awful it is and how we didn't do enough. And you'd tell me not to be silly. And I'd still feel bad. But here's the oddest thing: you're not here to tell me, so I'm telling myself. And it's making sense.'

★

'The police received a letter from someone called Gavin Jones. This Gavin bloke sent a copy to me too.

'It seems the guy has quite a history. In and out of children's homes in South Wales. A string of convictions.

'He says *he* found the drugs on the boat. He says he tried to sell them to the men.

'I think they might believe this Gavin. I think you might be off the hook.

'He says it was all his doing, and you tried to talk him out of it at every step.

'When the police got to the island, the gangsters were in the water, swimming for their lives.

'So Goofy's vanished. With Dad's motorboat. We've been round his bedsit. Looks like he's been, grabbed a few things and scarpered. The police can't find him anywhere. But if Goofy doesn't want to be found, they'll have a job, won't they?' She laughed. 'I guess you're not surprised to hear that. I'll bet you're rooting for him. I imagine he's gone back wherever he came from. Or somewhere new. Who even is he anyway? I mean: Goofy. What is it with you bloody surfers and your stupid nicknames? He's someone's son, right? Has he got brothers or sisters? I bet you don't even know. Boys are strange.'

★

The next day:

'Christ, Jake. Why did everything have to fucking fall apart? It was all . . . safe, good, secure.

'Perfect Hannah Lancaster. Perfect life. I had a home. I had a future.

'The storms came and buggered it all up.

'*You* buggered it all up. Dad did a lot too. But definitely *you*. What were you thinking?'

She had an urge to punch him. Which was sick. But she clenched her fist and put it over him and shook it at his face, then laughed wondering what a nurse would think if she passed the window, seeing her raise a fist at someone in a coma. Yup. That was pretty twisted.

She laughed again. Too much. But knew Jake would laugh too.

'Go on, then,' he'd say.

And she would. She'd punch his shoulder.

'Didn't even hurt,' he'd say.

And she'd punch him again.

'You'll have to try harder.' And she'd punch him again. And he'd mock-sneer: 'Pathetic.'

She didn't punch him. She held his hand and said: 'I miss you.'

And watched him, a good half-hour before she spoke again.

'It's all broken now. Blown apart like a straw house in a gale.

'Well, Jakey boy, these storms have caused a lot of damage. One thing has unravelled after another.

'Everything's undone. Everything.

'I feel naked and numb. But . . . here's the weird thing . . . free. There's nothing left to lose now, you see . . .

. . .

. . .

'Apart from you, of course.'

She cried. Then checked her phone. Phoebe would be waiting in the car outside, ready to take her home. Her new home. She stood, leant over, and kissed Jake.

'No chance.'

The voice was barely there.

Had she imagined it? She looked at his face, but his eyelids were still and his mouth unmoving.

'Jake?' she whispered. 'Jake?' She thought she should call a nurse, or press the emergency button. But she didn't, as if the words she'd heard were a spell, not yet completed, and she was afraid to break it.

His finger, an inch from hers, jumped. Barely, the tiniest movement. His eyelids twitched and opened. He saw her.

'All right, babe,' he said.

Hannah leant over and put her forehead to Jake's.

She closed her eyes. Tears ran down her face, and fell on his stubbled cheek.

Jake

THE TAXI DROVE down the lane.

The late season grockles had gone. The windows of the cottages were dark, and the grass on their lawns had grown long.

His family waited outside their home: Mum holding Beano on a lead, Sean skulking in the doorway, Hattie waving madly.

As Hannah helped him climb out of the taxi, Jake took in how everything had changed just while he'd been in hospital.

The lawn was mowed to stubble, and the Wendy house painted blue. Its door was open, and it was full of logs.

The border by the wall was exploding with autumn flowers. The burning sun of orange devil, soft, purple lavender and other, new plants that he didn't know. The veg patch had been freshly dug too.

'Late for planting, isn't it?' he said.

'Winter greens,' said Hannah. 'Free food for cold months.' She carried his bag inside and he hobbled slowly behind, wondering. Was Hannah staying that long? Had she planned that far ahead?

Inside, a hand-painted banner hung over the kitchen doorway: *Welcome home, Jake.*

There were balloons, candles and flowers in a vase on the table. The sideboard was bare and scrubbed, and the walls had been painted white.

And there was space.

'Where *is* everything?' said Jake.

'Car boot,' said April.

'Make any money?'

'Not really,' said Mum. 'But we didn't half get rid of a lot of stuff.'

'Did you fix those shelves too?'

'Sean did that.'

'Nice. All right, bro?'

'All right,' said Sean, his hands in his pockets.

'You gonna give me a hug?' said Jake. Sean just shrugged.

'Supper's grilled mackerel, spuds and salad,' said Hannah. 'Those fish are a good price right now.'

Jake's mouth watered from the smell. He sat down, and Hattie fetched him a beer. It tasted better than any he'd ever drunk. Maybe better than any beer anyone had ever drunk.

They all sat watching him, like some alien that had landed in their house. The same way they'd looked at Hannah, the day she'd first come round for tea.

'Jesus, stop staring. I'm fine, guys. Really.'

'How do you feel?' asked April.

'All right.'

'No brain damage, then?' said Sean. 'Like we'd notice.'

'Sean!' said April.

Hattie gasped, and threw herself at him. Jake put a hand on the top of her head. 'I'm fine, little sis, ya hear me? Fine.'

'Can you remember what happened?' said April.

'Not really. I remember the boat, heading out. The rest is gone.' That wasn't exactly true. He had pictures in his head. A man with a gun. The whales. Cutting a net. But only snapshots, no video. 'Any case, I'm sure Sean will fill me in.'

'Yeah, I got the whole thing taped up here.' Sean pointed at his head. 'All the gruesome details.'

'Were you scared?' said Jake.

'Nah,' said Sean. 'It was a blast.'

They ate and drank and talked, mostly about all the work that had been done on the house. How Hannah had organised them all.

He waited for the bomb-drop questions about cocaine, about guns, about Hannah's dad. But they didn't come. Maybe now wasn't the time. Not with Hattie there.

'What's the news on the rent?' he said.

'I'm paying some,' said Hannah.

'You can't do that,' said Jake. 'Mum, tell her.'

'I have. When I refuse the money, she goes and buys groceries instead and says it's rent.'

'I can't stay and eat for free,' said Hannah, 'so deal with it.' She stuck out her tongue. 'Besides, I've got a contract. A water-quality survey. I have to travel round the beaches collecting water and testing it. Beano loves it.'

'Not exactly Hawaii, is it?' said Jake.

'There's time for that,' she said, and smiled. 'One day.' Under the table, her toe stroked his ankle and slid up his trouser leg. He felt a warm glow, a tingle. It was affection, but he felt a stirring too, from the touch of her flesh on his.

'Sean's doing shifts down the shop,' said April. 'We're coping. Besides, all this . . . shenanigans, it makes you stop and think. All that money stuff. All the stuff that stops you sleeping at night. I don't worry about it, at the moment. Isn't that crazy? Maybe it takes something like this to make you see what matters.

'Anyway, we're coping. We don't have to move out. We'll manage. It's going to be hard, but the money . . . it's not important.'

'Mum, of course it's important.'

'Jakey. My son. I almost lost *you*.' She reached over and grabbed his hand. She couldn't speak then. She grabbed a napkin and wiped a tear away. Hannah cried a tear too, just from seeing April. Hattie too. Sean stuck his fingers down his throat. April laughed and smiled as she choked her words out.

'We're here, together. And you're alive and well. What else matters, son? What is there to worry about?'

There was so much to deal with. Not just the money, but

the police and the inquest. He'd be back to hospital for scans too. There was *plenty* to worry about.

But . . .

There was Hannah, with the warmth of her foot on his skin.

There was Mum, crying tears of joy.

There was Sean, chomping on food that wasn't pizza, and enjoying it.

There was Hattie, feeding crispy mackerel skin to Beano.

He looked out of the back-door window, to the porch. There was his board. Waiting for the day he'd get back in the water.

He looked at the chair in the corner, wedged between the fridge and the wall, the one Goofy always sat on. It had books on the seat and a dishcloth hanging off the back.

'I don't deserve you lot,' he said. He raised his bottle, the others raised their glasses, and everyone clinked. 'It's good to be home.'

Then it was his turn to fight back tears.

Sean glared in horror. 'Jesus, dude. Get a grip. You done with that?' He pointed his knife at Jake's half-empty plate.

'Sure.'

'I'll finish it,' said Sean. He grabbed it, and shovelled what was left of Jake's dinner on to his own plate.

Something twinged in Jake's mind. A sound-memory. Gulls' cries. Because he'd been thinking about Goofy.

'*I'll finish it.* That's what he said,' said Jake.

'Who?' said Hannah.

'Goofy. Before I passed out, that's what he said. *I'll finish it. I'll cut her free.* He meant Little One. She must have still been alive.'

There was a knock at the front door. Soft and slow. Hardly there.

'I'll get it,' said Hattie, leaping up. They heard the front door creak open and a low voice speak. April and Hannah craned their necks to hear. Beano nosed his way through the door, and barked.

'Who is it, love?' asked April. Hattie came back.

'Hannah,' she said. 'It's your mum.'

Hannah

AS SHE WALKED through the dark hallway, Hannah looked back at the thin light visible through the kitchen door: the orange glow of happiness. Then she turned her gaze to the figure framed in the open door. Mum didn't have any make-up on and the skin round her eyes was baggy and puffed with worry and tiredness. But she was stroking Beano, and that was putting a smile on her face.

'Hello, Hannah,' she said.

'Hi, Mum.' They hugged. Mum clung a while, feeling small and withered in Hannah's arms. The Mum-hen who had cared for her with soup and sandwiches was now just a shadow.

'Would you like to come in?' said Hannah. 'I'm sure April wouldn't mind. She'd like to see you.'

'Right. Of course she would. The wife of the man who

almost got her son killed. No, Hann. We need to talk. Just you and me.'

'She's not like that, Mum. None of them are. Please come in.'

Mum shook her head. She walked into the garden, away from the house. Hannah followed and Mum turned, clenching her hands tightly.

'Please come home, Hannah. We miss you.'

Hannah's insides churned. When she spoke, her voice trembled.

'I miss you too, Mum. Every day. It's just, with Dad . . . you know? I don't see him the same way now. He's not . . . Dad any more.'

'Don't say that. Please don't say that.'

'The last argument . . . It was intense.'

Mum bit her lip and shuffled, looking unsure of herself.

'He's trying to do the right thing,' she said.

'How?' said Hannah.

'He's making a plea bargain.'

'To save his skin.'

'No. The house will be sold; his businesses will go into liquidation. He will go to prison whatever he does.

'He doesn't have anything left to lose, Hannah. Only you.

'At first he was going to play the innocent, pretend it was all Rocky, that he never knew anything about the drugs. But he's changed his mind. He's telling the police everything. You see . . . whatever you said to him on the cliff that night, well, let's just say I think he knows it's the only way he's ever going to get you back. By making things right . . . or as right as they can be under the circumstances. Will you see him?'

Hannah shook her head.

'I can't forgive him, Mum. Jake almost died. What he did, with those men, it was wrong.'

'I can't blame you for feeling that way. But what Jake did, or tried to do. That was wrong too. Wasn't it?'

'Well, yes, but . . . Can *you* forgive him, Mum?' said Hannah.

'Not if I lose you,' said Mum, with a weak smile. 'He's a fool, Hannah. A foolish man, and now a very poor one. But I still love him and I know you do too. Is there any chance you could come home?'

Hannah wavered, looking for hardness in her heart and not finding it. Mum continued.

'I guess I'm like that whale's mother, calling her. She couldn't leave her daughter, could she? I've dreaded this, Hann. The time when our girl grows up and leaves. Every mum does. You going to Hawaii was the end, in a way. But this is far worse. He'll be in prison. And with you gone . . .' Mum shook her head, as if she couldn't imagine the future. Hannah saw it, though. The painful emptiness in that house, till it was sold. And then what?

'Oh, Mum.' She reached out and hugged her.

'Maybe you could come and see us?' said Mum. Hannah thought of how she'd left. The badly packed bags, filled with shaking hands. Dad drinking whisky in the lounge. His heavy presence like a brooding monster in its lair. How she'd wanted, *needed*, to get away from that. Had he changed since then? She'd believe it when she saw it.

But there was Mum. And she needed Hannah.

'Yes, I'll come and see you,' said Hannah. 'Then we'll see. I guess.' She looked back at the house. April was there, in the shadow of the door.

'Come in,' she said. 'Have some tea.'

'No, thank you,' said Mum. 'I have to go.'

She looked down the lane at the Range Rover, parked on the side. A figure was sitting in the driving seat, hunched in shadow.

'Is that Dad?'

Mum nodded. The car was facing away, but he would be able to see her in the mirror. Hannah took one step, then another, her legs moving by themselves.

She stopped, and Dad got out. He looked worse than Mum, stooping and broken.

They stared at each other. A while.

Then she ran to him, and hugged him. She couldn't help herself.

'This is going to be hard, Hannah,' he said. 'I'll be in prison. For quite a while.'

'It will be hard, Dad. But . . . we'll get there.'

He kissed the top of her head.

'Yes, we'll get there. Will you ever forgive me?'

'I don't know, Dad,' she said. She didn't. But she did know she loved him, whether she wanted to or not.

He gently lifted her arms from his shoulders.

April and Mum came up behind her. Hannah stood aside.

They all looked at each other. Not knowing what to do, or say.

'We should get off,' said Dad when the silence got too long, too awkward.

'Really?' said April. 'Because I think we could all use a drink, don't you?'

Hannah grabbed her parents by the hand, and pulled them into Jake's house.

Jake

TWO DAYS LATER Jake had an appointment with the police.

'You okay?' said Hannah, when he left her at the desk.

'Yes,' said Jake. A lie.

Sergeant Junkett led him to the interview room. He limped through, using his crutch. The room was square and simple. Empty, apart from the recording equipment, two chairs and a table. With a file and a notebook and pen on it. All the kit you needed for a confession.

'Thanks for coming in,' said Junkett. 'Have a seat.' He opened the file and read what was inside, then picked up his notebook and pen. 'This is entirely voluntary. This is all we'll need you for. At this stage, anyway. You'll probably be called as a witness. We'll need your account of what happened on the islands. Your brother will need to make a statement too, but I don't think he'll be required to attend court. Is that all clear?'

'Yes.'

'Good. Why don't you start at the beginning?' Junkett sounded serious, but kind too.

'I . . . I don't know *where* to begin,' said Jake. He sat in silence, looking at the notepad and Junkett's pen.

After a while, Junkett put the pen down. He leant forward.

'Don't look so worried. This —' he pointed at the recording machine — 'isn't on. You're not in any trouble. We just want to put the pieces of the jigsaw together. These men, you see: one of them's wanted up London way for all sorts of nasty stuff. They're quite a catch for us. So *anything* that will help the case against them is going to be incredibly useful.' Junkett paused while he opened the file and read.

'This . . . Gavin Jones. Who says he found the boat and the drugs. The men were after him to try and recover the drugs. You and your brother were engaged in some kind of whale rescue when the men caught up with you. Is that right?'

'Yeah . . . I guess so.'

'You guess so?' Junkett frowned at him. 'Why don't we start with Gavin? And please, *please*, don't worry. Like I say, we just want to put the picture together so we can nail the bad guys.'

'What about Goof . . . I mean Gavin? What will happen to him?'

'Oh, well. Let's just say he'll need a lawyer. If we ever find him.'

'You won't find him.'

'Do you know his whereabouts?'

'No.'

'Well, if he does get in touch with you, the best advice you could give him would be to hand himself in. I'm, er, assuming he *didn't* involve you, or let you know what was going on?' Junkett gave Jake a knowing look.

Jake took a breath and had a good look around the room, preparing himself. There was another chair, in the corner. It reminded him of the one at home, in the kitchen.

He'd already decided what to say. He hadn't told anyone, he'd just made a promise to himself when he'd sat at the kitchen table, looking at the empty chair.

'I knew all about it,' said Jake.

Junkett picked up his pen. 'Go on.'

Jake paused. This was harder than he'd thought it would be.

'Look,' said Junkett, trying to reassure him again. 'We just want the truth.'

'Then that's what you'll get,' said Jake. 'Because I've told enough lies to last a lifetime. Goofy . . . sorry, Gavin, didn't find the stuff. I did. I was the one who tried to sell it.'

Junkett put his pen down and his hand up. A stop sign.

'Er, okay, Jake. Before you say anything further, I should tell you, you might be liable for prosecution. You might give me reason to arrest you. I'd advise we bring in your lawyer before you say anything else.'

'There's no point. I won't say anything different to what I'm going to tell you now.

'I'm going to tell you everything. The boat, the deal, how we got rid of it. All of it, apart from one thing. There was one other guy involved, and a girl. And I'm not going to tell you who they are, no matter what. Other than that, I'll tell you the lot. It was me, you see, not Goofy. So, yeah, get a lawyer later, arrest me if you have to. Whatever. But for now, please, just listen.'

★

The truth came off Jake in waves.

It was a weight he was tired of carrying.

Junkett looked at him evenly the whole time without judgement, without pressure.

★

When he was done, Jake said: 'What now?'

'You're going to tell me again. With your lawyer present. We'll prepare your statement.'

'I mean what will happen . . . to me?'

'With your full cooperation and no previous? Hmmm. Maybe a suspended sentence. But maybe not. I don't know. It's possible you could do a deal for your testimony. Like I say, these guys are serious. They are who we're after. Not a surfer so starry-eyed in love that he did the most monumentally stupid thing he's ever done.' Junkett smiled. His eyes twinkled.

★

Two days later, Jake received a text from a number he didn't recognise.

Having a great holiday, it said. *Hawaii's off the scale. I'll catch one for you.*

Jake hit the palm of his hand on his head. *Of course*, he thought. *The weed! Goofy must have sold it . . . And gone travelling.*

Come home, he texted back. *It's safe . . . 'Gavin!'*

Then, a minute later, he sent another.

Come home, mate. Just come home.

Hannah and Jake, Jake and Hannah

HANNAH CONTINUED WITH her work. It required collecting samples of water and seaweed, every day, at intervals along the coast, wherever it was accessible. That meant a lot of climbing and scrambling. Beano loved it, and Jake too. He couldn't always follow Hannah because of his leg, but he was happy to sit on rocks and cliff tops, and wait.

One day, after Goofy had dropped them at Whitesands, Hannah stood thigh-deep in the sea, cutting seaweed off a rock. Jake sat with Beano, high on the rocks.

He fished her phone out of her bag when it rang, and took the message.

'Hannah!' he shouted, waving. 'That was Steve. They've been seen.'

'What, who?'

'Orcas. Killer whales. Off the cliffs near Penford, by one of your research mob. I *told* you what Goofy said about Little One was true. She's alive.'

She told herself not to get excited: there was no way anyone could know Little One was alive, even if orcas had been seen.

'When? How many? What direction were they travelling in?'

'Don't know. Apparently the guy saw black whales, a long way offshore.'

Hannah looked out to sea, as if she might see them, if they were there. She took hold of her heart and calmed it.

'They probably saw basking sharks, or maybe dolphins,' she said. It happened a lot. People saw one thing, and thought they saw another.

She waded back to the rocks.

'Shall we go and check?' said Jake. 'Just in case?'

'Sure.'

They went to the cliffs near Penford. The point there gave them a good view up and down the coast, and a long, far sight over the ocean.

They sat for a long time, scanning the deep green for black fins. The storms were gone and the water looked calm, although darker, under the autumn sky.

They didn't see whales. There were no jagged waves or coal-black birds to trick her. Just endless sea.

Word got round that whales had been sighted. There were rumours. Reports. Sightings. Calls.

But they only ever found out hours or days later. They

always arrived too late. The sightings of dark fins were always a way offshore. The glimpses were brief and the details vague.

The two of them agreed: the rescue had been on the news, and now the community was seeing shadows, desperate for proof the rescue had been a success.

They stopped searching. There was too much else to do; to sort out.

★

On the day she finished the project, they took a walk up to the cliffs. It wasn't more than a mile, and Jake could handle that.

The plan was to have a picnic and talk about the future. About work, money, where they were going to live. Even about Hawaii, though it'd be at least a year before they could go.

After hot pasties and chilled beer, they left Beano snuffling scraps off the rug and went and sat at the cliff top.

They didn't talk about the future. They watched the sea. Long swells were rolling in, gulls riding air streams, and slate clouds creeping across the sky.

Hannah breathed the sea-cooled air and leant against Jake as if he was a rock. The vastness of sea and sky made her dizzy.

'Strange, isn't it?' said Hannah.

'What?'

'The sea. It's always the same, but always different.'

'That makes no sense.' He poked her in the ribs with his elbow.

'It does,' she said. 'The sea was there before the mines were built.' She pointed along the cliff to the grey ruins. Granite blocks littered the ground. Some of them had split in two after falling in the storms. Older ones were coated in moss and grass. 'Look, Jake. The rocks are crumbling back into the land they came from. It'll take hundreds of years. Thousands. Then there'll be no sign they were ever here. The sea was there before, it'll be there when they're gone.

'Doesn't it blow your mind that all that's going on, churning away, even when we're . . . I dunno, in town, shopping or something? It's always the same. But always different too. Currents and tides and swells and wind and weather change. Every day, every second.'

'You're a bit deep, Hannah Lancaster. And weird. Anyway, I kind of get what you're saying. The sea *is* a weird place, a mystery.'

'It's not a place, it's not a mystery. Mysteries can be explained. The sea is . . . I don't *know* what it is . . . I'll never know. It is not a thing that can be known. It can only be experienced. I think that's true. At least it's what I feel. I've been thinking a lot, after everything that's happened. With you, with the whales. There's a lot that can't be understood, or explained. Maybe you just have to experience it. You can't know everything. Like us looking for Little One. She's gone, Jake. She might be dead at the bottom of the sea, or she might be chasing fish off the Scillies. We don't know. We'll never know. All we know is, we did the right thing at the time. But even that . . . it might have been the *wrong* thing. She might have died. I mean . . . there's things you can't control, things you can't understand. Am I making any sense, Jake? Tell me.'

'No. You are definitely weird.' He tapped his head. She laughed, and shoved him with her hand.

'But you know what I mean?'

'Yeah. Life throws stuff at you. Storms, like. All you can do is hold on.

'Anyways, thought we were meant to talk about our future? Money and stuff.'

'I don't feel like it today. You?'

'Nah.'

He gave her a peck on the cheek, then took her hand and squeezed it. Their lips locked, their arms snaking around each other's bodies. His hands began exploring and undoing. She pushed them down and away, once and then twice. But soon her hands were not pretending to fight any more, and they were finding his skin. Her breath was hot and quick.

'Not here,' she said.

'Why not?' he replied. But she stood up and refastened her jeans and shirt – buttons and zips that had magically come undone.

Hannah returned to the rug and started throwing things into the basket. She wanted to get to the car. To the house. To somewhere. Quickly.

She was bent over on her hands and knees as she worked, her hair hanging loose around her neck. She was teasing him with the sight of her, waiting for him to grab her. Then she'd wriggle from his grasp and run to the car, or some hidden den in the mines.

She looked back. Jake was standing, pointing at the sea.

'What is it?' she said.

'Come and see.'

Straight below, a hundred metres out, a fin broke the surface. A plume of misty breath shot into the air, then the orca sank back into the dark. Hannah held her breath.

Another fin broke the oil-green. And another.

Three whales, travelling fast. Big fins. Adults. They were shallow enough that she could just about see their bodies. Shadows in the water.

They came up every twenty seconds as they moved down the coast. Then the fins all broke the water at the same time, curved, and returned, following the cliff.

'Why are they coming back?' said Jake.

Some hundred metres down the coast, in the direction the whales had come from, a smaller shadow was gliding through the shallows, moving slowly. Its dorsal fin broke the surface. It breathed, and dived.

The older whales came back, circled the younger one, then went on ahead of her again. They repeated the pattern. Moving ahead, coming back, moving ahead, coming back. Waiting for the younger whale each time.

'Do you think that's her?' said Jake.

'Yes,' said Hannah. 'Yes, I do.'

They watched, till the whales had journeyed far down the coast, and they couldn't see them any more.

Acknowledgements

This footnote to a book is usually called 'acknowledgements'. But that's a dry word. For me it's about saying a very big and heartfelt 'thank you'.

So . . . *thank you* to Nick Lake, my editor, and Catherine Clarke, my agent. If I said, 'They know their stuff,' I'd be making a very big understatement. They're also both whip-smart and really, really nice people to work with. I could go on . . .

Thanks also to Julia, Lucy et al at the Bath Spa MA, and the gang of writer friends I made there. It's a while since I left, but the MA continues to shape my writing. If you think you have a book in you, and you need some help getting it out, there's nowhere better to go, in my opinion.

I have worked for the charity Whale and Dolphin Conservation (WDC) for a while. (Find out more at www.whales.org.) I'm lucky enough to have seen whales and dolphins in the wild, many times, and to have worked with some amazing 'whale-heads'. As you can imagine, this influenced Hannah's story quite a lot. I have tried to be as realistic as possible in the descriptions of whales, and the details of the rescue, but if there are any inaccuracies or mistakes in the text they are entirely mine.

As for Jake's story: some years ago, after a spell of savagely violent storms, WDC had reports of dolphins washing ashore in Cornwall. We duly sent two researchers to assess the scale of the problem, and to find out the cause (illegal pair trawlers, it turned out). The researchers spent a lot of time patrolling beaches and hard-to-get-to coves. And guess what they found?

The police reckoned the haul had a street value 'running into millions of pounds'.

You can see the local BBC report here: http://news.bbc.co.uk/1/hi/england/cornwall/7235851.stm

Of course, the researchers informed the police immediately, but I had the thought at the time: What if you didn't? What if you were stupid, or desperate enough to think you could cash in? And what might be the implications of doing something like that?

That was the spark of the story that became *Storms*.

Finally, *Storms* is not a sequel to my first book, *Kook*. It's a stand-alone novel. But it *is* set in the same fictional location and even features some of the same characters. If you enjoyed it, and were intrigued by the boy Hannah meets at the house on the Cape, then check out *Kook*. It's his story.